CW01637535

THE IMAGE

A thousand dots of silvery light floated above her in a glacial mist. Then the fragments of light slowly moved towards one another, relentlessly forming a gleaming shaft – slender, pointed, coming closer. She must run. But flight was impossible – she was strapped down. As she strained against her bonds, they grew tighter, stronger. Suddenly the mist cleared and the horror was poised above her, its deadly image now sharp in every detail. It was a hypodermic needle, its wicked point only inches above the body she knew was her own, but had lost all power to move. Strong blunt fingers gripped the needle, fingers of pale flesh for which there was no hand, no arm. The needle hovered, and then suddenly plunged towards her . . .

'No!' The word burst from her and she was suddenly wide awake. It was a nightmare . . . thank heaven! But as the days wore on, and the vision became part of her life, day and night, night and day, Karen knew that this terrifying picture was no fantasy. Part of her 'new' eye held THE IMAGE

The Image

Charlotte Paul

CORONET BOOKS
Hodder and Stoughton

Copyright © 1980 by Charlotte Paul Reese

First published in USA 1980 by
Warner Books Inc.

Coronet edition 1981

British Library C.I.P.

Paul, Charlotte
The Image – (Coronet Books).
I. Title
813′ .52 [F] PS3531. A8519

ISBN 0 340 27271 6

The characters and situations in this book are entirely imaginary and bear no relation to any real person or actual happening

This book is sold subject to the condition that it shall not, by way of trade or otherwise, be lent, re-sold, hired out or otherwise circulated without the publisher's prior consent in any form of binding or cover other than that in which this is published and without a similar condition including this condition being imposed on the subsequent purchaser.

Printed and bound in Great Britain for
Hodder and Stoughton Paperbacks, a
division of Hodder and Stoughton Ltd,
Mill Road, Dunton Green, Sevenoaks, Kent
(Editorial Office: 47 Bedford Square,
London, WC1 3DP) by ©ollins, Glasgow

*To the selfless doctors
and medical specialists who
encouraged, informed and corrected me
during the conception and birth
of this book.*

The Image

One

Dickie looked into the eyes of his lover and saw in them the conflict between guilt and desire more exciting to him than the most delicious sexual technique. The man who had come to terms with himself and could love another man without suffering would never arouse Dickie like this man who, even in the final ecstatic moment, was haunted by a sense of doing wrong.

"Happy?" he whispered, smiling into those wide-open tormented eyes. "Was it a good loving?"

Silence. Playfully, Dickie ran the tip of his tongue along his lover's lower lip. This was the moment he enjoyed most. When it was all over. When the groping hands were still, the hungry body sated, and he could watch his lover's guilt come flooding back. Now Dickie's feeling of power reached its peak, for he knew that despite the self-hate he could, if he wished, arouse his lover again. But did he want to? No, not really. He had other plans for the rest of the afternoon.

He pulled himself up onto one elbow, pressing his chest against the other man, and with his free hand caressed and teased first one nipple, then the other. He laughed softly as he felt the shudder his lover could not suppress.

"You don't like me any more? You don't like Hero?" he murmured. "Well then, farewell, my sweet Leander. Until tomorrow. Or the day after tomorrow." His fingers slid down to the navel, and gently tweaked soft hairs lying damp against the skin. "Or the day after the day after tomorrow, if I'm not busy. But first, dear one, the surprise you promised me."

With a sudden movement his lover sat up and brushed Dickie's hand aside. "I saw you with Alan."

For an instant Dickie was afraid that this time he had said too much, or at least had said it too soon. Getting his "surprise"—a euphemism they had both fallen into, so much more acceptable than the word "fix"—was important, as important as the expensive gifts and generous allowance this unhappy but extremely wealthy man exchanged for love in the afternoon. But it was only the usual jealousy. "You saw me with Alan? Of course you did, M'lord. He's the family accountant." Dickie grinned impishly. "I've done business with him for years."

"Dinner at the 410?"

"We were hungry."

His lover jumped to his feet and reached

for his clothes. "Damn you," he said huskily. "Damn you! *Damn* you!"

Maybe he *had* gone too far. Dickie slid off the bed and gave his lover's bare buttock an affectionate pat. "Don't let's quarrel. Not over old Alan. By the way, I told him about my lovely Triumph. He was envious."

"No doubt." The man began to put on his clothes.

"No, really. He does know quite a lot about bikes."

"I'm sure he could afford to buy you one."

Dickie stepped in front of him, both arms to his sides, palms up in a gesture of submission, forcing the now fully dressed man to confront his naked body. Would he turn away, walk out of the room? No. His calculation had been right. His lover's eyes fixed hungrily on Dickie's blue-violet eyes with their long lashes, his sensuous mouth, then moved slowly down the length of his body. "You're cruel," he said. "Beautiful and cruel."

"Do you want me?" Dickie whispered. "Look." He touched himself softly. "I could."

"Oh God . . ."

The cry of pain was echoed by the strident ring of the doorbell. Dickie's forefinger flew to his mouth. He shook his head in an urgent signal for silence. The bell rang again. After a long pause the quiet was broken by the demanding sound of knuckles rapping on a wooden door. Dickie let minutes pass after the last knock before he relaxed and sat down on the edge of the bed. The possibility of someones' discovering him in the arms of a lover didn't particularly concern him. What distressed him was the thought that his lover might flee through the back door before he had delivered the surprise. To his relief, the person on the other side of the door soon gave up and went away. Enough of the teasing, much as it amused and excited him. He looked up at his lover and bestowed his sweetest and most childlike smile. "Please, Daddy. My surprise."

The brooding eyes seemed to darken. "You'll get it. But first . . ." the voice broke off.

Both mind and body yearned for the gift this man had brought, but this was no time to show his eagerness. Love, only love, with subtle overtones of gratitude. . . . Dickie took his lover's hands in his own, gently turned them palms up, and kissed first one palm, then another. "Yes? But first?"

"I want to dress you."

Dickie exhaled softly. He had known the answer, but he loved to watch what happened to the man's face when he was forced to say it out loud. "Yes, Leander. Yes . . ."

Through half-closed eyes Dickie watched his lover pick up each article of clothing and go through the slow, silent ritual that had become the next-to-the-last act of their lovemaking. The hands moved deliberately, deftly. Dickie rarely felt admiration for another human being, especially not for a lover so plainly possessed by his need for the gift of love-making Dickie enjoyed withholding even more than granting, but something close to admiration stirred in him as he let himself be dressed. The act was more servile than if his lover had knelt to wash Dickie's feet.

But there was dignity in it, too. A silent statement in the slow movement of his hands saying that for all this self-abasement he was not completely lost, that this handsome, distinguished-looking man had his limits and could not be pushed beyond them. Today the eyes burned with a degree of love-hate Dickie had never seen in them before. Was he really *that* jealous of good old Alan? That was a good card to hold for future games.

Fully dressed in his jeans and shirt, Dickie smiled expectantly. The anxiety he always felt until the dear man actually delivered the surprise melted as his lover carefully rolled back Dickie's left sleeve. Dickie responded by reclining on the bed and extending his arm, palm up so as to offer the veins on the soft underarm. Now his lover's hands were swift. He drew a small packet out of the inside pocket of his jacket, opened it and laid the contents on the bed. Dickie looked lovingly at the familiar paraphernalia and closed his eyes in anticipation of the beautiful feeling that would soon course through him. Sensitive as Dickie was to anything that hurt his body—a scrape or cut deep enough to draw blood actually made him sick to his stomach—the familiar sting of the hypodermic needle and the slight pressure as it was withdrawn were pleasant sensations, mentally if not physically. For a moment he remained with his eyes closed, waiting for the first faint mist of euphoria to drift across his mind. "Ah," he murmured, still smiling. "Ah . . . Dear love . . . Dear Leander . . ." The promised surprise had been given, the gift received. Dickie was ready now for the last act—the regretful parting, the farewell kiss to seal his promise that he would be at home to his lover later in the week.

Dickie opened his eyes. "Thursday?" he said matter-of-factly. "Here, of course. Same time?"

"Who were you expecting this afternoon?"

Dickie frowned impatiently. His lover's jealousy had to be tolerated, but at this point, when he was, in a sense, home free, it was a little bothersome. "What do you mean, dear one?" He tried to make it light but his tone was distinctly peevish.

"You know damn well what I mean. Who was that at your door?"

Dickie shrugged. "I haven't a clue. My sister, maybe. She's come to town. Maybe she heard that little brother has joined the drug culture and decided it was up to her to show him the light."

"Sister?" His lover's laugh was edged with hysteria. "*Sister!* I may be half-crazy but I'm not a complete fool."

"Oh, *really.*" Dickie's head tilted sideways in a look that was both flirtatious and defiant. "You know there's no one else . . . no one like you . . ." he added with just enough emphasis on *you* to prolong his lover's agony. Arousing his lover's jealousy, feeding it, knowing when and how to quiet it—these were skills Dickie cultivated to an art.

"No one like me." A simple, flat statement. The anger seemed to subside. The tone of voice was reflective, as if the man was studying his own image in some interior looking glass. "No, I suppose not. No one who can assure you of a steady supply." He glanced thoughtfully at Dickie's arm and then at the instrument on the bed beside him. "I've never disappointed you, have I?"

The storm had passed. And thank goodness for that, Dickie mused, for the good feeling was mounting. He wanted to let it take him, to pick him up, lift him, carry him up, and out, and away.

"Thursday?" his lover asked. It was a voice Dickie hardly recognized. It was cold and empty. The usual undertone of anxious longing was entirely missing. Well, he liked that anxious, suffering sound, and he was going to have to hear it before he agreed to anything. "That depends," Dickie said, and noting the instant pain in his lover's eyes, he said it again. Oh, he was feeling beautiful now! That depends, that depends, that depends . . . God, the feeling!

"On *what?*" The expression on the man's face was now one of pure malevolence, but Dickie was too far gone to notice.

"Depends on what, depends on what . . ." Dickie giggled, closed his eyes, lay back on the bed and let the laughter rise with the clouds of beautiful feeling. "Depends on whether. That's what. On whether. I promise. I'll call you. Yes, dear one, Hero will call you. If it's good whether . . ." He was soaring on a wind of silent laughter. "I mean, if it's good weather . . ."

His lover's answer came to him from what seemed a very great distance. "You are evil," the bitter voice said. "You are all the evil I carry around inside of me. You are an open sore, a bleeding, suppurating, foul-smelling sore that will not heal."

Oh, it was beautiful, Leander's rising anger, coming out in a crescendo like the roar of in-rushing surf. Another sound mingled with it. His own voice, Dickie's voice, bursting with joy, his laughter tangling with the other's fury in a whirlwind of sound as black as a witch's night. He could see his lover clearly, sitting there on the edge of the bed with that marvelous, that altogether heavenly syringe in his hand. He was aware of every momement, saw him fill the syringe, watched it come toward his arm, saw its gleaming shaft and felt the quick sting of the needle. But it was all far away, images seen through the wrong end of a telescope. Now Leander was leaning over him, Leander's mouth was pressed against his, whispering some words. Words without meaning. He lay very still, trying to force meaning out of what he saw and heard. "Good-bye. You won't torment me again. Not ever again. Dickie, Dickie . . ." He was standing up, he was turning away . . . Suddenly, through the warm fog, the meaning came together. A *second shot.* Dear Leander had given him a second shot! On the edge of consciousness, Dickie struggled to pull himself up. He would run. He would call for help. He would get to the telephone . . . Leander's powerful arm pressed him down, pinning him against the bed. His other hand picked up the hypodermic needle and mockingly held it in front of Dickie's eyes.

Inwardly, Dickie cried out, he protested, then he called, "I *will* love you!" But if there was an answer, it was far above him, somewhere at the top of the great black pit into which he was falling, not fast but weightlessly, like an autumn leaf slipping sideways as it drifts to the ground. The blackness rose to meet him, embraced him, and slowly drew him down forever.

The man did not know how long he stood beside the bed, looking down into the wide-open staring eyes. Dickie was dead, but Dickie's eyes somehow lived.

He heard a voice—his own voice—in a retching sob as his body finally reacted and bolted through the bedroom door and across the living room. He came to his senses as the apartment door clicked shut behind him, and from there to his car his pace was unhurried. Once inside the car, he fell back against the seat exhausted. He knew that he would never escape from the betrayal and the terror in Dickie Brewster's eyes.

Two

The sun was setting. Its last warm glow rippled like a sheet of molten gold across the surface of Lake Washington. On the deck of her houseboat on Portage Bay, Karen Thorndyke squinted against the light and tried to bring the scene into focus.

To the right, one of the Montlake Bridge's neo-Gothic towers was barely visible. A little to the north of the bridge, the metal monster of the Husky stadium grandstand reared up darkly behind a pale green grove of poplar trees. To the left, the geometric shapes of the University District's high-rise business buildings were silhouetted against the fading sky. And directly across the lake stood the tall gray University of Washington hospital with the red brick buildings of the medical school clustered at its base. Karen saw it all dimly, remembering it more than seeing it, as if on that day four years ago when she moved into this little floating cottage she willed her failing eyes to make a photograph for the future.

Hers and her friend, Jennie's, were the last two houseboats of twenty tied up to either side of a long, narrow walkway, each resting on rafts of cedar logs. No. 134 East Sutherland Street was the post office designation for this floating white clapboard house that rose and fell with the water level of the lake, and groaned and dipped when a bad storm struck from the north.

Being farthest from shore, with no other houseboat between her own and the open water, Karen enjoyed the best view, a view that had been a kind of sensory radar through which she could detect the stealthy approach of blindness. Once the conical green copper roof of the Montlake Bridge tower had been in distinct contrast to the gray structure it capped. Once she had been able to read the numeral "49" on the World War II Navy shop vessel anchored on the other side of the lake, now housing laboratories for the University's School of Oceanography. The rhythmic movement of their long oars as the Husky crews skimmed past on practice runs. The families of feathery gray-green goslings, paddling furiously after their Canadian geese parents. The graceful flotilla of sailboats and yachts, burgees flying, in stately parade on Opening Day, the first Sunday in May. These and all the other sights of spring, with the leafing of trees, the bursting blossoms, the return of the hummingbirds, had become dimmer every year until now colors were fogged and shapes were blurred. She had thought how ironic it was that the only resident of East Sutherland, other than Jennie Karras, with an unimpeded view of the lake was, at this point, recording the scene through sounds. The strident but neighborly honking of the Canadian geese who had made themselves so much a part of the Portage Bay community that they never migrated. The distant hum and whirr of automobiles speeding along the concrete ramps leading to the Evergreen Point bridge, a sound that reminded her of surf on an ocean beach. The quack of Mallards perched on the ends of float logs, boldly demanding to be fed . . . . These created her view from the houseboat.

But not forever. She had taken the plunge. She was committed to the course she once had dreaded. At any moment she would receive the telephone call telling her to admit herself to Mathews Memorial Hospital as quickly as possible.

Earlier in the afternoon the next-to-the-last call had come, an alert advising her that the final summons was only a few hours away. For a moment, panic had swept over her. But the tranquil, hushed mood of the lake at twilight had diverted and soothed her. Fear had subsided, or rather she had managed to eject it so that it was outside herself, a separate entity she could analyze and cope with.

She inhaled deeply, pulling the fresh clean air into her lungs and releasing it slowly. It would be wise to go back into the house, nearer to the telephone. If it rang while she was out on deck, she would have to thread her way through her substantial collection of planter boxes, flower pots, and glass jugs with ivy—a jungle of green and flowering things to which she kept adding as if to defy the actual dimensions of the deck. Like all houseboaters, she was a compulsive gardener. Jennie was as driven as the rest of them, though Jennie, brought up in one of Seattle's few treeless and gardenless neighborhoods, had never planted a seed nor pruned a bush when she lived on land—unless one counted her not-so-successful attempts to grow marijuana in a window box. She and Jennie were co-authors of the Sutherland Principle: The desire to grow things increases in direct proportion to the decrease of available space in which to grow them.

Karen moved cautiously across the deck, avoiding earthenware pots, miniature rose bushes, a redwood table and deck chairs, the black iron hibachi, opened the French doors between the deck and living room and went inside. She paused there, enjoying the warmth and the fragrance of wood smoke still lingering from last night's hearth fire. As if to say good-bye, her eyes moved around the room from one familiar and beloved object to the next: the Franklin stove, and beside it, the battered copper washtub loaded with cedar kindling; the sofa and two chairs, slipcovered in her favorite shades of blue, turquoise, and purple; her grandfather's long mahogany bookcase which stood at a right angle to her work table by the picture window overlooking the lake. In the corner was her most treasured object of all—the tall, old-fashioned artist's easel her grandmother had given her on her fourteenth birthday.

Her parents had been loving and, because of their concern about her fading eyesight, had discouraged what they called her "unrealistic" hope of becoming an artist. She had held to her hope stubbornly however, and was aided and abetted by her grandmother.

Karen smiled at the memory of the old lady she was said to "take after." Automatically her gaze lifted to the big gilt-framed mirror above the easel. Large gray-blue eyes in a small face framed by long copper-colored hair—that was all she could make out. As misty as it was, the face in the mirror looked distinctly frightened. Karen made a face at her image, determined to dispel the fears that lingered at the edge of her awareness, then turned away and sat down in the armchair next to the telephone. In spite of her anxiety, or perhaps because of it, she felt drowsy.

Three weeks and two days ago her name had been placed on the Eye Bank waiting list. Eight days ago she had been notified that she had moved up to number ten and should not leave the city. One day—no, correction—twenty-nine hours ago she had been called into the doctor's office for her last pre-operative examination.

Now, at almost any moment, the final call would come and the waiting would be over. She would pick up the small suitcase already packed for her two-week stay in the hospital, phone for a taxi and be transported to Mathews Memorial on the magic carpet of a Yellow Cab. And there, she mused, the blinding fog will lift. I will be able to paint, perhaps quite differently, for the colors will be true and the shapes clearer. I will see the numerals on my wristwatch, and know when Jennie hangs new curtains in her kitchen window. For the first time I will truly appreciate every detail of these beautiful surroundings. The glistening expanse of blue water, the snowcapped peak of Mount Rainier, the masses of rhododendrons in full bloom in May. And faces! I will see faces! Eyes, chins, dimples, moles, smiles, frowns, tears. The face of Dr. Adam Stewart. I will really *see* Adam Stewart....

Karen rested her head against the back of the chair and closed her eyes. She was smiling. And musing on the past.

She was the most eager pupil ever to set off for a first day in grade school. Sack-lunch in hand, she skipped merrily down the driveway to board the school bus without a backward glance. But she was a subdued little girl when the bus deposited her in front of her home that afternoon.

"They all laughed at me," she explained. No tears, just an honest report. "There was a big picture on the wall. I said, 'Oh, look at the cute little pigs!' That's when everybody laughed. It wasn't pigs. It was kittens."

Her mother's brimming eyes had troubled her almost as much as her classmates' ridicule. "But it's all right," she added quickly. "The teacher moved me up to a front seat. Right by her desk. I can see everything fine now."

Karen had gone through school and college sitting in the front row. From the age of six she wore glasses, with frequent changes of prescription. But she was determined not to be left behind. She had a quick mind and the gift of a photographic memory. When words on the blackboard were indistinct, she guessed at them, and her guesses were usually right. Because she saw everything through a mist, she developed an acute sense of hearing. Thus, she adjusted to her handicap because she accepted it. And the deterioration of her eyesight had been so gradual that for years her ability to compensate had almost kept pace.

After graduation from the University of Washington, Karen obtained an interesting and reasonably well-paying job in the blueprint department of a Seattle aircraft factory. By that time regular glasses were useless, but contact lenses made it possible to work with large drawings.

She also decided to rent the houseboat on Portage Bay. For the first time in her life she was not being suffocated by the overprotective attitudes and gestures her failing vision seemed to evoke in others. She felt self-sufficient and very proud of going it alone. Her painting reflected her happiness. Although her eyesight was too poor for small figures and fine detail, she began experimenting with larger, bolder strokes. She even joined a car pool and every fifth week took her turn driving to the factory.

But everything changed when Karen went to the State Patrol Office to renew her driver's license. Her sight had diminished so over the past year that she could no longer read the letters at the top of the chart.

Losing her driver's license was a numbing shock, for it meant she could no longer share the responsibility of the car pool. She realized how totally dependent she would have to become on others.

The bleakness of the future became even clearer the day she went shopping for a new spring wardrobe. It had been almost a year since she had browsed through a downtown department store. She was back at the houseboat in an hour, empty-handed.

"What, no loot?" Jennie sang out from the adjoining deck.

"I didn't see anything I liked."

"Balls," Jennie said cheerfully. "Don't take off your jacket. We're going shopping together." It had been so like Jennie to guess that she had fled from the Bon Marché because she couldn't read the price tags or sizes, and she couldn't force herself to ask a sales clerk to read them for her.

And then the inevitable occurred. Karen's supervisor called her into his office and explained that, after careful reflection, he had decided she was no longer able to handle her work.

The day of the big decision—the day she decided to consult an eye surgeon—was stormy, but it had begun auspiciously with a phone call from the New Look Gallery with whom she had left some of her most recent paintings. Karen had felt misgivings about the paintings, even as she'd dropped them off, for they reflected her new style, which in her own mind was an admission of her dimming vision. At the time she had told herself she was just suffering from stage fright, since she hadn't yet exposed herself to outside criticism of her new technique. With the loss of her job, however, her outlook had become increasingly more gloomy.

So she had braced herself for disappointment when she heard George Manzo's voice on the phone, and was all the more amazed when she heard the paintings pronounced, "Absolutely superb, my dear." The gallery owner went on to say, "The beauty of it is that we've already received offers on two of them, and we hope you'll allow the gallery to bid on one of the others."

Karen was thrilled with the news. Selling one or two paintings wasn't going to support her, but it was no small step toward financial independence for a jobless—and unemployable?—young woman. It had provided another crumb of hope that the surgery, so long postponed "for just another year" was not going to be necessary.

She felt light-hearted for the first time in months. A celebration—a small one, anyway—was definitely in order. She thought of calling Jennie but remembered seeing her and her detective boyfriend, Doug Cooper, leaving the float together. No matter. In the mood the gallery's call had invoked, solitude was not lonely. First, a fire in the Franklin stove, its warmth and brightness in contrast to the cold gray world outside. And then a glass of wine to be sipped slowly while she listened to the tape of the book that had come in the morning mail.

There was plenty of kindling in the dented copper washtub but the cordwood was stacked on the deck. Karen put on her raincoat and a pair of cotton work gloves and opened the sliding door. For a moment she hesitated. The prevailing winds came from the south, so that the colony of houseboats was shielded by Capitol Hill, rising above Portage Bay to the south. But today's storm was blowing down from the north and was far more violent than it had appeared from the refuge of her living room. Angry waves pounded the float on which the houseboat rested, and broke over the deck in great plumes of icy water. But if she wanted a fire, she would simply have to get the firewood.

Karen stepped out onto the deck. Instantly, wind-driven rain hit her face with such force that she blinked hard and rapidly, with the result that the one contact lens she was wearing popped out and dropped onto the deck. "Damn!" she said out loud, recognizing the futility of trying to find it. Without the corrective lens, her right or "good" eye was as sightless as her left. It didn't matter, really. She could get to the woodpile and back with her eyes closed, as indeed they might as well be, she thought with the familiar mixture of resentment and acceptance her near blindness often aroused.

She left the French door open just enough to be able to push it all the way back with her foot when she returned with an armload of wood. Squinting against the rain and sightless without her contact lens, she did not see her little spaniel puppy jump out of his basket, squeak through the narrow opening and, the feathery stump of his tail wagging furiously, follow her along the rain-washed deck.

Waves were slamming against the houseboats like the wakes of passing ships. Lifted to the crest, dropping into the trough, lifted again, the floating cottages strained against their moorings. Karen moved cautiously along the deck, stumbled once or twice when the floor seemed to drop out from under her, but each time she caught herself and continued to the back of the house where the split alder logs were stacked.

She could do little more than distinguish light from dark. With rain stinging her eyes, she loaded her arms with firewood and was turning to retrace the slippery course back to the living room when a maverick wave smashed against the float. She stumbled and struggled to right herself. Completely off balance, her feet skidded, the wood flew out of her arms and she fell backwards against the woodpile, arms flailing uselessly. Another vicious wave struck. The houseboat shuddered and dipped. Karen was thrown clear as the stack of alder logs collapsed and fell away from the supporting wall of the house. A few logs skated across the deck but most of them dropped in an irregular mound, almost concealing the body of the spaniel puppy Karen had not seen, though he had been standing just behind her.

A high keening voice rose above the slap of the waves and the drumming of rain. It was a disembodied sound, more human than animal, the pitiful lament of a baby almost too weak to cry. Karen froze. On hands and knees she crawled toward the sound. Her hands moved swiftly along the edge of the murderous mountain of wood, stopping when her fingertips touched and identified the little dog's silk-coated hind legs.

"Inky!" Karen's cry echoed the puppy's dying wail. Frantically she removed the logs, crying, "It's all right, Inky. You'll be all right, puppy. . . ." But the little spaniel wasn't crying any more. He was panting heavily, his tongue protruding from his open mouth. A violent shudder rippled through his body. His head jerked back, his legs thrashed and the spasm ended.

Like a sleepwalker, Karen lifted the puppy and carried him into the house. For a long time she stood at the window, hugging the lifeless form against her breast as if to warm and comfort him. The day had brought her new hope that she could continue to live alone and support herself without risking major surgery. The day had also brought death.

Finally the wind died. Sea gulls were settling on the dark surface of the lake. The puppy in her arms was cool. Blood dripping from his mouth had collected in a small, glistening pool at her feet. Night was falling. She must bury him now, while there was still light.

She was standing beside the small patch of raw earth below the end of East Sutherland Street when two familiar figures, dimly seen through a blend of tears and raindrops, hurried down the slope. Then Jennie's arms were around her, hugging her fiercely. Doug, looming bearlike over both of them, was taking the spade from her hand.

"I killed Inky," Karen said.

"The hell you say!" Jennie responded, though her own voice had a catch in it.

Doug growled, "Let's go inside." Without relinquishing the spade, he embraced them both, propelling them along the float and into Karen's houseboat.

"Have you anything worth drinking around here?" he asked.

"In the cabinet," Karen replied. "There should be some Scotch."

"Scotch!" he exploded with such dramatic disdain that Karen smiled and began to feel better.

"Just pour, you clown," Jennie said affectionately. "And then I want you to tell Karen the name of that opthalmologist your mother went to. I think she's ready to listen."

Seated across the desk from Adam Stewart, Karen had tried vainly to bring the doctor's face into focus. He was a big man, broad-shouldered, and he was fair-haired. That's all her eyes could tell her, but she responded instantly to his voice, which was low and modulated. As she answered his questions, the voice-portrait filled out. A quiet man, she decided. Thoughtful, strong, but full of laughter.

The doctor put down his pen and stood up. "So much for the personal questions. Let's adjourn to the chamber of horrors and have a look at your eyes."

The examination lasted for two hours. As she had learned about him through his voice, she learned through the touch of his hands. His fingers were so gentle she didn't flinch when they explored the highly sensitive area of her eyes. He had explained while they were talking in his office that Dr. Franklin Drake would operate, that Dr. Drake confined himself to surgery while he, as assistant, conducted all eye examinations as well as assisting during the actual operation. "I'm glad," Karen said impulsively.

"Glad?"

"That you'll be there. During the surgery." Silence from the tall man at her side. I shouldn't have said that, Karen thought. Too personal. Out of place for a patient talking to a doctor she's never seen before—ha! Can't really see even now. But the decision to go ahead with the operation, plus the strength and reassurance he was so magically communicating through his hands, was giving her a pleasantly light-headed feeling.

Examination completed, Dr. Stewart had seated Karen in a chair by his desk and sat down across from her. She listened attentively while he explained his diagnosis. Her eyesight was failing because of a progressive deformity of the cornea called keratoconus, or coning of the cornea. Such a condition tends to be congenital, so that it was rare to find only one eye affected. In her case, the left eye was already functionally blind. The right, or "good eye" by comparison, had been providing only limited sight and had been badly overworked because of the deficiency of the "bad eye."

Karen said softly, "The answer is surgery."

"The answer is surgery," he repeated. "In your case, I see no possible alternative."

"You mean I'm going blind. *That's* the alternative."

"Virtually blind. But that isn't acceptable, is it? Not a true alternative. For someone else, it might be. But from everything you've told me about yourself, I think your future—self-realization, really—depends on being able to see, and see *well.* You're an artist, right? How long has it been since you could really bring your paintings into focus?"

She couldn't suppress a rueful smile. "Never, if you're going to insist on my being honest. Even as a child I had difficulty. But I managed."

"I don't paint pictures, but I do look at them, and my guess is that your technique has been seriously affected. I should say, restricted."

"Perhaps. But I could continue to paint with the sight I have."

"Ah." He paused, and when he spoke again Karen could hear both amusement and sympathy in his voice. "Come on now. You had already made up your mind to undergo surgery when you walked into my office."

She laughed. "You're right, of course. Absolutely right. But I didn't say so."

"No. Not out loud." He clapped his hands together, dismissing the mind reader, bringing back the doctor. "Let's look ahead. Prognosis, excellent. Part of my job today was to look for pathological conditions likely to affect post-operative recovery. If you had infected tonsils, or sinus trouble, or any infection of the nose or throat, we wouldn't operate until the condition cleared up. But I'm happy to say that you're in blooming good health, and that's a big plus.

"Another plus—Franklin Drake is considered the best corneal transplant surgeon in the country. You couldn't be in better hands. Okay? First, we'll get that left eye fixed up. About six months later, we'll do the right one. I'll bet that eighteen months from today you'll be buying a new car, and I promise you, I'm a very conservative gambler." He paused. "Are you with me so far?"

"Absolutely," she said with more feeling than she intended to betray.

"Fine. Now here's the timetable. Today is March seventh. Today your name goes on the waiting list at the Eye Bank."

"Eye Bank?" The words jolted her, giving her a sudden glimpse of something she hadn't considered.

"Eye banks are a well-established part of the medical scene," he said reassuringly. "In Seattle there are twenty-five to fifty names on the waiting list at all times. Within two to three weeks your name will hit the top of the list and you'll get your new cornea."

"My new cornea . . ." Her voice broke off. Why hadn't she thought of this before? She'd always known about eye banks, but *her* new cornea, *her* new eye . . . to be united forever with a part of someone else's body. . . . The idea made her uneasy.

As if her feeling had been telegraphed across his desk, Dr. Stewart said quietly, "Tell me what's troubling you, Karen. It's the thing about the donor, right?"

"Yes. I'm sorry if I seem ridiculous. But when you said I'll be on the waiting list for about three weeks, suddenly I was thinking—someone I don't know has only three weeks to live, and I'll benefit from her death by getting her eye. Will I know whose eye it is?"

"You'll never know. And I urge you, Karen, to put that part of the procedure out of your mind. Concentrate instead on my instructions. I don't want you to catch a cold while you're waiting to be called. Eat balanced meals. The less caffeine and alcohol the better. When you've advanced to the number ten spot on the waiting list, you'll be asked to stay close to home. When you're second from the top, you'll come back to me for another, much shorter examination. After that, keep your suitcase packed. The eye deteriorates rapidly. We have to operate at once when a cornea becomes available. So you could be called at any time of the day or night. . . ."

In the armchair beside her telephone, Karen slowly opened her eyes. She must have slept, for the sky was dark, and yellow light spilled out of the windows of Jennie's houseboat. Karen looked at the silent telephone and came wide awake. At any time of the day or night . . .

She had tried not to think about it, but the chilling truth was hard to ignore. When the telephone rang, calling her to the hospital, it would mean someone had just died. Not peacefully, from old age, or quietly in a hospital bed as a result of a fatal illness. She had learned enough about eye banks to know that they matched the age of the donor and the recipient, and that they rejected any tissue that might be affected by disease. The eye Dr. Drake gave her would be that of a young, healthy human being. Where was her donor now, this healthy young person who always carried an Eye Bank donor card? What violent act, what fatal accident would make it possible for a part of the donor's body to become a part of hers?

Karen jumped up and started toward the kitchen, determined to keep the menacing instrument of the telephone out of her sight. She reached the kitchen door. Her fingers groped along the wall and found the light switch. Karen cringed when the light went on, as if it were a flash of lightning. At that moment, the telephone rang. It rang again, loud and strident, twice, three times, while she made her way back to it, and slowly, heart pounding, lifted the receiver.

Three

From the moment Martha O'Donnell decided she herself would go to the morgue to identify the body of her brother, she began to feel queasy. The fact of his death had shocked and numbed her, but death was an abstraction. A corpse, a dead body—that was visual, that was real. Dickie, cold and lifeless in some dark refrigerated storage room in the morgue? The thought devastated her.

Of course, Henry Garner, faithful friend and counselor, had offered to make the identification. "It's only a formality," he had emphasized when he broke the news of Dickie's sudden death. "There's no need for you to put yourself through such an ordeal. As your attorney, I can go in your place."

Half of her had wanted to cry out. "Yes! Please do it for me. I can't go there. . . ." But the other half had reacted soberly. "Martha, you *have* to go because you have to know for sure." That second side, the side that was always unwilling to give up hope, was the side that prevailed. "Let's go together," she had said. Then she ran to the bathroom and, leaning over the wash basin, waited for the waves of nausea to subside.

Martha accepted the chair the Assistant Medical Examiner drew up beside his desk and tried to make her hands rest quietly in her lap. The examiner was soft-spoken and solicitous. As usual, Henry Garner was completely poised. He could speak for her and that helped. But he could not *look* for her, and somewhere in this municipal repository for human beings who had died violently or alone, Dickie's body was waiting to be identified and claimed. She glanced at the door of the administrative office in which she was sitting and thought uneasily of the death-filled rooms which lay beyond. Repressing a shudder, she turned sideways in her chair, cutting off the view of the threatening door as she tried to concentrate on what Henry was saying. "Would you mind going over the facts, Mr. Ryan? The report I received on the telephone was rather sketchy."

"Not at all." Ryan picked up a report sheet and quickly reviewed the handwritten notations. "At six P.M. yesterday evening, Jasper Carter, a tenant of the Westminster Apartments on Creighton Boulevard, telephoned the North Police Station. He stated he was afraid something had happened to Dickie Brewster, the occupant of

Apartment 4-C. Apparently he and Brewster had made dinner plans for the evening, but Brewster didn't show up, didn't answer his telephone, or respond when Carter knocked on his door. Carter couldn't understand it, because earlier in the afternoon Brewster himself had suggested the evening on the town. So, after repeated efforts to rouse him, Carter reported his concern to the police. Two officers on patrol in the area went to the Westminster, and with the cooperation of the resident manager gained entrance to Apartment 4-C. Dickie Brewster's body was lying on the bed."

"His body," Martha repeated dully. "He was dead."

The medical examiner nodded sympathetically. "Yes." He paused and turned toward Garner. "I'm not sure how much detail you're interested in."

Garner nodded reassuringly. "The cause of death is, of course, our greatest concern. I've already told Mrs. O'Donnell about your tentative findings."

Martha tried to speak but couldn't manage more than a mute nod of assent. Her eyes moved from the examiner to Garner, whose strong features and commanding height gave her an immediate and much needed feeling of security. He said quickly, "At this point you're virtually certain that you know the cause of death, aren't you, Mr. Ryan?"

The examiner nodded. "The *apparent* cause of death. As you know, nothing is final until the Chief Medical Examiner signs the death certificate."

"Meanwhile," Garner prodded, "the apparent cause of death?"

"It is our tentative opinion that Dickie Brewster died of an overdose of narcotics."

Martha's fingers clutched the arms of her chair. "I tried to tell him, but he wouldn't listen. He . . . laughed at me." Her voice shook and was so low that Ryan turned questioningly toward Garner.

Garner said quietly, "Mrs. O'Donnell's reason for flying to Seattle was to urge her brother to enter a drug abuse program."

"I see."

"Can you tell . . ." Martha's throat ached with the effort to speak, but this time the words were clearly audible. "Do you know the time of death?"

"More or less. It will have to be confirmed by the autopsy."

"What time was it?" She paused, and repeated in an urgent whisper, "*What time?*"

Ryan checked his report sheet. "Four P.M., or a little after."

"I was there! At four o'clock. I heard Dickie's voice. I know I did, even though he didn't answer when I rang the bell or when I knocked. He wouldn't let me in or . . . or maybe he *couldn't.* . . . Oh my God," Martha continued in a choked voice. "He was dying, and I was on the other side of the door. . . ."

"That may not be the case, Mrs. O'Donnell," the examiner broke in. "The toxicological workup may establish that death occurred later than our on-the-scene investigators estimated. In any event, you had no way of knowing."

Henry Garner rose quickly and stood beside Martha's chair. "Martha, he's right. And given Dickie's . . . whims, it's just as likely he *wouldn't* let you in as that he *couldn't*." He placed one hand protectively on her shoulder, and said, "Are you sure you want to view the body? Wouldn't you prefer to wait here?"

"No. I'm going to do it. I *have* to do it."

"Well then. We've asked our questions, haven't we? Let's get it over with." Garner cast a meaningful glance at the examiner. "If that's all right with you, Mr. Ryan?"

"Of course." Ryan stood up and gestured toward the door Martha had been trying to ignore. "Give me a few minutes. I'll just check to make sure . . ." his voice trailed off, leaving the unspoken words to reawaken Martha's dread of entering those unknown regions. Make sure of what? That bodies were covered, that blood had been wiped up? The images were vague and therefore doubly frightening.

As if he sensed what she was feeling, Garner's comforting hand patted her shoulder. "This won't take long, Martha. And it won't be nearly as difficult as you think it will be. It'll just be Dickie. No wounds or marks. Nothing unpleasant. The body is intact. . . ." He paused, and frowning slightly, added, "Except for the eyes."

With Garner beside her, Martha followed the examiner numbly through the dreaded door, along a corridor, up a flight of stairs, down another corridor. Her feet kept moving, obedient to some part of her brain that was capable of functioning without her consent. Every step they took, every corner they turned, brought her closer to Dickie. God, how could she have forgotten about the eyes! A shudder ran through her body with such violence that she stumbled and nearly lost her balance. Henry's strong hand grasped her elbow. "Courage," he said softly. "It will be over soon."

They were there. Ryan opened a door, stood aside, and said, "This is the viewing room." *Here?* her mind shrieked. He's here! . . . Martha closed her eyes but her feet kept moving and Garner's arm guided her into the room. With nausea mounting, she forced herself to open her eyes.

But the room was as empty and impersonal as the corridor outside. It was a square, six-by-six cubicle with a large, heavily curtained window on one wall. Henry's hand tightened on Martha's arm. He nodded, and the examiner stepped to the side of the window and pulled a cord. Slowly the curtains parted.

Martha saw another freshly painted dimly lighted cubicle, empty except for a stainless steel cart bearing a body completely covered by a sheet. That was Dickie, that still, hidden form. An attendant in a blue jacket was standing alongside the cart. Out of the corner of her eye she saw the examiner's signal and watched, as if paralyzed, while the attendant carefully rolled back the sheet to reveal Dickie's curly blond hair, Dickie's smooth summer-tanned skin, Dickie's *eyes* . . .

The lids, sunken into the empty eye sockets, were only partially closed. Martha barely suppressed a cry of horror. From deep memories of her childhood a single distinct and terrifying picture shot to the surface of her mind. Her beloved doll, Peggy, her prized possession at the age of eight. Martha had liked to lower the life-size baby doll until the lids dropped and the lashes of real hair rested on her cheeks, and then, very slowly, Martha would raise her and watch those perfectly round eyes come awake. And then, that terrible day when she went to play with Peggy, looked down in the doll bed where Peggy lay . . . and Peggy had no eyes. There were two gaping round holes in her head. Two black, eyeless pits. She screamed, and screamed. . . . Her parents had explained that three-year-old Dickie hadn't really meant any harm, but even weeks later when Peggy had come back from the doll hospital with her eyes glued back in place, Martha had refused to touch her. . . .

All her remembered terror came rushing back as she looked at Dickie's face. A bitter, foul-tasting fluid rose at the back of her throat and still she stared, transfixed by her intense awareness of those dark, empty eye sockets. She knew the examiner had pulled up a chair for her, and felt Garner's arm guide her to it. She sat down heavily and rested her head against the back of the chair while Ryan's anxious voice kept repeating that there was a rest room right next door.

She shook her head. "I don't want to go to the rest room. I want you to tell me about his eyes."

Garner said quickly, "Let's talk about that later, Martha. I want to get you back to your hotel. We'll talk later."

"No," Martha said stubbornly. "I want to know, Mr. Ryan. Why did you remove my brother's eyes? Couldn't you have waited until . . ." She swallowed several times, fighting down a new wave of nausea.

The examiner sounded defensive. "Mrs. O'Donnell, the eyes have to be removed within six to eight hours of the time of death or they won't be fresh enough to be used for corneal transplant. We notify the Eye Bank after we find the deceased is carrying a donor card. The Eye Bank enucleators come immediately, remove the eyes, and take them back to the Eye Bank in Mathews Memorial Hospital. The transplant operation must be performed within thirty-six to forty-eight hours of the donor's death."

"Mr. Ryan . . ." Martha addressed the examiner without looking at him. Her gaze was still fixed on the two eyeless pits where Dickie's beautiful eyes had been. "Where are they now?"

"I beg your pardon?"

"Mr. Ryan, *where are my brother's eyes?*"

The examiner consulted his wrist watch. He spoke very softly. "Ten-fifteen. I can't be sure, of course, because we never know who receives the donated eyes, nor who the surgeon is. But it's safe to assume that right about now, some person who would otherwise face partial or even total blindness is receiving the gift of sight." He paused and then added in an even more gentle tone, "That's a priceless gift, Mrs. O'Donnell."

Garner said quietly. "Indeed it is. But you say you don't know who that person might be?"

Ryan shook his head emphatically. "We don't even ask. And if we did we would never be told."

Martha whispered, "I never, never want to know who it is."

Garner signaled silently. The examiner went to the window and pulled the cord, and the curtains came together like slowly closing eyelids.

On a less-crowded street, the man might have attracted attention, for he was walking aimlessly, his steps rapid at one point, slow, almost hesitant the next, and he had reversed his course more than once. Having parked his car and plunged into the stream of shoppers along Fifth Avenue, he couldn't remember why he had thought this would be the way to get control of himself. The full realization of what he had done was only now breaking through his numbness. He had killed. He was obsessed by that fact—and this seemed peculiar to him—not by the fear of being caught. He had tried to concentrate on the terrible danger he faced—tried deliberately to let that fear divert him—but the passion and the fury that had peaked in that terrible act still dominated his emotions. He had killed, but wasn't that killing justified? He had to believe that it was. Dickie Brewster had been a parasite who had bled other men before him and would have drained others after him . . . only now there would be none after him. . . .

The man stumbled and almost fell.

"Oh, sorry." He bent quickly to pick up the package he had knocked out of a woman's hand.

"Are you all right?" she asked, and he mumbled, "Yes, yes, of course," and hurried away.

Four

Dr. Adam Stewart looked down at the still form on the operating table and wondered why he was feeling so anxious about the outcome of this particular operation. He certainly didn't doubt his ability to play his own role as assistant to Dr. Franklin Drake—he was perfectly capable of performing the operation himself and had done so for two years before he decided that working as the great man's assistant would be an invaluable experience. Nor could the strange apprehensiveness he was feeling be rooted in doubts about Drake, who performed some hundred or more corneal transplants a year. Adam Stewart, age thirty-three, seated at the feet of the master yet daring to worry that the master's hand would slip? The idea was ludicrous.

There was one negative factor, duly noted when he had examined Karen Thorndyke's eyes, duly stressed in the prognosis he had submitted to Drake. The malformation of the cornea, or "coning" of the transparent tissue that is the windowpane of the eye, had advanced to a critical point. In her left eye, it was now less than one fifth of the normal thickness, and the right, or good eye, was almost as bad. In the hands of a lesser surgeon such extreme thinness would multiply the ever-present risk of doing permanent damage to the eye. But this isn't a lesser surgeon, Adam reminded himself. This is Dr. Franklin Drake. *The* Dr. Franklin Drake.

Aside from this element of danger, all omens were good. All pre-operative procedures had gone smoothly, from three o'clock that morning when she checked into the hospital, through the routine seven o'clock dosage of Valium, atropine and morphine sulphate, to this final countdown. Now the circulating nurse was tucking the girl's long copper-brown hair under the edges of a turban and he and the anesthesiologist were poised for Drake's entrance. For the third or fourth time, Adam's eyes traveled to the big clock on the wall. Two minutes to eight. Two minutes in which to reflect that this beautiful young girl was risking total blindness in her bid for total sight, and that however favorable the odds were when Franklin Drake was in charge, for the next hour her whole future—her career as an artist, the degree of dependency in her relationships with others—all these would hang in the balance.

At precisely eight o'clock, the door from the scrub room swung open and Dr. Franklin Drake strode into the surgical theatre. Adam never watched the great man at work without thinking how appropriate the term "surgical theatre" was. Every gesture, from dipping his arms into the antiseptic solution to securing the last suture, was part of a stellar performance. Not that Drake played to an audience, imaginary or otherwise. Even when he permitted medical students or other surgeons to observe a kerotoplasty —and hundreds of doctors had come to Seattle just for that purpose—he was totally absorbed by the operation. It was his elegant precision and the extraordinary delicacy of his strong hands that choreographed a performance so polished not a single movement could be improved.

As usual, Drake's signal to the anesthesiologist was a barely perceptible nod. The anesthesiologist immediately began the rapid sequence of preliminaries to general anesthesia.

For the moment, Dr. Drake as well as Adam were spectators. The anesthesiologist was the star actor.

He had already inserted a teflon needle into a prominent vein in Karen's arm. From a bottle suspended above the operating table, the lactated Ringer's solution was slowly entering the girl's body by way of the clear plastic tubing connecting bottle to needle. Now thiopental sodium, commonly known by the trade name of Sodium Pentathol, began to enter the bloodstream through a three-way stopcock in the tubing.

Adam watched with admiration as the skilled performance continued, swiftly and silently. Before he entered the operating room, the anesthesiologist had selected all the necessary drugs, drawn each dose up in its syringe, labeled each one and lined them up on a tray in the order of use.

With the Pentathol guaranteeing unconsciousness, the next injection was three milligrams of curare. The anesthesiologist paused, eyes focused intently on Karen's face. Forty-five seconds was usually enough for the Pentathol and curare to take effect. But individual response to drugs is highly variable. He was observing Karen's reaction, both to the amount of dose and the time it took her to react to it, rather than consulting the wall clock. Adam trusted his colleague's clinical judgment. Nevertheless, his own eyes strayed to the clock, seeking assurance that there was nothing unusual—and therefore nothing disturbing—about her response.

Forty-five seconds. Fifty, fifty-five . . . The anesthesiologist was reaching for the fourth syringe. Adam exhaled deeply. "Succinyl choline, eighty milligrams," his mind recited automatically as the drug was administered. The muscle relaxant would quickly paralyze Karen so that the tube through which she would receive oxygen for the next hour could be inserted into her windpipe.

Again the anesthesiologist paused. Adam took a deep breath and thought, "So far, so good." Now for the last step before the operation began.

Very gently the anesthesiologist slid the plastic tube into Karen's mouth and down the narrow tracheal passage to her lungs. With the tube securely taped in place, he decreased the oxygen to fifty percent, still a rich mixture compared to the twenty percent contained by ordinary room air. He then administered a second and truly paralyzing dose of curare. Small amounts of nitrous oxide and halothane would be added and, sometime while the operation was in progress, Karen would receive another shot of curare. But essentially, anesthesia was complete, and Adam could perform one of the assistant surgeon's functions in a corneal transplant, the extrabulbar block, "blocking" or paralyzing nerves to keep the muscles that move the eyeball from contracting.

He proceeded with the immobilization of Karen's eyelids by injecting several cubic milliliters of one percent Xylocaine with adrenaline, an anesthetic combination known as the O'Brien block. He then carried out Van Lent's block by injecting the same fluid along the rim of the bony orbit above and below the eyeball.

Now he was ready to introduce a single milliliter into the apex of the orbit, this to make sure that four of the six extraocular muscles that govern the movements of the globe were also immobilized. Although Adam had performed these blocks well over a thousand times, he was acutely conscious of the risk of accidental hemorrhage. But it all went well.

Adam could feel Drake's intent gaze as he took the sterile tonometer from the operating nurse. He measured the intraocular pressure and Drake's eyes flickered with satisfaction, for the pressure had dropped several millimeters. Adam had skillfully avoided the danger of hemorrhage and the stage had been set. He stepped back and looked directly into Drake's alert brown eyes. Now Drake was on his own.

The pupil of Karen's eye had been reduced to the size of a pencil lead by the use of powerful constrictors known as miotics. Once the razor sharp circular knife or trephine had penetrated the cornea, the underlying lens had to be protected. The overlying iris would serve as a shield, but Drake's surgical wizardry was an equally important factor. If the lens in Karen's eye was accidentally damaged, it would have to be removed. Both Adam and Drake knew that converting a corneal transplant into an "open sky" type of surgery could cause dangerous complications such as loss of vitreous, which in turn could result in secondary glaucoma, retinal detachment, intraocular infection, and even the loss of the eye itself.

Adam threw another anxious look at the wall clock. One hour from now it would be over. But for the unconscious girl on the operating table, it was undoubtedly the most crucial hour of her lifetime.

Dr. Drake was proceeding with the usual composure. He separated the eyelids with tiny lid retractors. The lids were now rolled back and held firmly in place; the eye was fully exposed and the lids could neither blink nor close. Adam noted that the wall clock showed that only two minutes had passed.

Dr. Drake adjusted the operating microscope. From now on everything he did to that bald and staring eyeball would be accomplished with the aid of this remarkable invention, so high-powered that a suture "thread," finer than a human hair, would be as distinct as a piece of string, and the tiny circular cornea, actually only one-third of an inch in diameter, would seem to be three inches across.

Adam watched Drake's gloved hands, fascinated as always by the absolute control of his long but sturdy fingers. Now Drake was holding the instrument which was the key to the delicate operation—the trephine, a hollow rod, razor sharp at one end. The donor eye was waiting in its sterilized container, a complete eyeball that the Eye Bank enucleator had removed from a corpse only hours earlier, "fresh material" as it was known by those who dealt with transplants every day. The circular blade that Drake would use to remove Karen's defective cornea would, minutes later, be the instrument for excising the cornea from the donor eye so that a perfect match was insured.

Adam had followed every movement of Drake's remarkable hands so many times that the slightest variation had the same effect on him as a police whistle or fire siren. That happened now. Without knowing what had tripped the alarm, Adam tensed, eyes moving anxiously from Drake's masked face to Drake's hand, now poised over the unconscious girl with the trephine blade only a bare inch above the wide-open eye.

The break in routine was so subtle it took Adam a second to identify it. Drake, the most self-confident surgeon he had ever encountered, had hesitated. For a moment so brief no one but Adam could have caught it, Drake had been immobile. As if time had stopped, and all movement suspended . . . . Ridiculous, Adam told himself, nothing had happened. Drake was already proceeding as usual, gently placing the blade against the eye so that it encircled the cornea.

This was the first cut, barely entering the cornea, for it was meant only to outline the area to be removed. Later the trephine would go deeper, actually penetrating the eye. Adam chided himself for his unreasonable flicker of panic. Just because the great man hesitated, for God's sake. Drake's hands didn't slip . . . . Adam stole a look at the wall clock. Three minutes for this first shallow cut. Drake had been at work for only five minutes. Fifty-five minutes to go.

Now Drake was dyeing the circular cut to make it more visible. He tore open a small envelope, carefully removed a piece of paper that was half-plain, half-impregnated with fluorescein. Holding it by the plain end, he dipped the treated end into sterile water and let the resulting fluid drop into Karen's open eye. Now the incision was colored green and much easier to see during the critical moments ahead. Two more minutes had past.

Drake was inserting threads inside the green dyed circle, two tiny sutures that would later help him lift off the bad cornea. Another two minutes for this delicate stitching. 8:19 by the clock. Drake had started at 8:10. Fifty-one minutes to go, and in the next five minutes, Drake would perform the most dangerous phase of the operation—the second cut with the trephine. But this time the razor edge of the blade would penetrate the protective cornea and enter the chamber behind it. You're going to be all right. Karen, Adam promised her silently, and had to suppress a crazy impulse to reach out and hold her hand.

Drake was applying the trephine to the previous shallow incision. He began to rotate it slowly, eyes fixed on the measuring device that told him how deeply the blade was penetrating, steady and cool though an error of only two-hundredths of an inch could mean a blind left eye for the rest of the girl's life. When the blade had cut through two-thirds of the skin-deep corneal thickness, he adjusted the angle so that the trephine sloped ever so slightly and then he continued his rotation. He stopped and very gently withdrew the blade.

A tiny drop of transparent fluid formed at one point in the perimeter of the incision. Drake exchanged the trephine for a pair of scissors with curved blades and dull points. By tilting the trephine as it cut around the cornea, he had bevelled the edge of the incision, a technique that insured a snug fit when the new cornea was put in place. The bevelling had left an uncut spot at the bottom. Now one hand would use the scissors to snip that last miniscule bit of membrane. The other hand, with the aid of forceps, would simultaneously give a gentle pull on the sutures he had stitched on the inside of the circle. It would be done in a fraction of a second, one short potentially fatal moment, when everything rested on Drake's unfaltering hands and cool head.

Instinctively Adam's gaze moved from

Drake's hands to his face, seeking reassurance. The surgeon's expression was hidden by the white gauze mask. Since his eyes were only an inch from the microscope's dual eye piece, it was impossible to read them for a sign of his true state of mind. Adam tensed as the forceps and scissors hovered above the vulnerable eye. They touched the eye. The movement of Drake's fingers was almost imperceptible as he pressed the scissor handles and pulled upwards on the hair-like suture.

Adam exhaled deeply. Drake had met the critical moment with his usual absolute control. Not that the operation was complete. For the next three or four minutes, Drake would be repeating the process of cutting and removing a cornea, but this time he would be cutting into the donor eye, a lonely, bodiless eye in a little styrofoam box, now looking up unblinkingly from its bed of wet cotton. It was relatively easy to excise a cornea when it didn't matter if the blade penetrated too deeply and injured the structures behind it.

Drake would then place this normal "window" of the eye in the tiny hole from which he had just removed the defective cornea and stitch it into place. Twenty to twenty-five minutes for that. Then Adam would drop in some antiseptic ointment, remove the lid clamps, close the eyelids, bandage both eyes, and the operation would be complete. In comparison with what Drake had just done, procedure from now on was nothing about which to get tense. A feeling of relief hit Adam like a narcotic high. The thought occurred to him that Drake was a better surgeon than he was because Drake wasn't quite human. Then he took a closer look at the surgeon's masked face. His forehead was exposed, and it was covered with beads of sweat. Dr. Franklin Drake was human after all.

Five

"It's a landmark day," Adam Stewart's low and beautifully modulated voice announced on the sixth morning after the operation. "I'm going to uncover both eyes. Then I'll cover the operated eye but leave the right eye uncovered."

Karen sank back instinctively in the hospital bed as the doctor's gentle fingers removed the metal eye shield and the bandages. For several seconds after all the covering was gone her body was rigid, her eyelids squeezed shut.

Dr. Stewart's voice, with a touch of amusement, said, "Come on now, Karen. Relax. Remember, I've examined the operated eye before, and I can assure you that the healing process has been proceeding on schedule."

He had indeed uncovered her "new" eye before. In fact, he had done this every day, starting a few hours after the operation when she was still groggy from the anesthetic. But each examination had been accomplished very quickly. She had seen nothing more than a blond head, a tanned face, and a strange pair of magnifying spectacles, before new medication had blurred her vision and fresh bandages once again covered her eyes. Today was to be different.

"Karen," he said quietly. "Open your eyes."

Her lids lifted slowly. Her eyes darted about the room. Everything was in focus—everything was crystal clear! For a long time she said nothing. It was as though the oppressive fog that had enveloped her for so long had suddenly dispersed.

Karen wanted to jump from the bed and dance around the room. But there would be time for that later. Now she had to be content to lie quietly, to let the healing process run its course.

Once again she looked around the room, her eyes resting on every object they encountered. Then she looked up, directly into the doctor's face. Straight nose, strong chin, a somewhat crooked grin. His eyes were a brighter blue than she had imagined. She knew she was staring, but somehow that seemed to be all right.

"Well," she said at last, smiling up at him. "You look almost as nice as you sound."

He laughed. "Thank you. That is, thank you, if you *like* the way I sound."

"I do."

The blue eyes were very blue, and very intent. "Well then, thank you again." He extended his hands. "Hold on. I'm going to pull you up."

When Karen was sitting up with two pillows supporting her back, he walked to the foot of the bed, rested both hands on the footboard and studied her face as if he was analyzing a particularly interesting specimen under a microscope. "It's a day to remember, isn't it? Seeing things clearly. For the first time in years, right?"

"For the first time ever. Nothing ever had sharp outlines. Nothing was as clear as it is now, even when I was a child. And bright colors and bright light hurt my eyes so that I had to look away."

"Then you won't forget this day."

Out loud she had replied. "I don't think so." But silently, in the secret place of her unspoken thoughts, she had whispered—I'll always remember the day I really saw Adam Stewart for the first time.

A solemn group of mourners huddled together around an open grave, chilled by a wintry wind and pelting rain. Dickie Brewster had few friends who suffered any real sense of loss at his death, and only half of those few who had attended the chapel service were hardy enough—or felt sufficient obligation to the other members of the Brewster family—to proceed from there to this bleak and windswept hilltop in Heatherfield Cemetery. With bowed heads they listened to the minister's prayers for eternal life, while rain drummed on their umbrellas, dripped from their raincoats and formed puddles around their rain-soaked feet.

In the chapel, they had stood out as individuals Martha could recognize and Henry Garner could name. But this shivering cluster of human beings, hidden by layers of raingear and completely roofed over by umbrellas, was made up of faceless and anonymous non-persons. Only one attracted Martha's attention, though she didn't know why. Perhaps because the figure was standing a little apart from the others, as if her—(or his) it was impossible to say which—as if grief was an emotion this lonely person could not share. Without even knowing for sure whether it was a man or a woman. Martha had a feeling, groundless but distinct, that he or she had not been inside the chapel.

The farewell rite was over. The minister slipped his prayerbook into the pocket of his raincoat. As if in slow motion, the silent chorus of mourners glided away across the rain-soaked grass. Martha gazed for the last time at her brother's casket, thinking with a curious detachment that the floral wreaths were especially pretty, glistening with rain. When she looked up, she noticed that the stranger who had stood a little apart from everyone else at the graveside was leaving in the same way—separate, and alone. She touched Garner's arm, and said "Who is that, Henry?"

Garner's eyeglasses were fogged. He took them off and squinted at the retreating figures. "Which one?"

"Walking alone, several steps behind the others."

Garner shook his head. "I can't even tell if it's a man or a woman from this distance. Why do you ask?"

"Just curious." She shivered and tightened her grip on his arm. "I'm ready to go now."

As they walked arm in arm away from the deserted grave, Martha's mind had already gone on to other things.

The man waited until everyone had gone before he returned to the grave. A grounds-keeper in work clothes and a black rubber poncho was already filling it in, but the picture of Dickie's casket being lowered in the cold, wet earth still kept flashing through the man's mind. Dickie had always hated the cold. On that rare day when the temperature had gone nearly to freezing, he had threatened to move to Los Angeles. God, oh God! He wouldn't be going there now.

The man's reverie was interrupted by the sound of muted voices. He turned quickly and saw a small band of mourners crossing the rain-soaked lawn on their way to another grave. Hurriedly, he pulled a wilted blue hyacinth from his raincoat pocket, fondled it, and then threw it on top of the freshly filled grave. The grounds-keeper looked up, blinked at him with raindrops dripping from his eyelashes and nose, and went back to his work. With his own face shrouded by his hooded raincoat, the man hurried away.

Six

A thousand dots of silvery light floated above her in a glacial mist. Then the fragments of light slowly moved toward one another, relentlessly forming a gleaming shaft—slender, pointed, coming ever closer . . . . She must escape! She must run. But flight was impossible—she was strapped down. As she strained against her bonds they grew tighter, stronger . . . . The mist cleared and the horror was poised above her, its deadly image now sharp in every detail. It was a hypodermic needle, its wicked point only inches above the body she knew was her own but which she had lost all power to move. Strong blunt fingers gripped the needle, fingers of pale flesh for which there was no hand, no arm. The needle hovered, and then suddenly plunged toward her . . . .

Karen's scream of terror erupted from the

deep, black abyss of sleep. Muted at first, it grew louder and more desperate as it propelled her from dark to light until, at the peak, the word, "No!" burst from her throat and she came fully awake.

She lay absolutely still, her good right eye staring up at the bedroom ceiling. She had escaped the nightmare, but the image that had pursued her from one level of consciousness to another was still lurking in the shadows, tensed and ready to spring again. She was trembling uncontrollably. The blood vessels in her neck seemed ready to burst with the pressure of her thudding pulse. But she was awake, *and she must stay awake*. It was the only way the dream's evil presence could be held at bay.

She turned onto her side, raised herself carefully on one elbow, rested a few seconds and then slowly brought herself up to a sitting position. As gentle as the hands of a healer, her fingertips explored the bandage over her left eye and the adhesive strips that taped it to her cheek and forehead. The bandage was still in place, but in her agitated flight from sleep the adhesive strips had loosened.

Karen reached for the bedside lamp and pressed the switch. The room filled with light, dispersing the shadows, routing the spectral dream. But something of the terror lingered, like an odor she could neither identify nor forget. She got out of bed, drew on a blue flannel robe and slipped her feet into woolly scuffs. Robe and slippers were familiar and comforting.

Somewhat unsteadily she made her way from the bedroom to the kitchen. What she needed now was a glass of hot milk. It had been her mother's prescription for sleeplessness and all of the lurking terrors of the night and it, too, seemed familiar and comforting.

Carrying the hot glass wrapped in a linen napkin, Karen walked into the living room and sat down by a picture window overlooking the lake. Most of the other houseboats in the Portage Bay community were dark, but a few residents spurned the well-regulated life, and light from their windows cast rippling reflections across the dark water. As she sipped, Karen felt gratitude for the healing power of the familiar scene, however faintly perceived with the blurred vision of her good eye. She was in her own home, in her own little floating cottage, in her own living room, with her old-fashioned easel and her aquamarine sofa and all her treasured possessions surrounding her like so many security blankets. Why was she still trembling?

She drained the last drop of milk and carried the glass to the kitchen, rinsed it and set it upside down on the drainboard. In this brightly illuminated center of her normal day-to-day routine, the nightmare receded even farther. The butter-yellow walls, the geraniums in orange and yellow pots on the windowsill, the aged black and chromium wood stove—these were real, not some imagined and rapidly fading dream image. With a grim effort she tried to recapture the frightful dream, to test its power against the pervading cheerfulness of the little yellow room. Nothing remained of the vision except a blurred impression of an enveloping fog, strong fingers, something metallic . . . with a deep sigh of relief, she turned out the kitchen light and walked back to the bedroom.

On the way to bed, her reflection was caught by the big Victorian mirror over the bureau. She paused, searching the face of the mirrored Karen for some remnant of the nightmare's terror. She saw a small, delicately sculptured face with a short, straight nose and slightly rounded chin. Her long hair, as red-brown as freshly cut cedar except for the streaks bleached by the sun, covered her shoulders like a cape. The Karen image smiled reassuringly, as if to say, "See? *I'm* okay, so *you're* okay. Back to bed, Karen girl, for a good night's sleep."

Karen took off her robe and slippers and sat down on the edge of her bed, suddenly reluctant to go back to sleep. Like a child trying to postpone the inevitable moment when mother leaves the darkened room and closes the door behind her, she went through the litany of Dr. Stewart's "Don'ts" for post-operative recovery from eye surgery. Don't bend from the waist to pick up objects on the floor. Don't cough or sneeze. Don't ride public vehicles such as buses; they often stop suddenly and could give a dangerous jolt. Avoid crowds, avoid lifting heavy or large objects, avoid slippery area rugs, overhanging lamps and lampshades. *Never* go into a dark closet, or walk along a dimly lighted hall or alley. The recollection of Adam Stewart's steady, calm voice was reassuring.

As Karen ran through the litany, she removed the perforated metal cone worn over the bandage for protection and carefully peeled the bandage from her eye, preparatory to applying fresh adhesive strips. She reached for the switch on the bedside lamp. The room was illuminated by the glow of the lamp—and with a suddenness that made her mouth fall open in a soundless scream of anguish, the awful dream-image sprang into life.

She was looking at a real lamp, a real bureau, a real door into the hall—but she was seeing, like a transparency superimposed on these familiar objects, the hypodermic needle of her dream. But this was no dream! She watched, paralyzed. Her heart pounded and her throat ached with its futile effort to cry out as, once again, she saw with awful clarity the needle slowly, slowly descending. . . .

The image was more terrifying in the lighted room than it had been in her dream, because now she could not escape it by coming awake. It was as real as the lamp on the table or the mirror on the wall. And hidden in the billowing mist behind the image were shapes and meanings as menacing as the glittering shard of metal poised above her.

Her stricken throat at last released a scream as Karen leaped away from the bed, ran into the hall and slammed the bedroom door behind her. Shivering, she raced from hall to kitchen to living room, turning on all the lights. Her head throbbed. Though her body felt cold to the bone, her forehead was hot and dry. She had fled the bedroom without her robe or slippers, but the thought of going back into that room made her shudder. From the closet in the hall she pulled three coats off their hangers. She wrapped herself in one of them, lay down on the sofa and covered herself with the others. There she huddled, wakeful and shivering. The image would fade . . . eventually she would fall asleep.

But sleep eluded her. By daybreak every nerve ending felt raw. She yearned for the sound of a human voice, something to distract her from the image that had been so vague and yet so threatening. Steeling herself, she rushed into the bedroom, snatched up the clothes from the Victorian rocker and ran back to the living room.

She dressed quickly, the urgency of her need for company growing as her fingers fumbled with the buttons and snaps. She had forgotten her shoes. No matter. She couldn't go back to the bedroom, not right now.

Barefoot, she stepped out on the deck. For a moment the beauty of dawn on Lake Washington reduced the terror of the night to a childish and only dimly remembered bad dream. But the reality of that terror rushed back. Shivering, she threw an anguished look at Jennie's houseboat.

To her enormous relief, the kitchen light was on. Jennie always awakened at dawn. She often bragged that, needing only a few hours sleep, she enjoyed two days of life to everyone else's one. Doug Cooper might be with her. As a police detective, he frequently kept hours as bizarre as Jennie's. If he was in the houseboat now, neither he nor Jennie would be the least annoyed by her charging in.

So Karen beat her usual cadence on Jennie's door and moments later was sipping strong black tea at the kitchen table while Jennie and

Doug, both in bathrobes, exchanged glances and let the minutes tick by in silence.

Doug spoke first. "You're looking a little peaked, and you don't usually rise with the morning sun. None of my damned business, of course, but let's have it. What's wrong?"

Slowly, as if every word was born in pain, Karen began to describe how she had been awakened and what she had seen. And then the dam burst and the words poured out, tumbling over each other as she tried to make the experience as real and as horrifying to them as it had been to her. When she finished, she saw she had failed.

Doug's rough-hewn kindly face shone with sympathy, but not with belief. "A bad night, huh, kid? A nightmare can scare the bejeezus out of you, but you're back in the real world now. What you need is a foundation for the coming day. Who wouldn't hallucinate on an empty stomach? Bacon, eggs, and toast—that's my prescription."

Jennie's right hand waved dramatically. Her complexion, so pale it seemed transparent under its delicate spattering of freckles, her slightly upturned nose, small mouth and merry green eyes—a face as Celtic as a harp, Doug often said—were the gifts of her unknown Irish parents, but her gestures came from the Greek couple who had adopted her when she was an infant. "I think I may know what happened," Jennie said. "I had some friends who were into LSD. One of them kept tripping long after dropping her last sugar cube. Don't forget—you've been through major surgery and you've been given some heavy drugs. I'll bet you were suffering a hangover from all that damned stuff they gave you—before, during, *and* after your operation. After all, you've only been out of the hospital for a few days."

Karen smiled, for they were both so in character. Doug, who put his most serious thoughts in the form of a joke. Jennie, who could recognize human distress with the sensitivity of a high-powered Geiger counter. But Jennie's solemn explanation said as plainly as Doug's wisecracks that neither believed the vision had been more than a bad dream. Doug set about frying bacon, Jennie whipped up scrambled eggs, and Karen made toast. By the time they had finished breakfast, Karen was beginning to doubt that anything unusual had really occurred after all.

Through her kitchen window, Jennie watched Karen cross the boardwalk between their houseboats, slide back the French door to her own houseboat and disappear inside. Still she stayed at the window, eyes fixed on Karen's door as if at the count of ten a terror-stricken scream would shatter the early morning calm.

Behind her Doug's voice said quietly, "I think you're more worried about her than you need be."

Jennie sighed and said, "I hope you're right."

"Your coffee's getting cold."

She went back to the kitchen table, sat down and took a sip. "Oof!" she said, setting the mug down hard. "It's cold!"

"That," Doug said amiably, "is more or less what I just got through saying."

"I'm worried about her."

"I noticed that. I am, too."

Jennie exclaimed, "But you don't *act* worried. You never do."

"Oh, I worry, Jennie. I worry a lot. I just don't have your flair for the dramatic."

"Go to hell." She reached across the table and gave his hand an impulsive squeeze. "Doug, seriously—do you really think this vision of Karen's was nothing more than a bad dream?"

"Seriously—" Doug shook his head. "No. If it had hit her just once, I'd call it a nightmare. But the same image appeared when she was awake. I don't think the second so-called vision was a dream."

"Then what was it? Look, I've known Karen for two years. She doesn't scare easy. And she's not crazy."

"But what you haven't seen before, Jenny, is Karen recovering from eye surgery. She's brave and she's sane, but she's also extremely sensitive. Look at her paintings. They're exciting because they're a blend of the real and the unreal. At first glance, you think, 'Oh, I've been there before!' but you keep looking and pretty soon you see that she's pulled you over the line into someplace that never can be."

Jennie's fingers tapped the table as if they were wireless keys spelling out her thoughts. "You're saying—alone on a houseboat in the middle of the night, the line between the real and the unreal can get a little blurry. Meaning—Karen's vision was a hallucination."

"Yes, I think it was a hallucination. Maybe caused by the drugs she's been taking. We don't know what she's been given or what she may be taking now. You might have guessed right about the influence of the medication."

"And if it isn't something she's been taking?"

"Believe me, Jennie, then even *I'll* act worried."

Jasper Carter pulled into the carport behind the Westminster and entered the building through the alley door. As an offering at the altar of physical fitness, he ignored the elevator and rapidly climbed up the stairs to his apartment on the fourth floor. His pace slowed as he passed the door to Apartment 4-C. For the past two weeks, Dickie Brewster had been lurking on the fringe of his consciousness, quick to invade his thoughts when some physical reality, such as the unused red Triumph in parking space 4-C or the empty mailbox in the vestibule, forced him to accept the reality of Dickie's death. Now his hand went instinctively to his coat pocket, feeling and identifying the outline of the key ring to which a key to Dickie's apartment was still attached. Perhaps he should have surrendered it to the police or to that sister of Dickie's, Martha whatshername. But he hadn't, not so much because of the implications as from a deep unwillingness to have it forcibly taken from him.

Jasper continued down the hall to his own apartment, pulled out his key ring, and stopped abruptly in the process of fitting the key into the lock. Damn it all, had sister Martha taken the trouble to water Dickie's plants? Jasper knew how fond Dickie had been of them, more genuinely caring of the plants, Jasper had often reflected, than he ever was of the expensive objects he so skillfully extracted from his friends. From his lovers, goddamn it. But had one of them ever been rewarded with the unaffected delight that glowed in Dickie's eyes when he saw the rare species of South African amaryllis Jasper had given him as a birthday present?

Jasper withdrew the key and walked back to the adjoining apartment. It was hardly breaking and entering, he thought, since Dickie himself had given him the key. He let himself in, closed the door softly, and for several minutes stood perfectly still. He had more reason to hate these perfectly appointed rooms than he did to love them, but torn as he was by such ambivalence he still wanted to remember them.

His gaze moved slowly from the black and red lacquered chest to the delicately carved teak screen, and on from object to object until it settled on the display of exotic house plants in the east window. They, more than anything else in the room, evoked Dickie's presence.

He hurried to the window and pressed the soil of each pot with his forefinger to test for dampness. Not the smallest crumb of dirt stuck to his finger. As he had thought. Sister Martha certainly had ignored the plants. Other things on her mind, he thought drily as he noticed that all the drawers in Dickie's desk stood open. Unlike her brother, sister wasn't neat, for the contents of the drawers had obviously been turned inside-out in haste. She apparently hadn't bothered to restore order when the search for Dickie's will or savings passbook—whatever it was she was looking for—was over. Jasper smiled, thinking how furious Dickie would have been at anyone making such a mess in his apartment.

In the kitchen, Dickie's brass watering pot with the long, slender spout was in its accustomed place beside the sink. In fact, everything in both kitchen and living room was just where it should be, except for the ravaged desk drawers. He filled the pot from the cold tap, added just enough hot water to achieve room temperature, and decided to start with the plants in the bedroom.

He paused at the bedroom door, vaguely aware that something in the scene was unexpected. Something had intruded ever so faintly. Like a whisper, a stealthy movement, warm breath . . . Breathing! It was the sound of breathing! He wheeled around and ran for the door.

The blow descended like a hammer. He grunted, took one or two stumbling steps, and fell forward, unconscious. The watering pot lay on its side, spilling its contents. The damp pool of water, soaking into Dickie's gold and blue Chinese rug, was as dark as blood.

He left the Westminster by the back stairs as he had often done after a date with Dickie. To arrive and retreat in stealth, his mind reeling with guilt and self-disgust—this had been his shameful pattern.

At the service entrance he paused to dry his upper lip and forehead with a handkerchief. His right hand darted into his inside coat pocket, seeking reassurance that the slim packet of letters he had taken from Dickie's desk was still there. It was. Mission accomplished, in spite of the intrusion of that young man from the next apartment.

God, how could he have been so naive as to write those letters! Like a lovesick adolescent.

Just how deadly the ammunition was he had put into Dickie's hands was clear from the first day they had quarreled. Over what? How ironic! Over good neighbor Jasper. Jasper Carter. "Jazz," as Dickie called him, when for no particular reason he revealed that "Jazz," too, had a key to the apartment. The scene was as vivid as a bleeding wound. Dickie's eyes, wide with pretended innocence, Dickie's voice cooing, "Dear Leander! He waters my house plants for me. You don't have to worry about old Jazz. He's never seen you, he doesn't know who you are. But you've seen him, remember? I pointed him out from the window. . . . But you're jealous." He had laughed quietly. "Yes, I see it in your letters. Such beautiful letters. Do you realize you're a poet?"

"You keep my letters?" he had asked, for the first time glimpsing the danger he should have been wise enough to anticipate.

Dickie's mouth had curved into the smile that seemed provocative at first, but that he had gradually come to recognize as deeply malicious. "Of course! I like to re-read them. I love them. They're so . . . expressive."

"Give them to me. You don't really want them."

"Oh, I do. I do! They're full of memories. I wouldn't think of giving them up."

Letters! When Dickie was alive they would have been enough to ruin him. With Dickie dead, they could have been his death sentence. Until he had realized that, he had been sure he would never again enter the Westminster. He would never have believed he could go back inside Dickie's apartment. God, he would never have believed he could kill! But now he knew more about himself. He knew that he would be able to do whatever he had to do.

Seven

There shouldn't have been anything terrifying about the office of Dr. Herman Markey, D.D.S. Dr. Markey had done Karen's dental work since her first check-up as a young girl. He was short, plump, bald, and smiling, as comfortable and familiar as the fading cretonne slipcovers in his waiting room. With hands that smelled of pine soap he adjusted her bib, tilted her chair, and directed a beam of light into her open mouth, all the while chatting about her eye surgery.

"One of Franklin Drake's jobs, was it? Fine, fine. You couldn't have gone to a better man. Remarkable surgeon. Wider, please."

Karen murmured an assenting "Mmmm . . ." She was in no position to reply that she had never actually talked to Dr. Drake and had seen nothing more of him than two intent, dark eyes above a surgical mask, briefly glimpsed before the anesthetic took hold.

"We don't usually work on someone so soon after that kind of operation," the dentist continued, probing the crevice between two lower left molars. "But a toothache's a toothache, right?"

"Mmmm . . ." Indeed it had been, and too severe to be ignored, even in the opinion of Dr. Stewart.

"Well now, Karen. You've got quite a hole in this second molar. We'll have to fix it up. But no point in hurting you," he chuckled. "Like I tell little kids when I have to give them a shot, a little ouch is better than a big ouch. Right? Did I ever say that to you?"

"Mmmm . . ." That and the rest of Dr. Markey's homely repertoire was as much a part of the scene as the cretonne slipcovers. Karen smiled inwardly at the big-ouch-little-ouch epigram which inevitably preceded a shot of Novocaine. Surely, after all these years, the kindly Dr. Markey should remember that the pain-killing shot had never bothered her. And yet, she noted with amusement, he was turning his back while he prepared it, just as he always had, shielding his patient from the sight of a hypodermic needle. She felt like reassuring him and decided against it. He was being thoughtful. To tell him it wasn't necessary might suggest that his kindness was a little foolish.

He turned around. His pink-cheeked face was smiling. He moved toward her, bent over her and, still smiling, slowly raised his hand. But suddenly it was no longer *his* hand. Instead it was those same strong, cruel fingers of her nightmare, and grasping a hypodermic syringe, descending toward her. The whole room went black. The smiling face vanished into a choking fog. The only light was the gleaming point of the needle coming near, hovering over her, moving down. Karen screamed. From far away the sound echoed as if from the end of a long, dark tunnel, a shrill and distant cry of terror.

Striking out blindly, her bare arm caught the dentist off balance. He stumbled against the chair. She felt the sting of the needle as it grazed her arm. Blind to everything but the pursuing vision, she leapt out of the chair, ran through the reception room and out into the corridor.

The elevators were at the far end. Sobbing, she raced down the hall. Frantically pressing the Down button, she looked back to see Dr. Markey burst through the open office door, the needle still in his hand, calling, "Karen! Come back! Karen—"

Another terrified scream burst from her throat. She abandoned the elevator and bolted through the Exit door. With the white bib still tied around her neck, she fled down three flights of stairs and out onto the crowded sidewalk of Fourth Avenue.

She heard protesting voices, saw curious, disembodied faces and staring eyes as she lunged through knots of pedestrians. She ran, tripped and nearly fell, caught herself, and ran on without any sense of direction, stumbling, falling, struggling to her feet, battering resistant bodies, slamming against the sides of buildings.

At the crowded intersection of Fourth and

Pike, she saw but did not comprehend the meaning of the red light overhead. At the curb a mass of people blocked her escape. Pushing wildly with both arms, she forced her way through the human barrier, barely missing the rear fender of one car, catapulting herself directly into the path of another.

A whistle shrilled. A strong hand dropped onto her shoulder. An arm encircled her and lifted her off the ground. She was too exhausted to struggle, too winded to cry out. She closed her eyes and wept.

She was being carried, then lowered carefully until her feet were firmly planted on the cement sidewalk and her back was braced by the cold stone wall of an office building. Someone's hands had a firm grip on her elbows, both supporting and restraining her. She opened her eyes, and looked up into the worried face of a Seattle police officer.

"Lady," he said gently, "you're going to get yourself killed. What's the trouble? Where do you want to go?"

She tried to speak, but couldn't. With tears rolling down her cheeks she tried again, and still the words died in her throat.

"Take it easy," he said. "Take it easy . . ."

She nodded. The third time she tried she managed to get out the name, address, and telephone number of Dr. Adam Stewart.

Adam Stewart looked into the pale, tear-streaked face of the woman on the other side of his desk and was struck by her beauty just as he had been the first time she came to his office. Her large, thickly lashed gray-blue eyes had first impressed him, which he supposed was natural—eyes were his business. But now he also noted how expressive her mouth was. And that her short straight nose and delicately molded chin gave her a classic profile. Each time he had seen her since that first visit and examination, something had been added to that initial appreciation of her beauty.

But it went farther than that. Her responses were quick, her bursts of laughter uninhibited; she had that rare poise—or was it serenity?—that enabled her to sit through a long silence without averting her eyes, twirling her rings or reaching for a cigarette. Adam hadn't had such an interesting patient in a long time. Quiet, thoughtful, introspective—Karen Thorndyke was all of those.

Why then, had she gone charging down one of Seattle's busiest streets, long hair streaming behind her like a jet vapor trail, dental bib flapping? My God, Adam thought, post-operative trauma? Sure. That was obvious. But something didn't fit. It wasn't like the woman who had just endured his careful examination of her eye in silence and was now waiting patiently for his professional opinion.

"No damage done, Karen. Your eye is fine."

Her posture, ramrod straight while she was waiting for him to speak, relaxed a little and she gave him a tremulous smile. But the eyes were still haunted.

"The luck of the Thorndykes," she said. "Which is more than I deserve."

Adam shrugged. "Let's not bother with the

mea culpas. Let's just say that the gods smiled down on you today and kept you from ruining one of Dr. Drake's star performances. But don't try a stunt like that again. The gods might be out to lunch." He paused. "I've seen post-operative trauma take many different forms—I warned you, remember, that you might experience some sort of depression or anxiety after the operation." He grinned. "But you've come up with something new. And no harm done, thank the Lord."

"You're sure?"

There was tension in her voice and in the direct unblinking appeal of her eyes. "Karen, your eye is fine. What makes you think there's something wrong?"

"Because it . . ." her voice broke off.

"Take your time. When you're ready to talk I'll be here."

She drew in a deep breath, exhaled slowly and nodded. Seconds passed as he watched her struggle for self-control. At last she looked at him directly. "This isn't the first time I've seen the image."

"Tell me about it."

Adam listened attentively, nodding from time to time as she described, in broken phrases, the image that had been haunting her ever since her operation. A strong hand, the white fingers and a needle. The point of a needle shooting off fragments of light as blinding as if she were trying to look directly into the sun.

"What you're describing is a recurrent nightmare, right?" Adam asked.

Karen shook her head so violently that Adam hurried to her side and restrained her with both hands. "No sudden or violent movements," he said urgently. "Rule three, remember?"

For several minutes he kept her head still with his hands pressed against her cheeks, conscious of her trembling and of the rapid pulse beat against his thumbs. Finally, he released her and sat on the edge of the desk. One leg swinging casually, he studied her upturned face. Until now he had pegged her as a person not easily frightened, but there was fear in her wide eyes. "Look. At the risk of sounding like a cracked record, I've got to say again that however upsetting this may be, it won't last. If you can trust my opinion, you can accept that as fact."

"But I *can't* accept what you're saying!" Hands gripping the arms of her chair, Karen leaned forward and cried, "Dr. Stewart, I . . . I think the vision has something to do with my new eye."

Adam frowned as he considered the disturbing implications of what she had just said.

"My new eye . . ." she paused, swallowed with difficulty, and ended her sentence in a whisper, "I think my new eye can see something that doesn't exist. I've been trying to understand it. I know there's no rational explanation—but I think it sees something the donor saw, something important to him."

Groping for a way to break the tension, Adam said lightly, "There *is* a superstition, a very old superstition, that says the eye retains a picture of the last thing it saw before death. Years ago the notion was given so much credibility that some of the murderers listed in the records of Scotland Yard were careful to shoot out their victim's eyes, for fear the eyes would reveal their identity. Of course, there's no scientific basis for such an absurd idea."

Adam saw too late that instead of relieving her of her fear, he had intensified it. Murderer, victim . . . *he* had spoken the words, not Karen. Why in hell had he brought it up at all?

But instead of reacting hysterically, Karen was nodding, as if he had just clarified a perplexing issue. "That's it," she said quietly. "That's the reason I'm frightened by the image. Someone in Seattle was murdered the night before my operation. This," her fingers rested gently on the lid of her left eye, "this must be the victim's eye. It's trying to show me something about the murder."

"For God's sake!" Adam stood up abruptly and went back to his chair. "Look, there's absolutely *no way* an image can be imprinted on the eye, least of all on the cornea. And the only part of your eye taken from the donor is the cornea. The cornea is simply a bit of transparent tissue, it doesn't *see* by itself. It's nothing more than a windowpane, a protection for the delicate photographic mechanism that lies *behind* it. It's so impersonal we don't even have to match blood types when we transplant it to someone else."

He opened his desk drawer and took out a pad of prescription blanks, deliberately ending the conversation. "Your neighbor, the woman who's been changing the dressings on your eye. Do you suppose she'd be willing to spend the next couple of nights on your houseboat?"

"Jennie? She's offered to, many times."

"Good. Why don't you ask her to stay with you, tonight at least." He scrawled a few words on a prescription blank, tore it off and handed it to her. "Can you stop in at a pharmacy on your way home?"

"Yes, of course."

"Take two at bedtime. One every four hours during the day."

"Tranquilizers?"

"Mild ones."

She looked down at her hands, which were entwined as if they were comforting each other. "You know, I was hoping you'd find something physically wrong with my eye. Something that would explain the vision and, being physical, something that could be corrected." She looked at him imploringly. "But the eye is fine?"

"Better than fine. It's a beautiful job."

She sighed. "All right, Dr. Stewart. I'll go home and take my pills."

"And call your neighbor."

She smiled. "And call Jennie."

There was a moment of silence, and then they both rose and crossed the office together. At the door Adam said, "I'd like you to call me if you experience another . . ." he paused then continued "another traumatic nightmare."

Without a word she opened the door, gave him a reflective smile, and stepped into the reception room. She had disappeared through the outer door when Adam became aware that Franklin Drake was standing just outside the entrance to his own office. He also had been watching Karen.

As Adam approached his colleague, the older man said, "Who was that?"

Adam couldn't suppress a smile. "One of your patients, Frank."

Dr. Drake didn't seem disconcerted by failing to recognize someone whose eyesight, maybe even whose life, had been in his hands. "When I see a girl as beautiful as that one, I wish I could remember all my patients. But I never do." He shrugged. With a touch of bitterness, speaking more to himself than to Adam, he said, "Perhaps it's just as well. I can't imagine what life with Priscilla would be like if I gave her any real basis for her jealousy."

Adam put his hand on Drake's shoulder. "If you have a minute, I'll give you something else to think about, Frank," and as they returned to Drake's office he described the bizarre trauma of Karen Thorndyke's "visions."

Franklin Drake had been far more concerned at not recognizing Karen Thorndyke than he had revealed to Adam, for the incident laid bare the unsatisfactory direction his life had taken. Once he had had warm relationships with all his patients, but no longer. There was no time to respond to them as individuals. They had no personalities—only eyes.

He could remember an earlier time, almost twenty years before, when he first went into practice, full of ideals both for his private and professional lives. Franklin Drake—master surgeon, devoted husband, adoring father.

Where had it gone sour? Priscilla's inability to bear children had undoubtedly been the root cause. He could understand her disappointment. In fact he had shared it, and for a long time sympathized with her. But their mutual loss had separated them rather than drawn them together. While he had filled the void with surgery, and with tennis, chess matches, and civic projects, Priscilla had channeled herself into an ever narrower course, living only for him and through him. The more she depended on him, the more possessive she became, the more he withdrew from her. Bitter and lonely, she had interpreted the growing distance between them as proof that he was involved with other women.

At one point her obsessions had brought her to the edge of psychosis. Because she was still rational enough to feel miserable, she had agreed to voluntary commitment in a private sanitarium. After six months, the doctors sent her home. Only there, they said, could she prove she could be a reasonable and reasonably happy person. With his help, of course, as well as weekly sessions with a psychiatrist.

Three months later, Priscilla had canceled those weekly appointments, though for several weeks she was able to conceal the fact and had lied elaborately when he would ask how a session had gone. He had often wondered if their marriage would have been saved had he insisted that she continue therapy. But he had not. Out of loyalty? Or out of weakness?

Tonight he was taking her to the opening performance of the Seattle Opera Company, a supper with other patrons to follow. Though she had protested at first, she had finally agreed to go. But from the moment he entered the bedroom to change into evening wear her chilly silence announced more clearly than words that she resented what she called being "trapped" into a promise. As he inserted gold cuff links into the sleeves of an expensive pale blue shirt, Drake felt a flash of envy for Adam Stewart, who was single, gifted, and young, starting out as he himself had done, with all options still open to him.

Priscilla came out of her dressing room, stopped abruptly to look first at her husband and then at her own reflection in the full-length mirror. "How have you kept so young-looking," she said peevishly. "No matter what I wear, you make me feel dowdy. Of course, the male of the species is always more colorful than the female."

He had heard this complaint so often that he responded automatically. "Nonsense, Priscilla. Your outfit is lovely. You're a handsome woman and always have been."

She turned her back to the mirror. "By the way, I'll wager that I've never met half the people who are going to be at the supper," she said bitterly.

"Oh, for God's sake!" He rammed the cuff link into place, closed it, and lowered his voice, now harsh with his effort to control it. "Don't quibble, please. You know perfectly well that we're both always invited to these functions. Whenever you refuse to go, it isn't because you weren't asked. For years I stayed home with you until I decided that if you have the privilege of refusing, I have the right to accept. Damn it, Priscilla, we've run through this dialogue so often I could recite both parts of it without missing a cue. As I said, I like your gown. The color is especially becoming."

Priscilla began to reply but held back, biting her lip and thinking, because it's gray. Like my hair. Like the real me. Gray, drab, a colorless blank in a colorful gathering. Would his woman be there? She wouldn't be mousy plain nor wearing gray. Perhaps, just perhaps, she and Franklin would give themselves away this time, and she would learn the identity of her rival.

Jennie knew the minute Doug arrived that something had disturbed him. He usually waved gaily as he walked past her into the kitchen of the houseboat. The homecoming kiss was bestowed when he came back from the refrigerator with a cold bottle of beer in each hand. Tonight was different. He came directly to her, pulled her into his arms and held her in a close, bearlike embrace for several silent minutes before he said, "We've got trouble, Jennie."

Her face was pressing so hard against his breast pocket that her retorting, "Huh! What else is new?" had a muffled sound.

"It's not really *we*. Not exactly. It's Karen. She's had another . . . vision, or psychotic episode or whatever the hell it is."

"Damn!" Jennie murmured. "Damn, damn, goddamn!" She broke away from him and dropped into a chair by the window. "What happened?"

"This afternoon an officer named Erickson came in from his beat and began telling another cop about a girl who was hellbent on running into the middle of traffic on Fifth Avenue. He got her off the street, calmed her down, and called a patrol car to take her to her doctor's office. I wasn't paying much attention until he mentioned the doctor's name. Dr. Stewart. Dr. Adam Stewart."

Doug had quizzed Erickson methodically, and just as carefully relayed to Jennie what he had learned about Karen's vision in the dentist's chair and her bizarre reaction. When he finished, Jennie got up without a word, made a silent trip to the kitchen and came back in a few minutes with two uncapped bottles of beer and a plate of *feta* cheese, spiced Greek olives and rye bread.

"I've got an idea, Doug," Jennie said. "I may not be a psychologist yet, but it seems to me that when people suffer from a deep-rooted fear they can't identify, the recommended therapy is to help them dig down and expose it, right? Like peeling off the layers of an onion, one layer at a time until you get to the core."

Doug nodded in agreement.

"So," Jennie continued, "if we can help Karen see through the fog surrounding her vision, the reason for her reaction to the needle will be dragged into the open and she'll be able to overcome her fear."

Doug helped himself to an olive, his brow furled in concentration: "That's a damn good idea. And you're just the person to help. You've got the most important qualification of all—your closeness to Karen. On top of that, you've got the tool that might be the right one for the job."

Jennie's eyebrows drew together and her eyes narrowed in an expression of skepticism.

"Either I'm smarter than I think I am or you know me better than I do."

"You took a course in hypnotism. You know the technique. Use it."

"Put Karen into a trance?"

"Start by accepting Karen's idea that her new eye does see, as she fears. Her hallucination is visual. She's a visual person, a painter. Okay. What if you put her into a trance, and suggest that she paint a picture of the image. It might take a few inductions, but maybe she'll be able to paint whatever has been lurking in that fog."

"And if she starts to paint the image and freaks out, what do I do?"

"Yell. I'll be in the next room."

Eight

The May night was warm and fragrant and a gentle breeze brushed the dark surface of the lake. At the foot of East Sutherland, the last street lamp cast rays as pale as moonlight into the cul-de-sac where the long wooden float with its twenty satellite houseboats extended out over the water at a right angle to the shore.

Walking arm in arm with Adam, Karen paused at the lake's edge, arrested by an odor so pungent it seemed to reach out of the dark to demand her recognition. "Smell that!" she exclaimed. "Isn't it wonderful!"

Puzzled, Adam said, "Smell what?"

Karen drew the scent into her lungs and released it with a sigh. "Balm of Gilead," she said, disappearing into the shadow and returning with several small, dark leaves. She rubbed one between her fingers and held it under Adam's nose.

"Mmm . . ." he murmured. "So that's balm of Gilead. No wonder the Turks used it to treat cuts and burns."

Karen dropped the leaves and slid her hand back under his arm. "You know, Adam, for an illiterate surgeon—*your* words, not mine—you amaze me."

Adam laughed. "You're still groggy from discovering that I really do love opera."

They walked slowly along the float between the parallel rows of cottages with dark or shaded windows, their footsteps on the bare wood ringing out rhythmically in the surrounding silence. At the door to Karen's houseboat, Adam said, "The Turkish uses for the balm of Gilead are only a small part of my store of irrelevant and uncorrelated information."

"I don't doubt it." Karen spoke softly, aware of the dark windows and sleeping neighbors. "Okay. Go ahead. Amaze me again."

"I also make one hell of an omelet."

Karen slid open the French doors, flipped the wall switch, and drew Adam into the living room. This was the third time they had spent the evening together, but until tonight he had said good-bye at the door and left with nothing more than a friendly handshake. The first time she had liked his restraint and even considered it a compliment. It was a refreshingly genteel contrast to the men she had known, who assumed an unmarried woman living alone in a houseboat would like them to stay for breakfast. After their second date and another sexless parting at the front door, she decided that Adam had developed a firm policy for social contacts with women patients, possibly as a result of a bad experience with one of them. But tonight he was actually inside the house, and by his own initiative—looking much too big for the little room and saying, "Where's the kitchen?" She felt a surge of happiness. She could still feel a certain aloof quality about him, but at least this evening wasn't going to end as abruptly as the others.

She followed him into the kitchen. Among her potted geraniums and copper pans hanging from the ceiling he looked even more like a friendly red-headed giant who had dropped in to meet the folks in Lilliputia. "Do you use an apron?" she asked, feeling absolutely incapable of wiping the smile off her face. "Mask? Gloves? Sutures?"

He shook his head. His blue eyes moved systematically around the lemon-yellow cubicle. Humming, he opened the refrigerator, gave the contents a quick evaluation, and nodded his approval. "Good. And look what I found—a chilled bottle of *Chablis grand cru.* Now if you'll pour two glasses of this excellent wine"—he handed her the bottle—"I'll line up the solid stuff."

In companionable silence, Karen poured the wine while Adam assembled his ingredients—eggs, milk, a green pepper, bacon, cheddar cheese. Grinning, he accepted a glass, and lifted it. "To operas and omelettes, but not necessarily in the order named."

They both sipped, and then he said, "Young

woman, you're too much of a distraction. Please remove yourself from the combat area while the general is doing his thing."

Karen lifted her glass in a salute and walked back to the living room. The French door stood open. She crossed the room with the intention of closing it, but the summer-soft air was too compelling. Such a beautiful night should not be ignored or rejected by a closed door. With the idea of arranging chairs by the picnic table so that they could enjoy their midnight supper outside, Karen walked around the corner to the wide front deck where the view of the lake was unobstructed by other houseboats and they could sip their wine and savor the omelette as detached from the rest of the world as if the houseboat were a ship at sea.

She opened two folding armchairs, set them at opposite sides of her small cedar table and noted that there was probably enough light coming through the picture window, unless she wanted to add a candle or two for atmosphere. And perhaps she would, for the night seemed to have grown darker in the ten or fifteen minutes since she and Adam had walked down the float together. In fact, much darker, as if the purple sky had dropped and dense shadows were pressing in from all sides.

She stood at the outside edge of the deck, fenced in by the series of foot-high planter boxes that had been her concession to a landlord who insisted his tenants weren't safe without some kind of railing.

With a growing sense of unreality, she peered into the dark. It was too dark and it was growing cool. She leaned over the flower boxes, looking down into the water just as the clouds parted and the moon shone through. And there, for the first time, she found light. Somewhere in the depths of the lake, light seemed to be floating upward like a phosphorescent orb rising slowly from the murky bottom. It came nearer, growing steadily brighter, until the watery light was so intense it dazzled her eyes. She tried to close her eyes, to turn away, to call out, but instead she was drawn to it, closer and closer, hypnotized by the horror of the slowly emerging vision.

Yes—there it was again! The shard of light, the wicked point, the deadly needle . . . Her throat constricted by a scream that she couldn't release, Karen struck out at the image. She toppled over the flower box; she was falling. The burning light was enclosing her, drawing her down. She was crying out but there was no sound. Slowly, mercilessly, the dark water closed over her head.

When Karen regained consciousness, she was lying on her bed. Adam's shadowy figure loomed over her, a presence more than a person. Except for a pale streak cast by a light in the hall, the bedroom was dark, so she could not see his face. But she groped for and found his hand. "I saw it again. It came up from the bottom of the lake."

"It's all right, Karen. It's all right." He straightened up and would have withdrawn his hand but she clung desperately to it. With his free hand he switched on the bedside lamp.

"We're both soaking wet," he said, in the reasonable tone of a parent soothing a frightened child. "I have to leave you for a minute but I'll be right back."

Reluctantly she released his hand but her eyes followed him as he went into the bathroom, turned on the light and closed the door. Shivering uncontrollably, she watched that closed door, fear of the image creeping back until the door opened and Adam reappeared. He was stripped except for a bath towel around his hips and he was carrying a second towel.

Karen neither spoke nor resisted as he undressed her and dried her body.

"I'm so cold," she whispered.

"I'm going to do something about that. Just lie quietly." Deftly he removed the damp bedspread and rolled her up inside a cocoon of blankets.

His concern was real, his hands were gentle, but the distance he had always kept between them was still there. He might have been wearing a business suit rather than a bath towel. He might have been in his office rather than in her bedroom. He had been as impersonal about stripping, rubbing and lifting her naked body as he would be examining her eyes.

"God bless synthetics," he said as he collected his dripping clothing from the bathroom and left the bedroom.

Seconds later she heard the muted hum of the clothes dryer in the utility room. The sound released a surge of emotion so strong and so unexpected that her hands tightened into fists. She was feeling much more than reluctance at being left alone after a bad experience. This was desire, a longing for Adam's body as real and physical as pain. She buried her face in her pillow. She had never felt such aching need as that laid bare by the sound from the utility room telling her that Adam was preparing to leave.

At the faint brush of bare feet on carpet, Karen turned over and opened her eyes. Adam was beside the bed, and he was holding two small, stemmed glasses, each nearly filled with a coppery-brown liquid.

"I found the brandy," he said, sitting down on the edge of the bed. "A great antidote for lake water. Here, I'll prop you up." Putting the glasses on the bedstand, he reached across her for the second pillow, pulled her up with one hand and with the other stuffed the pillow firmly behind her back.

He handed her a glass and lifted his own in a toast. "Cheers!"

Karen answered with a nod and a smile, for she knew her voice would betray her if her eyes hadn't. She took the brandy in small eager sips, praying silently that the moment of emotion would pass so that she could sound as cheerfully impersonal as he did.

"Not too fast," he cautioned her.

"Adam," she said urgently. "Adam . . . please put down your glass."

Something changed in his eyes, but he didn't move. Impulsively she took the glass from his hand and put it beside her own on the bedstand. She saw rejection in his face and in the stiffness of his posture, but she had plunged and could not stop her fall. Throwing her arms around his neck, she pulled him down and clung to him as if she were drowning.

He would not make love to her, she knew that, but the abrupt motion with which he broke free shocked and paralyzed her. She stared up at him, heart pounding wildly, as he put both her arms under the covers and tucked the edge of the quilt firmly under her chin. "I'm going to see to it that you eat something before I leave. You rest while I go make that omelet and I'll be back shortly, bearing food."

For several minutes Karen lay perfectly still. Inside its casing of blankets her body throbbed with self-awareness. She felt every inch of skin—the tender patch at the back of her knees, the sweat-damp crevass between her breasts, the trembling ache in her groin. She visualized Adam returning with two plates of food, setting them down and carefully rearranging the blankets so that she could sit up and eat without bringing her body out of hiding. Damn you, she said out loud, with a flash of anger directed more at herself than at him. If my body is to be discreetly hidden, I myself will do the hiding. She threw back the bedclothes. Teeth chattering, she went first to her clothes closet, then to her chest of drawers. When Adam returned with their late supper on a tray, she was thoroughly clothed in pajamas, bathrobe and slippers, sitting up very straight in the chair by the window.

While they ate, Adam talked about the opera they had seen that evening, as if nothing unusual had occurred between their return to the houseboat and the creation of a cheese and bacon omelet. Cheerful, friendly, but aloof—that was the man who had pulled her from the lake when she was struggling with her demon image with such desperation that she had almost drowned. And now he wasn't going to talk about it. But when they had finished eating and he produced two cups of hot coffee laced with rum, she rebelled. "It was the vision again."

"Yes. You told me."

"The same vision. A needle with a gleaming point, coming at me. I can see the fingers holding the needle, but the rest is foggy. Someone is *there*. There's a face. But I can't see it."

He simply nodded.

"I know you're thinking I'm suffering from some sort of delusion. But please. I'm *not* insane." She paused, looking at him searchingly.

He was frowning. Because he was worried? Or because he found the whole subject distasteful? He shook his head. "Look, Karen, your believing in this so-called vision, your insistence that it means something—it bothers me. It bothers me very much."

Looking directly into his eyes, Karen said, "I can't pretend with you. I don't want to pretend, anyway. So, much as you'd like me to do it, I can't just sweetly change the subject and agree that the image of the needle has nothing to do with my new cornea. The truth is . . ."

Her voice broke. She set down her empty cup on the table beside her chair and for several moments studied her hands as if she were organizing an argument—or gathering courage to say something she knew would condemn her. At last she said, "I've been living with this, and I have to face it. This transplanted eye ties me to the person who gave it to me. There *is* a meaning to my vision. It's incomplete. It's vague. I'm absolutely sure there's more to it that I haven't yet been able to bring into focus. I'm equally sure that I *must* find out who the donor was—that would be the first step. The next will be to figure out what sort of—don't shake your head when I say it, please—what sort of message my new eye is trying to pass along to me.

"When you told me about the old superstition—that the eye of a murder victim retains the image of the murderer—that's when I realized that my eye is showing me the murder weapon. So the vision is going to keep right on haunting me until I've seen and understood all of it, until I *see* who the killer was and expose him."

"You'll never be able to find out who the donor was, Karen. Give it up. It's a brick wall. A dead end."

Stubbornly, she pursued him. "But couldn't you get the information from the Eye Bank for me?"

"No one can get that information."

She finally nodded her defeat. "I suppose you're right. But tell me the truth, Adam," she begged, "do *you* think I'm losing my mind?"

The moment of hesitation was barely discernible. Karen told herself she might have imagined it because his voice sounded positive when he said, "Of course not. The operation was more of a shock to you than either of us realized. Your reaction is unusual, and unusually severe, but at this point I'm sure it's run its course. . . . Well, it's high time for me to be on my way and for you to get some sleep." He took her empty cup, leaned down and kissed her lightly on the forehead. "I'll clean up and turn out the lights. You get to bed. And stay home and rest tomorrow. Doctor's orders."

When he left the bedroom, Karen jumped out of her chair and closed the door. From the bedroom she could see the French doors in the living room. Tonight, of all nights, she did not want to watch him leave.

Nine

Karen entered the administrative offices of the Eye Bank feeling a little like a pilgrim whose long journey to the healing shrine was about to end. Despite Adam's warning that it was impossible to discover the identity of an eye donor, Karen had telephoned the Eye Bank as soon as she had awakened. Adam, she decided, was hung up on medical ethics. By his own admission, he had never tried to trace the source of a donated eye. A pleasant female voice had said that Mrs. Wilkins, the director, would be free at two o'clock and would be glad to talk to her about the Eye Bank's history and its procedures.

The receptionist's welcome intensified Karen's feeling that the information she wanted so badly was within her grasp. "Miss Thorndyke? Yes, indeed. We've been expecting you. Would you like to go right in, please?"

Karen followed the smiling girl's gesture toward an open door with the name "Anita Wilkins" painted in modest black letters on the glass panel. Standing beside a large desk was a slender, gray-haired woman wearing an ice-blue blouse and matching wool skirt that fell in folds to the top of her stylish boots. "I'm Mrs. Wilkins," she said, coming forward with her hand extended. Karen grasped it gratefully. The director's clear, intelligent eyes and strong handshake drove out the last lingering fear that she had embarked on a hopeless mission.

"So you're interested in the operation of the Eye Bank," the director said, as she drew up a chair for Karen and returned to her own seat on the other side of the desk. "History and procedures, I think you told my secretary."

"Well, yes." In view of the friendly reception, Karen felt a little ashamed of a subterfuge that had seemed necessary when she telephoned for an appointment. Should she just blurt out her real purpose in coming?

"I can give you copies of some newspaper and magazine articles that will fill you in on the history, which goes back to 1944 when a Dr. Paton helped to organize a kind of clearing house for donated eyes. There are now eye banks in cities all over the country—I'd estimate about a hundred, though I haven't seen any recent figures. So if one bank can't supply a cornea, another bank can often meet the need. But as I said, I'll give you some reading material. I get too enthusiastic when I start talking about eye banks, and I talk too much."

Karen laughed. "Not as far as I'm concerned, believe me. I'm deeply interested." She paused. Perhaps this was the time to ask the all important question. Karen drew a deep breath and decided to plunge. "So eyes are sent from one area to another. And eyes donated to the Seattle bank are shipped to other cities. But in the case of a patient who received a corneal transplant right here in Mathews Memorial Hospital—where would that eye come from?"

The director's eyes rested on her thoughtfully for several seconds before she said, "Have you had a corneal transplant?"

Karen nodded, relieved to be arriving at the central question. "Yes. Yes, I have. About a month ago."

"Dr. Drake?"

"Yes."

"Wonderful. Very few men in the country can equal him. Now tell me, Karen. Your curiosity about the Eye Bank is understandable. I'm delighted that you want to know more. But is there some aspect of the project that's of particular interest to you?"

Karen looked directly into the woman's clear and perceptive eyes. "I want to know my donor's name."

"That's out of the question," the director said quietly.

"But *why?*"

"Even the surgeon doesn't know where the material comes from, and he doesn't ask. It's of no importance."

"But surely you keep records," Karen insisted. "I know you try to match the age of the donor with the age of the recipient. You can't do that if you don't know how old both are. And you must know a lot more than that."

"We do." The director leaned back in her chair. Now her voice was more patient than cordial. "Some donors are patients who die in local hospitals. Others are the victims of violent or unattended deaths, donors whose corneas come to us through the County Medical Examiner's office. In both cases we have records of names, addresses at the time of death, cause of death, and, of course, age. We need all this in order to determine the suitability of the cornea for a transplant operation. As for the identity of the *recipient* . . ." She looked searchingly at Karen and said. "In the case of eyes received from the Medical Examiner, we know the age and sex of the recipient. But as to the *name* of the recipient, or where and when the transplant is performed—no, indeed. We don't know that. It's not important that we do. In fact, we learned a long time ago that it's important that we do *not* have that information."

"But *why?*" Karen exclaimed. Adam's repeated, "Impossible," was sounding in her ears and the frustration it had created in her was flooding back full force. "Anyone who receives a cornea is bound to feel deeply grateful to that person." She fell silent, struggling against a mounting sense of helplessness. "Someone gave *me* a gift. Isn't it natural that I would want to know who that person was?"

"My dear girl . . ." The director sighed. "You may feel so. Perhaps it is. But in my experience —and I've been connected with various eye bank organizations for almost twenty years—the recipient either doesn't think about it at all, or very definitely does *not* want to know. No one likes to reflect on the fact that someone must have died in order to provide material for the transplant."

"Mrs. Wilkins, I *am* thinking about it. I can't help it. So I might as well know who my donor was."

"Even if I knew, I couldn't tell you. Because it's not my decision. It's Eye Bank policy." Her voice was firm, but her eyes were sympathetic. Karen watched those eyes, seeking in them some indication that she might relent. Silence hung between them, while the director waited for Karen to leave without being asked to, and Karen tried desperately to think of an effective appeal. During that wordless hiatus, Karen noticed that the director's eyes moved away from her face, focused on something at the far side of the office, and then came back to her face.

Karen stood up, thanked the director for her patience and turned toward the door. The only object the director's glance could have turned to was a bank of gray metal file cabinets. She shook hands with the director, stopped at the reception desk to pick up the promised Eye Bank literature, and left. She had almost lost hope by the end of her conversation with the director. But during those last few seconds before her retreat from battle, hope was reborn. However desperate her plan, there might be another way to win.

In the hospital cafeteria, Adam and Karen sat down at a corner table with cups of strong black coffee. For the first time since she had startled him by walking into his office in the opthalmology wing, Adam asked what she was doing in Mathews Memorial.

"I went to the Eye Bank. I had a long talk with Mrs. Wilkins."

"Did you. And what was the purpose of that?" He was obviously displeased.

"I asked her to tell me who the donor was."

"That was way out of line, and Mrs. Wilkins is a busy woman." He paused, frowning, and then added, "What did she say?"

"That she has quite a lot of information about the donors, but very little about the recipients. And that there's no way of matching them up. Plus, because of Eye Bank policy . . . well, you know, she repeated what you've told me all along."

Adam murmured a non-committal, "Mmm" and sipped his coffee.

"But there *is* a way." Karen spoke quickly, instinctively trying to get it all out before he could dismiss her idea. "There are file cabinets in the director's office. I'm convinced they contain the Eye Bank records. You told me Dr. Drake performs about a hundred corneal transplants a year. Which means that, on the average, he operates once every three days. The records must contain the name, address and cause of death of the person who donated a cornea on April third—I was called to the hospital the night of the third, remember? The age and sex of the recipient would also be in that file. Don't you see? Who was the donor on April third, whose eye was used April fourth for a transplant to a female, age twenty-six?"

Adam said irritably, "It's not that simple. Drake *averages* one operation every three days, that's true. But he can operate only when fresh material becomes available, and that doesn't happen with such predictable regularity. There have been times that Drake has done three corneal transplants in one day."

Karen grasped his hand. "Adam, listen. *You* know if Dr. Drake did more than one transplant on April fourth."

Adam's answer was a reluctant nod.

"Well? Did he?"

Adam shook his head. "No, he did not."

"There!" Karen paused, choking back her eagerness. Adam could have lied, and didn't. Or else he knew she would be able to check his statement. "I need your help," she said, her voice tense and low. "As an eye surgeon, you would certainly be permitted to look through those files."

"Undoubtedly."

"But you won't. Because of ethics."

Adam hesitated. "That, in part. But not that alone. I don't want to help you pursue this fantasy. I want to exorcise it."

Karen sighed. "Oh damn. All right. You win." She smiled. "Thanks for the coffee anyway. I had to try. . . ." She stood up, slung the strap of her handbag over her shoulder and flipped a renegade lock of copper hair back from her face.

He rose and followed her to the cafeteria's outside door. "I wish I didn't have that damn dinner conference tonight. There's a new spot on Lake Union I . . . well, tomorrow night. Okay?"

She smiled up at him. "Very much 'Okay.'"

"I'll phone you tomorrow."

The glass door closed between them. After a few steps Karen looked back. He was still at the door. She waved cheerfully and proceeded along the sidewalk toward the bus stop. There she stopped, waited a minute or two and then looked back once more. Adam was no longer standing at the door. She walked quickly to the corner, turned right and continued halfway around the block, where a cement ramp led down to a service door into the Mathews Memorial Hospital's basement.

If the man hadn't been looking out the window, he would not have seen her entering the hospital through the basement door. The gods were watching over him. . . . That's what Dickie had said so often, even when the gods voted against him as they did the night Dickie insisted they go to a chic gambling hall some fifteen miles outside the Seattle city limits.

"The gods are watching over me tonight, Leander. I know I'm going to make a killing. Come on, give, dear one. I know you always carry gobs of cash. Your lovely bankroll will make me rich and you richer. More important . . ." his large eyes widened in an expression as deceptively innocent, and as seductive, as the soft curve of his lower lip. "More important, it will make me happy and, sweet Leander, that means I'll be in a mood to make you happy, too."

Once again he had been manipulated. Dickie

had taken all his money, and had lost it all, too. When he refused to ask the house for credit, Dickie became petulant and started a nasty scene. Dickie could be vicious when he was thwarted. It had always surprised him that someone so beautiful could be so evil.

But for once, he hadn't changed his mind. So Dickie had stalked off and attached himself to better prey. He had wanted to run after him, to plead with him, but he hadn't. Even in that offbeat back room, far from the clubs and restaurants patronized by his friends, he couldn't risk drawing attention to himself.

Enough of such maudlin thoughts. Dickie was gone. What was left now was self-preservation, and it appeared that his luck was changing. Like a gift from Olympus, the gods had allowed him to see the girl sneak into the building. They had given him an opportunity to finish this ugly business once and for all.

Ten

Karen had no specific plan, only a stubborn determination to achieve her goal. Now that she was inside the massive block-square structure of Mathews Memorial Hospital, she realized how woefully unprepared she was. Burglary, she reflected wryly, just isn't my line.

Her immediate problem was that she knew nothing about the hospital floor plan, except that the Eye Bank administrative offices were on the sixth floor west, and that her room had been in the east wing of the same floor. As to the uses of the other floors, she was totally ignorant. On her way in to report for the operation at two o'clock in the morning, she had hurried through an emergency entrance, seeing nothing clearly. All she could remember of her departure was Jennie's strong hand under her elbow and a seemingly endless walk through a maze of corridors. But here she was, stealing into the nether regions of a medical center complex so confusing that, according to Jennie, there were street signs wherever two corridors intersected.

Spotting the cement ramp from the street to the hospital basement had been a happy accident. When she hurried past the bus stop she had no scheme other than to circle back and somehow gain entrance without going through the lobby where Adam might see her.

Now she stopped just inside the basement door, noting with relief that she was alone in a concrete passage leading from the unmarked exit into a wide, brightly lighted corridor ahead. For the moment she was safe. Voices, footsteps, the opening or closing of a door would echo in a place like this, giving her plenty of time to slip out the door through which she had entered.

She leaned against the cold cement wall and tried to collect her thoughts. It was probably safe to assume that the Eye Bank offices operated on a conventional nine-to-five schedule. Since they were located in an area quite separate from hospital wards and operating rooms staffed around the clock, they would certainly be vacant between quitting time and, say, eight o'clock the next morning. So, first and foremost, she must avoid the sixth floor until at least 5:30 to allow for any conscientious staff member who might have decided to stay late. It was now five minutes to five. For the next thirty-five minutes, she must remain inconspicuous.

She considered waiting in the lobby by the main entrance. The advantage of the lobby was that it was both large and crowded. There, among the multiple sofas and chairs, gift and flower shops, book and newspaper stands, where no amount of soundproofing would completely subdue the cacophonous blend of ringing telephones, public address system announcements, the breathy swish of revolving doors, and the insistent murmur of a television show no one was watching—there among the decibels and anxious faces she would be nothing more than another visitor. But there was the chance, slight as it might be, that Adam would come through the lobby on his way home, rather than going directly to the basement parking lot.

Perhaps it would be safer to wait in one of the small lounges upstairs. On Sixth East there had been an area where visitors often waited if the patients they had come to see were not ready to receive them. There must be similar sitting rooms on other floors. Yes, she decided. The upper floors were the lesser risk.

Karen drew in a sharp breath. Elevators! She had come within an ace of leaving this temporary hiding place in search of the central elevator system that would take her to one of the upper floors. Her pulse fluttered with the realization of how close she had come to making a serious mistake. Almost everyone in the ten-floor hospital traveled by elevator. To ride one would be as foolhardy as knocking on the door of Adam's office to see if he was still in the building.

She advanced as far as the main corridor and forced herself to walk slowly as she passed closed doors marked with various letters and numerals as indecipherable to her as a foreign code. Boiler rooms, machine rooms, or whatever, no one came in or out before she reached the end of the corridor where a sign in big black letters read STAIRS. She thought she heard footsteps behind her, but when she looked back the corridor was empty. She pushed the heavy metal door, slid through it and closed it carefully so that it wouldn't slam.

A narrow cement stairway rose in front of her, turned sharply back on itself and continued its steep ascent up the dimly lit hollow core of a stairwell that apparently opened onto every floor from the basement to the roof. Karen felt as short of breath as if she had just crossed the finish line in a long, hard race. She paused for several minutes, and then slowly began to climb.

Once again she thought she heard footsteps. But this time she was certain that they were keeping pace with her. When she went fast, so did the pursuing steps. When she slowed down, they slowed, too. Her heart began to pound. The combination of fear and physical exertion seemed about to overwhelm her. She could not risk blacking out. She dared not turn around to see who was behind her. At the same time she was afraid not to. And the footsteps were coming closer.

Suddenly, on the seventh floor landing, the door to the stairwell burst open and a young man in a white coat came tearing out in an obvious hurry to get downstairs. When he noticed Karen, he slackened his pace, gave her a curious but appreciative look, and then continued down, two steps at a time and whistling. His merry tune grew fainter and fainter, and then she heard another heavy stairwell door open and close, and he was gone.

At the eighth floor exit, Karen paused, struggled to regain her composure, listening. She was alone in the stairwell—instinct told her that. Whoever had been climbing the stairs behind her had changed course when the young man in the white coat appeared. Was it her imagination, or had the presence of a boisterous third person kept her pursuer from catching up with her? Or was it all just coincidence?

Karen's mind whirled with questions for which there seemed to be no answers. Suddenly she felt that she would be safer in the hospital corridor than in the stairwell. Cautiously, she opened the door.

There would be other and better times, other safer opportunities. But as the man retreated through the busy hospital corridors he kept thinking—I must make my opportunities. I cannot wait for chance, or for the whim of a divine power.

He had already come to realize that he would do whatever he had to do. Now he saw that he could not wait for the right moment. Time was running out. And she was somewhere in the hospital.

Wide corridors ran to the left and right of the elevators. Karen advanced only a few feet when all her senses came alive with a Proustian remembrance of things past. She had been here before. And walking toward her was a man in a business suit who seemed to belong in this dim and distorted moment of *déjà vu*. He approached briskly, smiled as if he had seen her someplace but couldn't remember where, walked past her and rang for an elevator. When he was gone Karen proceeded cautiously down the hall to the T-intersection where a wide main corridor led off to the left, and there she stopped abruptly, remembering. The operating room. Surgery. Post-operative recovery rooms. Straight ahead of her, not twenty feet away, was the tall figure of Dr. Adam Stewart.

She stiffened. As if in a dream, she tried to turn and run and couldn't move. His back was toward her and he was engrossed in conversation with a young man in a starched white jacket who was looking past Adam, right at her. Did he recognize her? If not, why were his eyes focused so steadily on her face? The nightmare paralysis broke. She turned quickly and fled back to the exit door. Pulse thumping wildly, she mounted the stairs to the ninth floor.

She was alone in the stairwell, at least for the moment. Then, above her, a door opened, a heavy footfall rang out in the hollow stairwell. All her determination to keep her head and think things through was swept aside by a sudden surge of panic. She ran down the stairs, heels clattering, faster and faster, down, down, fleeing the pursuing footsteps until she could go no farther. Gasping for breath, she plunged through the door into the basement, ran down the corridor, turned left, ran on, turned right, ran again. . . .

The man heard the approach of the hospital cart and caught himself just in time. She was up ahead, still running. The staccato rhythm of her heels on the concrete floor echoed the length of the corridor. From another direction the rumble of the cart was growing louder, mingling now with two male voices—hospital attendants, probably, or more likely, since this hall led to an outside loading area, two men from a mortuary on their way to their hearse. In either case, they had come between himself and the fleeing girl.

He turned quickly and ducked back around the corner. Though he was panting from the excitement of coming so close to her, he had enough control of himself to realize that now the risk was too great. As if it were mocking him, the half brick in his pocket pressed against his flesh. His hand closed over it convulsively. Dickie would have scoffed at such amateur bungling, and at his naiveté in thinking that he could crush her skull so that she would appear to have died from falling downstairs. "What late late show have you been watching, dear Leander?" The teasing voice was as clear as if Dickie were standing beside him. Angrily he pulled the brick out of his pocket, dropped it as if it burned his palm, and ran toward the elevator that would deposit him, like any other visitor, in the hospital lobby on the first floor.

Directly in front of Karen, a pair of wide doors stood open, revealing a concrete platform some three or four feet higher than an outside loading area. A hearse was backed up to the platform with its rear doors swinging wide.

Karen stared into the shadowy but empty interior, and for the first time in her headlong flight stopped long enough to listen. Men's voices, the sound of a rolling cart—they were right behind her, trapping her between themselves and the open hearse.

Miraculously, Karen's panic subsided as suddenly as it had overtaken her. She stood perfectly still, calm and clear-headed, as the cart rolled past her bearing a body covered with a sheet. Two men in white jackets lifted the stretcher and slid it into the hearse's open maw. "Leave the damn thing here, Jerry," one of the men said with a brusque gesture at the hospital cart. "We've got another pick-up and I don't feel like doing it on my own time."

The second man slammed and latched the door, both climbed into the front seat, and they were gone.

Slowly, Karen retraced her flight until she found the short passage through which she had originally entered the hospital basement. It was, after all, the safest place to wait, for it was not in the stream of ordinary traffic. What if someone did come by and notice her? Well, she had lost her way trying to find the exit to the parking lot. She looked at her wrist watch. In a few minutes, she would be inside the Eye Bank's administrative office and no one would ever know she had broken into it—if she kept her head.

In one of the smaller conference rooms off the mezzanine of the Olympic Hotel, Adam Stewart and Franklin Drake were sipping Scotch and soda while waiters distributed Dungeness crab cocktails and latecomers hurried to the portable bar to fortify themselves for the meeting about to begin. Their conversation was, as usual, almost entirely shop talk. Once during their four-year association, Drake had had just enough to drink, and just enough pressure from his unhappy marriage, to talk about himself. Adam knew Priscilla Drake as a somewhat austere woman. She was difficult to communicate with because at all functions, social or otherwise, her gaze was directed in such relentless pursuit of her husband's movements that she spoke very little and listened less. Drake had confided that she was possessive, jealous, suspicious to the point of paranoia so severe that at one point in the marriage he had been forced to put her in an institution. He had blamed their childlessness, and the fact that years ago there had, indeed, been someone else. But after that brief moment of confession, Drake had never made more than an occasional allusion to his personal life.

It was even a little unusual for him to refer to a particular patient, except in terms of his or her surgical needs. But he did tonight, with a definite gleam of interest in his eyes. "By the way, Adam. How's that beautiful girl doing?"

Adam knew that he was speaking of Karen. "She's fine. Progressing nicely."

In his own ears, the unqualified conviction of his answer had a false ring. He wondered if Drake had given any thought to what Adam had told him about Karen's visions.

"Well," said Drake, "she certainly looked fine today."

Startled, Adam realized that Drake was still

talking about Karen. Today . . . had Drake seen them in the coffee shop? Nothing wrong with that. But Drake might also have witnessed Karen's visit to the Eye Bank offices. For the first time, it occurred to Adam that the loyal Mrs. Wilkins, always conscientious in her guardianship of Eye Bank policy, might have reported Karen's unusual request. And this thought made him uneasy. "You saw her today?"

Drake finished his Scotch, set the glass down on the bar, and turned to appraise the doctors who were beginning to take their places at the table. "What? Oh, the girl. Yes. She was in the hall when I left this evening."

Drake dismissed the subject with a motion toward the banquet table. "Let's sit down while there are a couple of free chairs. I want to talk to you about the Merchant case."

It was surprisingly easy. Karen simply climbed the stairs from the basement to the sixth floor, walked into the now vacant administrative section of the Eye Bank and straight into the director's office. Clearly, everyone had gone home. The corridor and all the rooms on both sides of the hall were dark.

She groped her way across the outer room, past the secretary-receptionist's desk and through the inner door to the director's private office. There, fading twilight shone through windows so that she didn't have to worry about bumping into furniture, but all the illumination in the world couldn't help her open a locked filing cabinet without a key.

Once more she thought ruefully of how

poorly prepared she was. At least she should have anticipated her need for a flashlight. It was beginning to get dark, and it was obvious that she couldn't turn on lights in an office that was supposed to be closed for the night without attracting attention. As for tools—a fingernail file and a half-dozen hairpins were the only metal objects among the miscellany at the bottom of her handbag.

There were two filing cabinets, both apparently controlled by a lock located above the top drawer. Her fingers were exploring one of the small metal circles when she heard footsteps, distant at first, but steadily approaching along the main hall. She searched the room desperately for a hiding place. There was a narrow door in the wall beside the filing cabinets. She opened it, and in the dim light made out shelves stacked with reams of paper and other clerical supplies. She slipped into the narrow space between the shelves and the door just as someone flipped a switch in the outer office and a shaft of light pierced the gloom of the director's inner sanctum. She closed the door, wincing as her body was jammed between the door and the hard edges of the shelves.

Ears tuned to every movement on the other side of the door, she quickly recognized that the unseen person was a janitor. Wastebaskets were picked up, emptied into a bag that rustled, and noisily set down again. A vacuum cleaner made a fast sweep of the carpet. Footsteps, rustling plastic trash bag, and vacuum with squeaky wheels retreated to the outer office.

More faintly, she heard the same acts repeated. Someone was going through a nightly routine, probably starting with the director's office because it was the last of the series on both sides of the hall. Now she understood that the office door had been left unlocked to speed the janitor's rounds. Ten to one, she thought, the person will lock the door when leaving the office. She prayed that the door would at least open from the inside. When work begins in the next office, it will be safe to come out. But much safer, she decided, to stay right here until the janitor had gone over the whole area and moved on to another wing.

Time seemed to stretch out interminably while she waited in the total blackness of the closet prison, aching with the pressure of the shelves against her rib cage and unable to read her wrist watch.

When at last she dared, Karen stole back through the outer office, cautiously opened the door and peered into the dark corridor. It was silent, vacant, and almost as black as the inside of the storage closet. She tested the doorknob from the outside. The janitor had locked it. She closed it again quickly, and went back to the director's office. Both excited and frightened, Karen tried the top drawer of the director's desk. It opened smoothly. Methodically her fingers explored the interior. She was about to give up when she felt some keys. Two small keys, hanging on a metal ring to which a cardboard identification tag had been tied with a string. Suddenly she felt even more daring than she had when she launched herself on this search by impulsively passing up the bus stop. Risk or no risk, she had to have light.

She flicked on the brass desk lamp. The first object she saw was a stack of cards, fluorescent red in color, imprinted with large black letters: HUMAN EYES. Handle With Care. Repressing a shudder, she picked up the keys that lay next to them. On one, the word "Files" was written in pencil on a little cardboard tag. She decided to leave the light on. If someone noticed that this office was illuminated, it would be someone who knew that the janitor was at work at this time of night. In any case, it was a risk she had to take.

Rapid inspection of the first file cabinet revealed nothing. Halfway through the second, Karen came upon the donor files, clearly marked, arranged once in chronological order and cross-referenced to a second set of index cards catalogued by name. In her excitement her usually acute sense of hearing failed her. If she heard the approaching footsteps, their significance didn't register until it was too late. Suddenly a key was being inserted into a lock, and she heard the faint sound of a door brushing the carpet as it was pushed open.

She tried frantically to get back into the supply closet. A strong hand caught her by the shoulder and pulled her back into the room. Blinking against the light, Karen looked up at the intruder. It was Adam.

"I tried to reach you at home. No answer. I phoned Jennie. She said you were going to have supper with her and she was worried because you hadn't appeared."

Karen looked at him steadily. "I owe her an apology."

"You owe *me* an explanation!"

"Are you sure that's necessary?" Karen pointed to the open drawer. "There. The names of donors. You understand me well enough to have guessed that you'd find me here. Why can't you understand why I have to do this?"

Adam's voice was tense with his effort to keep it under control. "I thought we had settled all this."

Karen shook her head. "*I* didn't say it was settled. I simply gave up trying to talk to you about it. Look . . ." She lifted several files out of the open drawer, carried them to the director's desk and set them down within the circle of light cast by the desk lamp. "*This* is the way to settle the issue. You're here legitimately. You have every right to check through donor files. You match up the date of my operation with the information about the person whose eye was used that day. If I'm wrong—if the donor died of natural causes—okay, just say so. You think I've got some sort of obsession. You're right, absolutely right. I *am* obsessed. But you can help me overcome it. Just read these files, and tell me the truth."

Adam frowned but he went to the desk, sat down and began to go through the chronological listings.

Karen stepped back and waited, as silent as he.

At last he paused, went back to the beginning of an entry and read it again. "I'm sorry.

There's absolutely nothing here to suggest that the donor of your cornea was murdered."

Karen said quietly, "I don't believe it."

"Don't be so goddamn stubborn!" Adam slammed the palms of both hands down on the desk. "I am *telling* you. Dickie Brewster. Age twenty-six. Cause of death—an overdose of narcotics. What the hell—even that's more than I should tell you."

"Overdose!" Karen exclaimed. "Wouldn't that affect the eye?"

Adam said coldly, "Death by overdose has no effect on the cornea, whatever. O.D.'s are among the best possible sources of young, healthy eyes."

"But don't you see?" Karen persisted. "Drugs are administered by needles. *Needles!* The last thing he—Dickie Brewster—saw was the needle that killed him. So I'm right!"

Adam lifted one hand. "Slow down. Addicts almost invariably inject themselves. This man's overdose was undoubtedly self-administered. If you want to call that suicide, okay."

Karen said quietly, "I'd like to accept what you say. I want desperately to get over these . . ." She stopped abruptly, afraid she was going to cry and determined not to in front of him. She continued, ". . . these hallucinations, as you call them. Actually you haven't disproved my theory. You've been describing Dickie Brewster as an addict." She pointed at the open file. "Does it state there that he was?"

"No," Adam admitted. "It simply gives the cause of death. Death by overdose."

"Which could mean one injection. One

deadly shot and one only. Given by someone who killed him deliberately. So the evidence fits my theory just as much as it fits yours."

Adam closed the file, snapped off the desk lamp, strode past Karen and dropped the folders into place in the filing cabinet. Maintaining a furious silence, he closed the drawer, locked both cabinets and dropped the keys into the top drawer of the director's desk. Then he turned to face her. "Look, I don't want to talk to you when I'm angry. Come on. I'll give you a lift home."

Throughout the drive to Portage Bay neither of them spoke. At the door to the houseboat, Adam broke the silence. "If you had any real proof, I'd go along with you. I do want to help you. Believe me. *I do want to help.* But I don't think humoring you is the way to do it." With that he turned and walked away. She watched him until she could no longer distinguish his figure from the shadows and then as she groped for her doorkeys, the tears she had managed to hold back in Adam's presence poured freely down her cheeks.

"You're eavesdropping," Doug commented as he joined Jennie at the window so that he, too, had a good view of the entrance to Karen's houseboat.

"I am not. I can't hear a thing. I'm a voyeur, and I'm a little worried about what I'm seeing. Adam Stewart's dumped Karen at the door and stomped off. She's obviously unhappy and fumbling with the doorkey as if someone had cemented up the keyhole. I don't know what's happened, but I'm going to haul her over here."

Karen came gratefully, admitted that she hadn't had any dinner, and at the kitchen table, while Jennie re-heated the moussaka, she told them how she had schemed to get into the Eye Bank files and what she had learned.

"So you see, it *is* possible to find out who a donor is. Mine was Dickie Brewster, age twenty-six. He died of an overdose of drugs. And it *is* possible that he was murdered. I'm sure there was more in the file than that, but Adam was angry and refused to tell me anything more. In fact, he seemed angry at himself for telling me that much."

"No doubt," Doug said drily. "When a doctor talks about medical ethics, he feels like Moses bringing the tablets down from the mountain. But of course he's right. You didn't have any business pulling a B and E in Mathews Memorial Hospital."

"Oh, shut up, Doug," Jennie said pleasantly. "Okay, Karen. So now you're sure that your new eye is trying to tell you something and that you've got to find out how the donor died."

"The name and age isn't much. But it's a place to start."

"You're dead set on this, are you? You don't believe Dr. Stewart's right, that it's just an unusual post-operative trauma?"

Karen shook her head energetically. "I can't accept that explanation. I know what I've got to do. As crazy as it may sound to both of you, I won't quit until I find out exactly how Dickie Brewster died."

Jennie turned to Doug. "I think it's time to tell Karen about your idea."

"Agreed."

"You're an artist," Jennie began. "All your senses are unusually sharp—hearing, sense of smell, your feeling for shapes and colors. But the way this sensitivity comes alive is through your painting, right? Anyway, the point is—and Doug is the one who put this thought together—the point is, your feelings, your experiences, maybe even thoughts you can't express in words, come out when you paint. So Doug suggested that you try to paint the image."

An involuntary shudder rippled through Karen's body. She dropped her fork and the deep blue of her eyes seemed to get even darker. "Paint it." The words came out like a sigh. "But there wouldn't be much to paint. The needle, the fingers—the rest is hidden. It's lost in a fog."

Jennie nodded as if no other response could have pleased her more. "Exactly! But the picture is all there, in your new eye. The *eye* sees the whole image, but so far hasn't been able to communicate all of it to you. It's as if your personal radar is getting only part of the message. Okay—maybe it *is* crazy to believe your new eye is, well, imprinted with an image, but let's go with that idea and see where it takes us. Maybe when you start painting, the fog will begin to evaporate."

"I'm afraid," Karen whispered. "Just thinking about it scares me."

Doug's hand reached across the table and covered hers. "At this point you may be more frightened of what's hidden than you are of what you can see. Bring it all out of hiding, and you might discover that it's not as terrible as you think it is."

"If I don't freak out and do something stupid."

"Number one," Jennie said firmly, "we won't let you. I'm going to be right with you when you start to paint, and Doug is going to be within shouting distance. Number two—this is Doug's second genius idea—before you even start painting, I'm going to get you so relaxed you wouldn't panic if a ten-pound hypodermic needle fell through the ceiling and began reciting Psalm 23."

Karen smiled tremulously at first, but in Jennie's freckled face there was such a funny mixture of the comic and the earnest that she began to laugh. "If I'm crazy, you are, too. How are you going to get me that relaxed?"

"Hypnotism," Jennie said confidently. "It's been done to me. I've studied it and done it to others."

"It may not work," Doug said. "But it's worth a try."

Karen was still smiling, but her voice was unsteady. "You're wonderful, Jennie. And so are you, Doug. I love you, both of you. But I need some time to think about this. Okay?"

Jennie blew her a kiss. "Anytime that you're ready, we'll be here."

Eleven

It hadn't called for any special powers of deduction to find out where Dickie Brewster lived. His address was listed in the Seattle telephone directory. But by the time Karen reached the vestibule of the Westminster, her determination began to flag.

It wasn't too late to turn back. Simply leave, walk out, take the bus home to Portage Bay. For a moment the decision hung in balance. *The human eye.* But wasn't it possible that the complete picture of Dickie's death could be put together, bit by bit? If so, almost anything she learned about him might hurry the process. She *had* to go ahead.

As she scanned the names on the double tier of metal mailboxes, the thought struck her that Adam would be almost as angry if he knew what she was doing today as he had been last night at discovering her inside the Eye Bank office. Why was he so opposed to her following the only possible course through which she could prove or disprove that there was a basis for the haunting image? She was puzzled and hurt by his reaction. He seemed determined to block her, to prevent her from discovering . . . discovering what?

Karen shook her head, as if to clear it of an uneasy thought. Adam was a physician, a scientist. She shouldn't read anything unusual into his opposition. Jennie and Doug were supportive, but sympathetic as they were, neither of them had accepted her conviction that her new eye had the power to lead her to Dickie's killer. For that matter, neither of them was convinced that Dickie had been murdered. Doug especially had a "show-me" attitude. Which made it all the more important that she carry through her idea of exploring the place where Dickie had lived. His name on a mailbox seemed to shout agreement. Dickie Brewster, Apartment 4C.

She tried the door from the vestibule into the lobby, and the foolishness of this errand hit her full force. What a stumbling amateur she was! The entrance was locked, as she should have anticipated. The door to 4-C would be, too. She had no reason to believe anyone would be in the apartment, even less reason to think she would be welcomed. Damn, she thought, and suddenly more determined than ever to pursue her unplanned plan, she pressed the bell for Apartment 4-C.

The sound of the buzzer rang out so sharply that she jumped, but she quickly pushed the door open and entered the building. With mounting excitement, she rode the elevator to the fourth floor, hurried down the hall to 4-C and tapped lightly on the door.

It was opened almost immediately by a pleasant-looking woman with bright blue eyes and skin that glowed as if she had just come in from a long walk in the cold. "Yes?" Her tone was neither hostile nor friendly. Just a little surprised, as if she had been expecting someone else.

"My name is Karen Thorndyke." It came out in a rush and a little breathlessly, but at least, Karen thought, so far I'm telling the truth.

The woman smiled. A polite smile, but it was enormously reassuring. Her clear eyes, her unadorned, soap and water complexion, and the tweedy green skirt and heavy white sweater she was wearing, gave Karen the impression of a direct and honest person who would be a sympathetic listener.

"I don't want to impose, but I must talk to you. For only a few minutes."

The woman stepped aside. "I'm going out soon. In fact, when you rang I thought it was someone else. But do come in, please."

She led the way to a sofa upholstered in gold velvet and sat down on one end, motioning Karen to take the other.

"I'm Martha O'Donnell," she said pleasantly. "Your name is . . . Karen Thorndyke?"

"Yes. I'll try to be brief. Mrs. O'Donnell, is it?" The woman nodded. "Are you a relative of Dickie Brewster's?"

Pain flickered in the clear blue eyes. "I'm his sister. And you? Did you know my brother?"

Karen shook her head. "No. I . . ." Suddenly her throat was tight. How to say, clearly and simply, why she had come, without sounding like a raving psychotic? "Were you and Dickie very close?"

It was an awkward opening. Frowning, Martha O'Donnell answered, "My home is in Dublin, Miss Thorndyke, and has been since my marriage ten years ago. For that reason Dickie and I have not been 'close,' as you say, at least not geographically."

"Please forgive me," Karen said quickly. "I know that was a personal question. But it's important, terribly important. I'll try to explain."

The other woman said coolly, "Please do."

"Did you keep in touch with him? I mean did he write a lot? So that you knew something about his . . ." Karen hesitated, groped for words, and finished weakly, ". . . about his life style?"

Now Martha O'Donnell's tone was distinctly antagonistic. "You offered to explain why you came. But your questions don't give me any sort of explanation." She stood up. "As I said before, I'm about to go out."

"Please!" The word rang out as urgently as a cry for help. Martha O'Donnell's expression softened. She sat down, nearer to Karen this time, and said quietly, "What's troubling you?"

For an instant Karen considered an approach that might meet the other woman's demand for an explanation. That she owed thanks to Dickie Brewster and to the person who, as next of kin, must have approved his donation to the Eye Bank. But she dismissed the thought as quickly as it came to her. It was true, but it was an evasion, a cheap trick, and the thought of using it repelled her. "Last month I had a corneal transplant. Your brother was the donor. And ever since, my left eye . . your brother's eye . . . has shown me a certain image. I think that my—my new eye can see what Dickie Brewster was looking at when he died."

Martha O'Donnell's face went chalk white. Her lips opened and froze in a silent cry. For several seconds she stared at Karen's left eye, her face contorted in an expression of such utter revulsion that Karen instinctively covered the offending eye with her hand. "Mrs. O'Donnell," she said apologetically, "I'm terribly sorry to upset you. It was a generous gift. I'm sincerely grateful. But I *have* to find out what happened. It's as if your brother was trying to tell me, trying to show me, through his eye . . . Please! I'm not hysterical. I'm not just imagining things. I *know* your brother was murdered. His eye has shown me how it was done. But who did it? And why? I need your help. . . ."

The paralysis broke as Martha O'Donnell's stricken thought was finally released and she gave a long, thin wail. "He poked out Peggy's eyes! He was only three years old and he poked out her eyes!" Her voice rose hysterically with every word. "Do you hear me? *Do you hear what I said!* She didn't have any eyes! There were two big round holes, two dark, empty eye sockets." Tears of grief poured down her cheeks.

Now it was Karen's turn to reach out to

comfort her, but Martha O'Donnell recoiled at the touch of her hand.

Karen withdrew her hand, shocked by the torment she was causing. She hesitated, feeling both ashamed and helpless in the face of anguish she seemed only to make worse with an awkward attempt at consolation. She stood up and crossed the living room, reluctant to leave the grief-stricken woman alone.

Behind her, the hysterical sobbing began to subside. Karen retreated quickly then and closed the door to 4-C behind her. She could never again seek help from Martha O'Donnell. But more than ever she was convinced that she must not abandon her search until she knew what Dickie's eye was trying to show her.

The young man was standing in the hall just outside the door of the adjoining apartment. Both arms were holding large paper sacks brimming with groceries, while his right hand fumbled with a door key. He looked up as Karen approached.

Dark eyes studied her with frank curiosity. He must have seen her leaving Dickie Brewster's apartment. He may even have heard Martha O'Donnell's hysterical cries. He would like to know what I was doing there, Karen thought, and he's making no bones about it. Dickie Brewster's next door neighbor. Perhaps her luck was changing.

She stopped and smiled. "Here. You rescue the groceries. I'll unlock the door."

He smiled, showing extraordinarily white even teeth, and dropped the key ring into

Karen's open palm. "I was afraid you were going to ask me for change of a dollar."

Laughing, Karen inserted the key and opened the door. "I'd like to talk to you."

"*Well!*" He stepped inside, lowered both sacks to a small loveseat, straightened up and rubbed his palms together. "My first proposition of the day."

"I'm serious."

"Ah . . then you better come in and sit down. I never attempt any serious thinking on my feet."

"Serious, eh," he said again, as he led her into the living room. "In that case, how about a short one? I happen to have a keg of brandy tied around my neck."

"If you have some wine . . ."

He went to a sideboard in the dining area and returned with two stemmed glasses filled with white wine. "To your very good health," he said, lifting his glass. They sat down across from each other. Karen was still undecided as to how she should open this unusual conversation when he said cheerfully, "It's about Dickie."

She nodded. The statement was remarkable for its frankness, but hardly in the realm of ESP. After all, he had seen her leaving Dickie's apartment.

"By the way, I'm Jasper Carter. Who are you?"

"Karen Thorndyke."

"Did you know poor old Dickie?"

Karen shook her head. The direct approach? The whole truth and nothing but the truth? No, not quite. She had tried that with Martha

O'Donnell. Nevertheless, she could still be as frank as he, and whatever she did reveal could be true. "I never knew him. In fact, I've never seen him. How long did you know Dickie Brewster?"

"I was living in this apartment when Dickie moved in next door. That was three years ago, take or give a little."

"You were good friends?"

"What's that? I mean, what's a *good* friend? Oh, hell. I know what you mean. It's just that Dickie wasn't a particularly good person. But yes, we were friends." He paused, dark eyes focusing on her with a look of unabashed appraisal. "Whereas you didn't even know him, so you couldn't have liked or disliked him. But more to the point, *why* do you want to know about Dickie?"

"I'd like to know the circumstances of his death."

Jasper Carter shrugged. "That's not privileged information. The police know it, the coroner knows it. It's a matter of public record. He O.D.'d."

"I know. But how?"

Again Carter's shoulders rose in a gesture of indifference. "How? He shot up once too often, I suppose. Or too much."

"Did you see him the day he died?"

Carter nodded.

"Was there anything unusual? Did he seem excited or upset? Was he with someone else?"

Carter raised one hand. "I surrender, dear. Look, I'll tell you how it happened, at least the part I know about. About two o'clock that afternoon, I saw handsome Dickie in the carport. He was pulling in and I was going out. He'd heard about a new spot near Pike Place and he said we ought to try it. I said okay, how about six? He said make it seven, he had an afternoon date."

"Excuse me for interrupting . . ." A date on the afternoon of the day he died. Another person to be sought out, to interrogate. "A date? Do you know who she was? Can you give me her name?"

Jasper Carter laughed outright. "Dear and beautiful Karen. Did I say anything about a she?"

"Well, no." Karen looked at him steadily, cataloguing this new fact.

Carter leaned back in his chair and said to the ceiling, "Dickie Brewster was one of the most beautiful *and* most expensive fags in the greater Seattle area. I'm letting no cat out of *that* bag. Dickie would have told you the same thing himself."

"So you were going to meet him at seven, right? Please go on."

"Yes. Well, not much more to it. I got back to my apartment about six-thirty. Showered, changed clothes, threw back a neat Scotch, knocked on his door a little after seven. No answer. Maybe he was in the shower. I banged harder. Still no answer. I went back to my apartment and phoned. No answer. Phoned again fifteen minutes later. Didn't like it at all, so I called the police. Two cops showed up and got the manager to let them in. Dickie was on the bed and he was gone. *Gone.*"

There was an emotional quality to Carter's

voice that hadn't been there before. For all his facetiousness, Jasper Carter had evidently cared for his neighbor. And since Dickie Brewster had been a homosexual, Jasper had quite possibly been one of his lovers.

A jealous lover, perhaps, angered because Dickie had an afternoon date with someone else? Angry enough to pretend he wasn't angry at all, so that when he met Dickie Brewster that evening, Dickie, unsuspecting, would have let him into the apartment, perhaps allowed his former lover to give him the shot, not knowing it would be deadly. . . . Karen repressed a shudder. She had always been highly imaginative. It was the quality that made her paintings so distinctive. But she wasn't painting, she was hunting for the truth of what had happened to Dickie Brewster on the afternoon of April third. She mustn't let her imagination run away with her now. "Was Dickie an addict?"

"I suspected it. I never knew for sure."

"His . . . date, the afternoon he died. Did you know him?"

Carter broke into scornful laughter. "God, no. I stayed out of dear Dickie's affairs."

"And Dickie never talked about him?"

"Dickie *bragged* about him, my dear. There's a very expensive motorcycle down in the carport. A present from Leander. Oh, yes, they had pet names for each other. Dickie was Hero. His loving sponsor was Leander. Very classical, right? 'I read it in the story-book, that, for to kiss his dear, Leander swam the Hellespont—and I will swim this here . . .' And a very jealous Leander, too, I gathered from some of Dickie's comments. Something else Dickie bragged about. He *adored* jealousy. It excited him. It was an emotion he was incapable of feeling, but how he loved to arouse it in someone else." Carter paused and gave Karen a rueful smile. "Your glass is empty. Let me fill it."

Karen rose. Perhaps it was her over-active imagination, but disturbing thoughts were beginning to come together. There was the persistent vision of the hypodermic needle. Plus the possibility that the overdose was not an accident, and not self-administered, as Adam had insisted. Mix these ingredients with Dickie Brewster's penchant for jealous lovers—Leander, who had a date with him the afternoon of his death, and Jasper Carter, whom Dickie may have discarded in favor of a man who could provide a very expensive motorcycle. Nothing really meshed, but suddenly Karen didn't want to be alone with Jasper Carter. With great difficulty she managed to say thanks and good-bye in a casual tone of voice, to walk slowly to the door, and walk just as slowly down the hall to the elevator, though she sensed that Jasper Carter was out in the hall, watching her. When she reached the vestibule on the ground floor, she ran. Out into the street, down the street, away, away, and never looking back.

In Apartment 4-C, Martha O'Donnell was at the telephone talking to Henry Garner. "I'm all right now, Henry. No, no. I've calmed down. I'm fine, really, but I thought you ought to know about this girl. I don't know *what* she might do. I tell you, she's mad! To actually believe that her eye can see what Dickie saw . . . . Wouldn't *you* call that insane?"

Henry Garner reassured Martha that he would check into the matter and lowered the telephone with a deep sigh. Even in death Dickie Brewster could be a disruptive factor in his life. As the family lawyer, Garner had become enmeshed in Dickie's escapades countless times—from paying off fifteen hundred dollars worth of long overdue parking tickets to getting Dickie released from jail and persuading the judge to dismiss disorderly conduct charges.

Garner grimaced as he thought of the last time Dickie had sent him an SOS in the middle of the night. He had wrapped the car he was driving around a tree and called Garner from a phone booth on the highway. When Garner arrived to give Dickie a ride home, he discovered Dickie and his two passengers sky high on whatever drug was currently Dickie's favorite. But Garner could have dealt with that. What he couldn't deal with were Dickie's friends—both dressed in women's clothing with grotesquely made-up faces. For the entire ride back into town the two had mockingly made passes, both verbally and physically, at Garner. Dickie had found it all very amusing. It became a subject he delighted to bring up, and not always when they were alone.

And now it seemed that he still wasn't through with Dickie.

In Apartment 4-D, Jasper Carter was pouring himself a double Scotch. He drank it in two gulps, put the glass down and gently touched the back of his head, as if the swelling and tenderness were still there. Getting slugged was something he ought to have reported to the police, but there were several things the local fuzz didn't need to know.

Most particularly he didn't want them to discover that when he called them the afternoon Dickie died, he had already been inside the apartment, and that getting the manager to admit them had been a farce. A necessary farce, since under the circumstances, it seemed wise not to mention that he had a key. But that omission had trapped him. He couldn't report that he was attacked inside 4-C. Nothing felonious about watering the house plants. But the cops' next question would have been—how did you get in? That one he couldn't answer without contradicting what he had told them the evening they found Dickie's body on his bed. He had lied then, just as he had lied to the inquisitive Karen Thorndyke a few minutes ago. It was his story—and he was stuck with it forever.

Why in hell had he kept the key anyway?

He poured and drank another Scotch, slipped the key to 4-C off his key ring, and pushed it deep into the soggy contents of the garbage pail. Now to drop it down the chute to the basement incinerator . . . and the last physical bond with Dickie Brewster would be gone forever.

Twelve

When she left the Westminster, Karen had no intention of telling Adam Stewart she had been there, but on the way home she began to see such concealment in a different light. However aloof he might appear at times, at other times his interest in her was so intense it couldn't possibly be called impersonal. Whatever feelings were behind his professional mask, he had become important to her. Do patients always fall in love with their doctors, she thought, or only with their psychiatrists? In any event, *she* was emotionally involved, whether or not he was and to deceive him did violence to her own feelings. It was illogical, even disloyal to be suspicious of his motives for opposing her search.

When she reached her houseboat she was surprised to find Adam leaning against the railing and tapping his fingers impatiently.

"I was just about to give up on you and go back to the office," he said with a smile. He leaned down, and when he arose he held out a colorful bouquet of anemones to her. "My peace offering. I hope you'll accept it."

With a delight that she hadn't felt for a long while, Karen took the flowers and led Adam inside. They poured tall glasses of lemonade and took them out on the deck. Karen, feeling guilty for having doubted him, told him about her bewildering conversation with Dickie's sister Martha and her meeting with Jasper Carter.

Adam listened without interrupting, which in itself seemed a sign of sympathy. More ashamed than ever of her earlier decision to hide things from him, she said, "Adam, you haven't once said that I'm stubborn, or that my vision is the result of post-operative trauma, or that this is all an irrational obsession."

His voice was tinged with irony. "Did I really say all that?"

"Several times. Especially when you were angry."

"Not really angry. Frustrated. This image you see—I can't cope with your belief in it. When men can't cope, they get angry."

"You don't sound angry now," Karen said hopefully. "Or are you just being patient with me?"

He reached across the table and took her hand. "To the extent that I've been patient, I think I've taken the wrong approach. Patience may be a virtue, but it's too damn passive in a situation like this." He paused, as if to sort out his words. There was a distinct hardness in his voice when he went on. "I'll be blunt. I fear for you, Karen. For both your physical and emotional health, if this thing continues to haunt you. Yet I'm glad you told me about your trip to the Westminister, and I hope that you'll continue to talk to me about the image, to tell me everything about it. Perhaps in the process something will surface that will give us the clue to ridding you of this damn hallucination. And I want your promise that you won't confide in anyone else."

Karen asked curiously, "Why not?"

Adam's response was curt. "You tried to this afternoon, didn't you? When you talked to Martha O'Donnell. You saw her reaction."

"She got hysterical, but not because of me. It was about something Dickie had done."

"Granted. But that was triggered by your extraordinary statements about her brother's eye. Face it, Karen. You terrified her because she thought—well, you said it yourself—she thought you'd gone mad. And that's exactly the reaction you're bound to get if you insist on telling people about your new eye."

Karen sighed and took her hand from his. "You may be right, Adam. But let's not talk about it anymore today."

When they finished their drinks, Adam stood to leave. "I'll call you later. Meanwhile, remember your promise not to discuss this with anyone else."

Karen said quietly, "I didn't promise, Adam."

After he left, Karen's gaze moved to the old-fashioned easel in the living room. A blank canvas faced her. Were Doug and Jennie right? Could it cast light into the dark corner of her mind where some unidentified but distinctly painful thought was fighting for recognition? She knew she would have to try.

Doug was in Karen's bedroom with two cans of cold beer and the May issue of *Sports Illustrated.* In the living room, Jennie drew the drapes across the picture window to shut off the familiar view, for any distracting sounds or sights would make it harder for Karen to concentrate on Jennie's signals. Then she asked Karen to take her favorite chair, while she herself sat a few feet away in the chair she invariably took when she dropped in, and therefore the spot Karen would subconsciously identify as "Jennie's chair."

She began in casual, relaxed tones, explaining the two distinct parts of hypnosis, what the textbooks call trance induction, or putting the subject into the hypnotic state, and trance utilization, or evoking potentials beyond the learned limitations of the subject. The first step might be easier than the second, she pointed out.

But, Jennie emphasized, Karen was an excellent subject. For one thing, a good relationship between the hypnotist and the subject is absolutely essential, that certainly existed between them. "You trust me," Jennie said confidently. She made it a statement rather than a question, since it was meant to establish the hypnotist as a secure and positive force.

"Oh, yes. More than anyone I know."

Jennie smiled. "I'm glad. That's important. And we've got something else going for us. Hypnosis usually refers to the process through which the subject becomes capable of improbable or uncommon acts, things he or she wouldn't do awake. You're a good subject because the so-called improbable thing I want you to do is not far outside your normal or conscious behavior. You're a painter. When you're in a trance, you're going to paint a picture. Only you'll go beyond what you would paint if you were not in a trance."

Karen smiled. "No crystal ball? No revolving lights or shiny fountain pens?"

Jennie noted with satisfaction that in spite of Karen's teasing tone, there was no tension in her voice. "We don't need gimmicks. That's for vaudeville. Okay. Now, I'm going to sit in your chair, Karen. I want you to come and sit in mine."

By allowing the person in command to occupy her place, Karen had accepted that person's power to tell her what to do; resistance to later shifts had been greatly reduced by her willingness to make this one. And "command" was the key word. Jennie would repeatedly use imperatives—"*Be* comfortable." "*Be* relaxed."

"I think you're ready now, Karen," Jennie said. "It's time for you to go into a trance."

"Yes. Fine."

Closing the curtains had been the first step in helping Karen become disengaged from all sources of stimulation other than Jennie's voice. Their easy conversation had produced a degree of relaxation that further shut off channels of distraction. There was one more step.

"You're sitting in a comfortable chair. You like the chair. You're relaxed, so relaxed, so comfortable. Now your eyelids are beginning to feel heavy. Heavier and heavier. Your eyelids are fluttering. They're beginning to droop. Slowly, very slowly. Your eyes are closed now. You cannot open them. You're warm and comfortable. You're breathing deeply . . ."

Jennie continued to talk in an even but completely natural tone of voice. There was nothing clinical or impersonal in her relationship to Karen; she spoke in intimate terms. "You're perfectly comfortable, aren't you, Karen? Just nod if you are. Lovely. Relax all your muscles. Even your lips, your jaw. You're doing beautifully. Beautifully. And it's beginning to happen. What a warm, pleasant feeling. The feeling lifts you, it carries you . . ."

After five or six minutes Jennie paused, as she would do deliberately and repeatedly while inducing and prolonging the trance. Pauses, sometimes lengthy ones, or raising her voice, or repeating a gesture such as flexing the fingers—these could all become messages that would affect Karen's susceptibility to Jennie's suggestions. Then Jennie continued with the same soft flow of words, reassuring and encouraging her, allowing her to assimilate one level of suggestion, then gently pulling her on to another.

"Slowly, deeper and deeper. Your hand is moving. It's lifting just a little. Lifting by itself. Your hand is lifting a little more. Now the whole arm. . . . The elbow is bending. . . . More, more, lifting, lifting . . ."

Again Jennie paused, longer this time before beginning again "Now I want you to put your arm down. Slowly, slowly, let your hands rest in your lap. I want you to go deeper and deeper asleep. *Tell me*," she said with sudden emphasis, "*tell me* that you will go deeper and deeper asleep. *Tell me* by nodding your head. Nod your head forward, slowly . . ."

Karen's head moved in the barest suggestion of a nod.

"Slowly, slowly, nodding forward. Still more, still more . . ."

Karen's head responded with a definite nod.

"Lovely, lovely. Now I want you to go deeper and deeper asleep. I'm going to count for you. One, two, three, four, five, six, seven, eight. . . . You are now half asleep." Jennie paused, waited a few seconds and then continued, "Eleven, twelve. . . ." At the count of fifteen, she said, "Three-quarters asleep. Almost there." At twenty, she said, "Take a deep breath. You are asleep, but I want you to be sleeping more and more and more . . ."

Karen was breathing deeply and evenly, by all appearances sound asleep. Until now, Jennie's suggestions had been positive. Lift your arm, bend your elbow, nod your head—Karen needn't be truly hypnotized to respond to such positive commands. The negative suggestion was a different matter. When Karen became incapable of a movement she was actually physically able to carry out, she would have reached the stage of a deep hypnotic trance.

Jennie said firmly, "Your hands are in your lap, Karen, but you can't move them. You're trying to move them, but your hands are too heavy. You can't lift them. They won't move. . . . Now I want you to try moving your hands. Lift them up. Are you trying, Karen? Nod if you're trying. Yes, yes, I see you nod. You are trying, but they won't move. . . . Now stop trying, Karen, and go deeper asleep . . .

"There is something I want you to think about. In just a few seconds I'm going to ask you to open your eyes. Because there is something I want you to do."

Jennie had brought Karen to the critical moment when the depth and usefulness of the trance would be given the first real test. The moment of truth, Jennie thought. Is she really in a hypnotic sleep or is she simply trying hard to cooperate?

"There's something I want you to do, Karen. I really *want* you to do it. I know you can do it. And I know you're going to enjoy doing it. Now, I want you to open your eyes."

Karen's lids lifted.

"You like to paint, don't you, Karen. You're a fine artist. You enjoy painting. That's true, isn't it, Karen?"

"Yes. That's true."

"Very good. Now your brushes and paints are laid out on the table in the corner, and there's an empty canvas on your easel. I want you to stand up and walk over to the easel, and I want you to paint."

It had taken twenty-five minutes to produce what appeared to be a medium trance, but would that be enough to enable Karen to do the "uncommon or improbable," a painting of the image that would reveal more than she had seen before?

To Jennie's vast relief, Karen stood up and approached the easel without hesitation. Jennie followed and stood behind her, close enough to be heard without changing the even pitch of her voice, but outside Karen's range of vision so that her physical presence would not dilute Karen's concentration on her painting. "I want you to start painting now," Jennie said softly. "You will paint the image. I want you to imagine the needle. A shiny, shiny, needle, very sharp. The light around it is so bright it hurts your eyes. The needle, Karen, the needle . . ."

Karen responded immediately. She squeezed paint onto the palette, selected a brush, and applied a series of long strokes, streaks of palest yellows sweeping downward at an angle from the upper left to the lower right corner of the canvas. Jennie had often watched Karen at work and recognized that she was painting differently now. Rapidly, with a kind of contained fury, as if her mind was a cauldron filled to the brim with the scalding image-memory and she must paint, paint, paint to keep it from spilling over.

In only a few minutes, Karen had produced a picture so exactly like the image she had described that Jennie suddenly felt as if a chilling wind had blown across her face. Karen stopped painting. The brush dropped from her hand. She stood, frozen, staring at the canvas. Jennie stepped forward quickly, flung both arms around her and turned her away from a painting that even to her seemed to exude some unspeakable evil.

Karen's mouth was open in a silent scream. She was struggling inside Jennie's tight embrace, her body caught in wave after wave of convulsive shudders. Doug was in the bedroom, she had only to call him. But should she? Wouldn't her shouted cry for help and Doug's sudden appearance be dangerous to Karen in her present state? Calmly, firmly, she said, "I want you to awaken now, Karen. I'm going to count again, but this time I'm going to count backwards. When I say *one*, you will wake up. You will come wide awake, and you will see a picture on your easel but you won't remember painting it. Listen, Karen, listen—twenty, nineteen, eighteen . . ."

At the word "one," Karen's body relaxed. Her expression was natural, only a little puzzled, as she stepped out of Jennie's embrace and looked into her friend's face.

"What time is it?" she asked. "Have I been asleep?"

"Yes, dear. Forty-five minutes, give or take a little. How do you feel?"

Karen smiled wearily. "A little tired." She glanced at her fingers, sticky with yellow and black paint, and at the brush on the floor at her feet. "Oh," she said, and turned toward the canvas.

Jennie called, "Doug? Would you come in here, please?"

Doug burst out of the bedroom, quickly took in the appearance of calm and slowed his pace. "Painting session over?"

Jennie threw him a heavily weighted look. "Karen's looking at what she did. I just woke her up, so actually she's seeing her painting for the first time."

"Mmm . . ." Doug picked up the implied SOS and moved up beside Karen.

Karen's face was pale, but she was studying the painting without any visible sign of hysteria.

"Well," Doug said amiably, "what do you think?"

Karen shook her head. "It's all there, just the way I've seen it. That's the trouble with it. It's *just* the way it's appeared to me before—nothing more or less. The needle is there, the fingers are there—and the fog is there, as usual, concealing most of the image. It didn't work, Jennie."

"Hey, wait a minute. It *did* work. You were in hypnosis, and you painted in hypnosis. That's damned good for the first time around."

"Don't be a quitter," Doug said, dropping an affectionate arm around Karen's shoulders. "Try it again. And soon."

"Nothing came out of the fog," Karen murmured. "Nothing."

All at once Jennie stepped closer to the canvas, squinting in fierce concentration at one small area.

"What's up?" Doug asked. "Get any closer and you're going to dip the end of your nose in the paint."

"Look," Jennie said earnestly. "Karen's vision has never appeared to me, right? But her description has been so exact that I think I could have painted this thing myself. But there *is* something new. It's faint, but it's there."

For the first time, Karen's expression was animated. "Where?" she asked, curiosity and apprehension fighting for control of her voice.

Jennie pointed to the middle of the upper half of the picture. "It's all fog, all gray and kind of turbulent, as if a cold wind had just come up."

Karen nodded. "Yes. That's the way it's always appeared to me."

"But look," Jennie insisted, her forefinger zeroing in on one small spot. "Right here, something is showing through the fog. It's just a little lighter, and it's got a definite shape."

Eyes fixed on the spot, Karen breathed, "Lord, Jennie, that *is* new. I've never seen that before. It's never been there before."

"What does it look like to you?"

Karen said without hesitation, "It's an eye. A human eye." She walked across the room and dropped into a chair by the window. Looking out across the lake, she said quietly, "But whose eye? Whose eye was Dickie Brewster looking into when he died?"

Back in Jennie's houseboat, Doug made a phone call.

". . . My friend Tim Ryan. Classmate, Roosevelt High and U of W," he explained to Jennie. "While I was majoring in right tackle, he took up permanent residence in the medical library. He's assistant medical examiner for the county. If Karen is determined to uncover the circumstances of Dickie Brewster's death, then Tim will know as much as anyone about it. At least he's bound to know more than Karen does. I made an appointment to drop in at the coroner's office."

"Take Karen with you," Jennie said. "This is her search. We can help her, but we can't take it away from her."

Thirteen

Assistant Medical Examiner Tim Ryan accepted the manila file folder his secretary brought to him and opened it out flat. With a cordial smile for Doug and Karen, who were seated on the other side of his desk, he said, "Glad to cooperate, Doug. Hope I can answer your questions. Fire away."

"Do you remember the Dickie Brewster case?"

"Not in detail. But it's all here . . ." He slapped the open file with the palm of his hand. "Demographic information, scene circumstance statement. Photographs. And of course, autopsy reports."

"The cause of death was an overdose, right? Heavy narcotics?"

"Right." He leafed through the various reports, picked up one sheet, studied it for a moment and said, "Brewster was in excellent health, if that's an appropriate term for a heroin addict."

"What were the circumstances of his death? I know your investigators always include that in their reports."

The examiner nodded. "They sure do." He picked out another sheet and scanned it quickly. "Responded to a call from police radio central. Apartment 4-C, the Westminster, Creighton Boulevard. Body sprawled out on the bed. Evidence that he had started to vomit. Probably choked on his own stomach contents." He looked up, addressing himself to Karen. "Our investigators aren't doctors, Miss Thorndyke, but they do know their business. However, in the case of a suspected O.D., the decision as to the cause of death is based on a complete autopsy. Every body cavity is opened. Tissue specimens are taken and studied in the lab. Bile, urine, blood, gastric contents are all tested."

"But if all that is done hurriedly?" Karen said.

"The posting pathologist isn't under any pressure for a quick decision. He does whatever he has to do. Meanwhile the body can be released to the funeral home, the death certificate can be signed and sent to the Department of Vital Statistics, and still the lab studies continue until we're absolutely sure we really *know*. The death certificate is marked 'Hold' and the line showing cause of death is left blank until we're completely satisfied." He gestured at the spread of report sheets, now fanned out in front of him like a deck of cards just before the magician says, "Choose one." "It's all here. And it all adds up. No doubt at all about the cause of death. *Or* the time."

Karen said earnestly, "Mr. Ryan, what did your investigators report about the circumstances of Dickie Brewster's death?"

"The circumstances?" The examiner threw a questioning glance at Doug, as if asking authorization to reply. The detective was known to him as a professional with legitimate professional interest. Miss Karen Thorndyke was unexplained and unofficial.

Doug nodded. "Whatever you can tell us, Tim. We already know Brewster died of an overdose. But maybe you've got some ideas as to *why* he O.D.'d."

"You mean was it an accident or a suicide?" The examiner paused thoughtfully. "That's a matter of conjecture. But in your line of work, Doug, you know as well as I do that there are relatively few true suicides. Accidental suicides —that's what these O.D.'s are. The average stuff is cut with various kinds of sugars down to three, four, maybe five percent. But every now and then, some stronger stuff is dumped on the street. If a user who's accustomed to the five percent dope gets hold of a mix with, say, fifteen percent heroin, he's had it. That probably happened to Brewster." He looked at Doug with a smile that bordered on the apologetic. "I don't often use the word 'probably.' "

"I know what you mean." Doug nodded reassuringly. "Listen, Tim. I'm not taking notes. I'm here as . . . well, you might say as a friend of the family. Another question or two and we'll split. Are you sure the overdose was self-administered?"

The examiner frowned. "No evidence that it wasn't. Almost impossible to tell, anyway."

"Could you tell where the fatal injection was given?"

"Oh yes, definitely. Obvious trace of fresh blood. A slight swelling."

"Was it in a spot Brewster could reach if he were giving it to himself?"

"Doug, there's hardly an inch of a man's body he can't get to if he's had the habit long enough to have to move that needle around. I've seen tracks in the soles of a man's feet." He examined the report. "Nothing unusual here. It was his left arm. Why? Are you thinking someone else gave it to him?"

"Just exploring the possibility."

Ryan shrugged. "Might be. A lot of addicts do it for each other."

"Voluntarily. How about *in*voluntarily?"

The examiner's frown deepened. "My God, Doug. Murder? If there had been the least suggestion of any force used, any marks or bruises, any sign of a struggle, the two police officers who were on the scene first would have reported it, and fast."

"Any drug hardware?"

"Oh, sure. The usual. A small tin box. A length of rubber tubing. A syringe and a small plastic baggie, empty but with a detectable trace of whitish powder. Which, of course, doesn't prove much, does it? Whether he shot it himself, or someone else did it for him?"

"You did say his body was sprawled out on the bed, right? Would that indicate that he was trying to move to get help, or maybe even get to the telephone?"

"It might or might not. You can't draw any conclusions from that. A lot of these drug abusers change their minds when it's too late. At first giving themselves a fix seems like a great idea, but then they begin to have trouble breathing. They feel flushed, the heart beats get irregular. About the time they lose all motor controls, they go into a panic. I would conjecture that Brewster recognized something was happening that had never happened before. Suppose he was trying to make it to the phone? That doesn't prove anything."

"No, I guess not." Doug stood up and extended his hand. "Thanks, Tim. Thanks a lot. Oh, by the way, I noticed pictures of Brewster in your file. Can you trust me with one of them? Just a head shot. I'll return it."

"Sure." The examiner shuffled through a half-dozen glossy prints and handed one of them to Doug.

Karen glanced at it and quickly turned away. "Mr. Ryan, please," her voice was unsteady, "may I ask one more question? You said Dickie Brewster had been an addict for several years. Isn't it true that a habit such as he had developed could cost him forty to fifty dollars a day?"

"Absolutely. Or more. Heroin addiction is a luxury."

Karen drew in a deep breath. "What do you conclude from that?"

"Miss Thorndyke, I'm not very good at 'let's suppose.' But I'd say that means he had plenty of money."

"Or else that he wasn't paying for his drugs. I saw his apartment. It was nice. But it wasn't the home of a wealthy man and the Westminster is not an expensive place. When we came in you said you couldn't remember his case in detail. But for the last half hour you've been studying his file very carefully. Does anything at all strike you as unusual?"

The examiner reflected for a moment, tapping his chin with a forefinger. "No. I don't think so. Except for . . . well, yes. I guess you might consider it unusual. The difference in the tracks."

"Tracks? You mean the needle marks?"

Ryan nodded. "Most addicts get their stuff off the street and they ordinarily shoot it under unhygienic conditions. The marks frequently get infected from dirty needles. Tiny microscopic bits of lint and dirt get imbedded under the skin and stay there. So a track is actually the tiny bump of scar tissue that forms when these dirty and infected spots heal over. A row of tracks looks like a very small fine-toothed zipper. Well, Brewster had plenty of them, but the newest marks were clean. After years of buying off the street, he must have been getting his stuff from someone who knew what he was doing."

Throughout the ritual of final handshakes, one thought buzzed more loudly than any of the others that had come into Karen's mind. Who had been giving Dickie his injections? The moment they were out on the street and walking to Doug's car, Karen said eagerly, "Doug, I've been thinking . . . but first, tell me what *you* think."

With a wry grin, Doug said, "Same as you. That Dickie's lover was rich, right? Jasper Carter told you he was extremely jealous. So we've added a few brush strokes to the profile of the killer. He was well-heeled, subject to fits of passionate jealousy. A man called Leander. Leander killed his Hero, probably in a jealous rage. Now all we've got to do is find out—who *is* this Leander?"

"Mmmm . . ." Karen stopped suddenly, turned to face Doug and said, "I have an idea. The motorcycle. The expensive gift Leander, whoever he is, gave to Dickie. Jasper Carter said it's still in the carport behind the Westminster."

"And you think we ought to go and check it out."

"Yes. Would you mind?"

In the Westminster carport, Doug exclaimed, "That *is* a beauty. A Triumph. One of their specials. You can't touch it for less than five thousand dollars." His hand ran over it like a trainer caressing his favorite race horse. In a small notebook pulled from his jacket pocket, he jotted down the serial number and other identifying details. "Okay, so now we've seen the bike. Which verifies what that guy Carter told you, but doesn't really tell us anything we don't already know."

"Maybe it could," Karen persisted. "We've got the serial number, the make and model, and most important, the license number. Isn't that enough to trace back to the person who bought it?"

Doug shook his head. "I can check with the Department of Motor Vehicles, but they'll give me the name of the registered owner, not the name of the purchaser. DMV doesn't know or care who paid for it."

"Damn."

"Never mind," Doug said cheerfully. "There's more than one way to find a polecat, as my grandpa in Chillicothe used to say. My first day off, I'll check out the shops that sell Triumphs. At this point, we're headed for Portage Bay. Jenny should be home by now."

When they turned into the cul-de-sac at the end of East Sutherland, Adam Stewart's maroon Oldsmobile was parked at the bottom of the slope. Karen stared at it in silence, aware that her pulse was thumping like a tiny drum beat at the thought of seeing him.

"Adam's?" Doug said laconically, as they walked past the car. "You have a date with him?"

Karen's quick laugh had a nervous undertone. "Well, he did say . . . that is, I don't know. Considering the way our last conversation ended . . ."

Doug put a hand on her arm. "Whoa. Slow down. Before you take off on a dead run, I want to know if you're going to tell him about going to the MEO's office?"

Karen's eyes were troubled. "You don't think I should?"

Doug's only answer was a noncommittal shrug.

"Please, Doug. You told me not to mention doing the painting to him and so did Jennie. You didn't say so, but I've got a hunch you both thought I was a fool to tell him about barging in on Dickie's sister and talking to Jasper Carter. Right?"

"Right," Doug said soberly.

Looking down the float to the houseboat where she knew Adam was waiting for her, Karen said quietly, "I've got to tell him, Doug. I don't want to lie, or pretend, or conceal—not the way I feel about him. He hasn't said so, but I know he thinks I'm mad, or at least half-mad, and that's why he hasn't even . . ." she paused, adding almost apologetically, ". . . hasn't touched me. Maybe by showing him that there *are* some unanswered questions about Dickie's death, he'll decide that I'm not a paranoid schizophrenic who any sensible man would steer clear of."

"Okay, kiddo," Doug said with gruff affection. "But why don't you bring him over to Jennie's and we'll spill the beans together. Everything, about the MEO and the motorcycle. Nothing, at least for now, about the painting sessions. I'll mix the drinks. Deal?"

Karen smiled up at him. "Deal," she said. "You're a good man, Douglas W. Cooper."

"One of Seattle's finest," Doug said, and they proceeded along the floating sidewalk to their houseboats.

Adam was standing at Jennie's front window, glass in hand and a thoughtful frown on his face. He listened to Karen's recital and Doug's occasional comments with the same attentiveness he had shown when Karen told him about her visit to the Westminster. But Karen knew Adam's polite silence in no way indicated belief or approval. She was braced for rejection, maybe even for the half-controlled anger that once or twice had threatened to boil over when she was being "stubborn."

To her immense surprise, when she finished her confession, his frown melted into a smile. "Thanks, Karen. I appreciate your telling me. You, too, Doug. I think you and Jennie know that I've been disturbed by these, well, visions of Karen's. However, I've got to agree with you that the best way to exorcise the demon is to track him down, meet him face to face."

Karen's laugh was spontaneous and free. "Oh my goodness," she murmured. "You don't know how I've been hoping that you'd say something like that. You actually mean you've decided I'm not a mental case?"

Adam's eyebrows rose quizzically. "Did I ever say you were?"

"Well, I . . ." Karen hesitated. Something in his voice or manner puzzled her, something just beyond her grasp. "I *thought* you did."

Adam left the window, put down his glass and took both of her hands in his. "All Scots are skeptics. They'd rather be wrong than naive."

"Maybe we learned something at the coroner's office," Doug said. "Maybe we didn't. But I've got an idea about how to take a closer look at the question of where Brewster was getting his dope."

Adam released Karen's hands and said curiously, "What have you got in mind, Doug?"

"The medical examiner found some evidence to prove that Brewster used to get his stuff off the street but that six, eight months ago, he began getting shots from someone who knew how to give them you might say, well, professionally. With a clean needle, clean paraphernalia."

"Yes, yes," Adam said with a touch of impatience. "What's your idea?"

"I've got some contacts with the street traffic. Time was when I knew local pushers by their first names. One old contact in particular might know where Brewster had been buying. Or more exactly, when he quit buying on the street, and maybe even why he quit."

"If you were able to get that information," Adam asked, "what good would it do?"

"I don't know," Doug said pleasantly. Giving Adam a long and appraising look, he added, "But I'm going to give it a try. I'll use your phone in the bedroom, Jennie. Why don't you sweeten our drinks while I'm making the call?"

Was the wink at Jennie as he left the living room a signal? Karen didn't know, but she did note that when Jennie went to the kitchen to refill their glasses, she turned on the little radio next to the sink and the room filled suddenly with a blast of hard rock from WKJR, drowning whatever sounds might otherwise have escaped from the bedroom.

Ten minutes later, Doug was back in the living room. He swallowed a generous gulp of bourbon and announced, "Well, that was a tough one, but I finally convinced him. He's a smart informer, believe me, meaning he's managed to keep his skin for eight years that I know of, maybe longer. Anyway, he's agreed to talk."

"How much?" Jennie asked drily. "If you're talking about the guy I think you're talking about, he doesn't hand out freebies."

"Two big ones," Doug replied.

"Hah!"

"It's inflation, sweetheart." He turned to Adam. "I think we can learn something about Brewster, providing you're willing to cooperate."

Adam said levelly, "Of course."

Doug's face showed his surprise at such a quick response. "He won't take a chance on being seen with me. I was in vice for a long time. Too many of those characters would recognize me and that would be very bad for Big Toby. He will talk to you. I set it up for tomorrow night at six, Doc Maynard's on Pioneer Place."

"That's fine. You said two big ones. Meaning two hundred dollars."

"Right. I'll raise it."

Adam shook his head. "Let me handle it."

Karen broke in eagerly. "I'm going with you, Adam."

"All right. If Doug doesn't object."

For several seconds Doug's alert eyes took inventory of Adam's face. "Well," he said slowly, "Karen won't bother him if she stays at the table while you and Toby get together. I've already told him your girl friend and Brewster's sister, who is concerned about what happened to her brother, might come along. I figured Karen would want to make the scene. What I didn't figure was that you'd agree to it."

Adam smiled. "Only because I knew she would insist in spite of my objections."

"Okay. Six o'clock, Doc Maynard's. Adam, you'll see a big guy, built along the same lines you are. Gray hair, scar across one cheek, probably wearing jeans and an old navy pea jacket. He'll go straight back to the farthest stool, or the last one with a vacant stool next to it. You stroll on back and give him that great dramatic line—'Doug sent me.' "

After Karen and Adam had left, Jennie sat down and began turning her glass from side to side like a fortune teller consulting a crystal ball. Finally she said, "Detective Cooper, let's have it. I can hear the wheels turning. What are you thinking?"

"That Dr. Stewart wants our little girl to believe he's finally seen the light and he's going to cooperate."

"But does he mean it? Or is he humoring her, because he really does care for her?"

Doug's shoulders lifted in a massive shrug. "First he tries to discourage her, hints that she's balmy, blows his stack when he catches her snooping inside the Eye Bank. Tonight he offers to ante up the two hundred and keep the date with Toby. That guy's an enigma to me."

"Agreeing to take Karen along without putting up an argument . . . that's a reverse play."

Doug said grimly, "I didn't mention it, Jen, but you ought to know. I'm going, too. I won't go inside Doc Maynard's or anywhere near Toby, but believe me, I won't be very far away."

"Big brother is watching."

"You got the picture, baby." He finished his drink and put down his glass.

"Doug, something else is bothering me—the painting. Adam let himself into Karen's houseboat. He could have seen the painting while he was waiting for her to come home. It's right there in the living room."

"It's facing the wall. There's no reason for the back of a canvas to attract his attention."

"I have a bad feeling about it, that's all."

"What the hell, if he did get nosy, what would he see? That Karen, an artist who often paints abstracts, is doing one that has something to do with her eye. He might guess that she's trying to paint her vision, but that doesn't tell him she's doing it under hypnosis."

"I repeat—I don't like it, I don't like it at all."

Doug put his hands under her arms, lifted her off her chair and set her squarely on her feet. He gave her a long, deep kiss and then said against her mouth, "Okay, so let's do something we both like."

"We haven't had dinner."

"Who needs it?" Doug murmured, and kissed her again.

Fourteen

It was five-thirty, and the informer wouldn't be on his barstool at Doc Maynard's Public House until six. Adam parked by a two-hour meter on the street paralleling the waterfront. To the west, a rose-gold sun was dropping behind the rugged Olympic Mountains, its last glow caught by the rippled surface of Puget Sound.

Adam inserted coins into the meter. "We've got a little time to kill."

"Let's walk around and window-shop." Karen laughed pensively. "The last time I came to Pioneer Square, my eyes bothered me so much I couldn't really see anything."

Arm in arm, they strolled up the slope of Yesler Way, where once ox teams skidded logs from the heavily timbered hill above the mud flats to Henry Yesler's sawmill on the bay. Now the foot of the skid road ended in a block of decaying hotels, a beer tavern, secondhand bookstore and an avant-garde art gallery.

They paused at the corner of First Avenue and Yesler. Pioneer Square lay before them, three thousand square feet of land, triangular in shape. In the 1889's and 1890's it was the center of the business district and the frontier town's answer to New York's Fifth Avenue, its prosperity rooted in the fact that Seattle was the jumping off place for the Klondike. But gradually the city moved away from the waterfront. Pioneer Square became a derelict, peopled by homeless alcoholics and displaced canoe Indians. Some buildings were razed to make room for parking lots. Others remained like ghosts of a forgotten day.

Now Pioneer Square was enjoying a revival. In its own way, it had become more chic than the *nouveau riche* district on the hill above.

Adam and Karen walked along the south side of the square, talking little, pausing often along the wide street. Well-dressed shoppers mingled with the young, the bearded, and the braless in the crowds drifting from boutique to boutique. The swinging doors of saloons that for twenty years had seen few customers other than winos and seamen now swung with a heavy traffic of prosperous business and professional men and women.

Back on the square, Adam and Karen proceeded along the east side of the triangle to the Pioneer Building, whose tall arched windows, ornate sculptured columns and intricate stone lacework made her the queen of Seattle's late

Victorian structures. Adam looked at his wrist watch. "It's almost six. Look, Karen, it's not too late to change your mind, take a bus back to the houseboat and let me handle this."

"We've already debated that, remember? And I won."

"Okay then, let's go in."

The bar of Doc Maynard's Public House ran the length of the room, its huge mirror and massive oak frame covering the wall all the way to the fourteen-foot ceiling. Square wooden tables and straight-back wooden chairs stood at comfortable distances from each other on a floor of black and white tiles. On the wall to the right, a huge photograph of the good doctor glared down from its ornate gilt frame, accurately expressing his feelings about an establishment that bore his name but served nothing stronger than beer and wine.

Behind the bar, a young man in shirt-sleeves looked up as Adam and Karen came in, gave them a friendly nod, and went back to arranging wine bottles on the shelf below the mirror. The only people at the bar were a man and woman sitting on stools near the entrance.

Adam guided Karen to a small table set against the wall opposite the bar. "This place is strictly self-service. What shall I get you?"

"Burgundy?"

Adam smiled. "I can't promise anything except that it will probably be red."

At a few minutes after six, the heavy front doors swung open, admitting a young man in jeans and navy blue turtleneck sweater.

Karen looked inquiringly at Adam.

"I don't think so," Adam said quietly. "Too short and too young for the man Doug described. And he isn't wearing an old pea jacket."

Karen whispered, "But he's coming this way."

The young man threaded his way toward their table, but continued past them to the back of the saloon.

Karen looked anxiously from the front door to the big marble clock and back again. At ten minutes after six, Adam said against her ear, "Doug didn't promise the man would be on time."

They were about to give up at six-thirty when the doors swung open to admit a big man in his fifties, wearing jeans and a worn pea jacket. He walked the length of the bar without turning his head, stepped up to the last stool and signaled the bartender.

Adam said quietly, "Karen, stay here."

Reluctantly Karen nodded assent and watched Adam's unhurried approach to the lone man at the end of the bar. She was too far away to hear what they were saying, considered moving to another table, and then finally decided against it. So far the conversation appeared to be relaxed. This was far too important to risk doing something that might spoil Toby's cooperative mood. She concentrated instead on their gestures and facial expressions, thinking how nice it was to be able to sense what was going on with the aid of her eyes instead of only her ears.

Both men had ordered beer, studying their brimming glasses as if the depth of the foamy head was their only serious concern. Their lips moved when the bartender was at the far end of the bar. They seemed lost in thought when he came near, or when a waitress emerged from the kitchen and poured coffee from a aluminum pitcher into the glass coffee pots at the end of the bar.

In a few minutes Adam's right hand slid inside his coat, a movement Karen understood because she had seen him tuck an envelope of twenty dollar bills into the inside pocket. He pushed the envelope along the bar. The informer looked at him uncertainly and in one swift movement whisked the money into his own pocket.

Now Adam's attention was fixed on the front of the saloon, where two rough-looking men in business suits were coming through the door. They took places at the bar and began to talk, seemingly absorbed in their own conversation but repeatedly looking over to where Adam and Toby sat. Adam switched his attention back to Toby and said something that brought Toby's head up like a hunting dog picking up a scent. For several seconds both Toby and Adam were motionless, and then the man in pea-jacket and jeans drained his glass, quickly slid off his stool, and walked to the front of the saloon and out the door. Adam's eyes followed him, but he remained on his stool with the beer glass still in his hand.

The solid thud of the massive doors closing behind the departing Toby set Karen in motion.

Adam hadn't moved. The informer was leaving though his conversation with Adam had obviously been too short to have covered the subject of Dickie Brewster. She grabbed her purse, jumped up from her table and ran out into the street in time to see Doug rush out of the alley and leap down the outside steps to the basement level of the adjacent building and through the entrance to the Brasserie Pittsbourg.

The picture was clear. Doug had probably come to Pioneer Place to watch over this rendezvous but had remained hidden so as not to send the informer into a panic. But the informer had taken flight, so Doug was chasing after him . . . Without considering the circumstances, heedless of everything but keeping Doug in sight, Karen burst through the same door into the restaurant.

A dozen astonished diners were observing Doug's departure through a door at the back marked LADIES ROOM. In her haste, Karen brushed against a waitress, nearly lost her balance, and dropped her handbag. Murmuring apologies, she picked up the purse and ran on.

The door she had seen Doug go through opened into a short, empty corridor. Straight ahead was a blank wall. Besides the door she had just come through, there was only one possible exit—through the door on the right marked "Ladies."

Calling, "Doug?" she opened the door.

A woman at the wash basin looked up curiously.

Karen gasped, "Excuse me! Did someone just come in here?"

"I did," the woman said icily. "And now you, of course."

Karen retreated hastily and stood in the corridor clutching her handbag, too mystified to think beyond the fact that minutes were ticking by and Doug, as well as the informer, was getting farther and farther away. She had seen him go through that door from the restaurant. Surely he couldn't vanish. And she was certain he hadn't deliberately eluded her. On the other hand, perhaps Doug hadn't seen her running after him . . .

Karen was about to obey the voice of reason and return to Doc Maynard's when she saw a narrow gap at the end of the corridor. What she had at first taken to be a blank wall was actually a large piece of plywood resting against the wall and not even nailed into place. She inserted her fingers in the crack, gripped the edge of the board and threw all her weight into sliding it to the side. On her third try, she pushed it back just far enough to slip sideways through the opening.

The single bulb above the entrance to the Ladies Room cast enough light to show her that she was in a small tunnel. The air was heavy with the blended odors of dust, mildew, and wet cement. Old boards lay in careless heaps on both sides of the unlighted corridor. The narrow passage down the center was so dirty she couldn't tell whether it was wooden or paved.

Cracked, uneven, like an old sidewalk. . . . But of course! This must be the underground city. Karen's schoolgirl history lessons came back to her. After the fire of 1889 a new city had been built on top of the burned out area. Many of the buildings had been left with original sidewalks anywhere from ten to thirty-two feet below the street level. Karen's class had thought it comical that if someone wanted to cross the street they had to climb a ladder from the sidewalk up to the street, walk across to the other side, then climb down another ladder. Eventually most of the merchants closed up their ground floors and moved their shops to the second or third floor.

The Brasserie Pittsbourg was in the basement of the Pioneer Building. That is, the basement *now*, but the street level when the building had opened for business in 1892. There was still an opening between the rear of the restaurant and the deserted underground, and that's where she was now. And so was Doug. For somewhere up ahead, far beyond the scope of the dim light from the corridor behind her, she thought she heard the hollow ring of footsteps. She ran toward the sound.

The man's head throbbed so viciously he was afraid he would vomit. If that started, it would take over and he would be too weak to carry out his plan. The attacks had started after he had killed Dickie, and this was the worst yet. As always, the pain struck when he became over-excited, and excitement had been building up from the moment he decided that he must kill the girl tonight. This time it burst without warning while he was hiding in the shadows at the rear of the Brasserie Pittshourg, waiting for her to come out of the Ladies Room. So near, so near. He couldn't let the pain inside his head defeat him now.

When he heard a door open he tensed, clutching his improvised weapon with both hands, repressing a moan as new shocks of pain burst at his temples and behind his eyes. Now, now . . . She must be in the hall outside of the Ladies Room. In seconds she would come around the corner. Light footsteps, step, step, step . . . Silence. She had stopped. He could imagine her standing in the hall, pausing to look for something in her handbag. He imagined he could hear her breathing, that he could smell her cologne. Why wait for her to come to him when in two or three strides he could go to her? A swift, killing blow . . . There might be one terrible second when he would see her staring eyes, when Dickie's eye, glowing at him like the jewel in an idol's forehead, would laugh at him for the last time. And then he would close her eyelids, and kill Dickie forever.

More steps. She was coming at last. But she didn't appear. Instead, he heard a rough sound, as if a door was resisting opening or was stuck in its track. There must be another exit. She was getting away!

He was around the corner in time to see her while she was still on the fringe of the pale light cast by the bulb in the ceiling outside the Ladies Room.

As he slipped through the narrow opening in the hallway's dead end, she disappeared into the darkness but he could still hear her footsteps. This was far better than what he had planned.

The dark was his protection and his blessing. He wouldn't have to suffer that last, hideous staring gaze in Dickie's dying eye. It would be over soon. Her footsteps echoed along the black passageway. All he had to do was to follow that sound.

Fifteen

The dirt-encrusted and rubble-strewn sidewalk became harder to follow with every step until finally the darkness swallowed her completely. *Now* what? Karen asked herself. If she hadn't been able to overtake Doug when there was some light to see by, what were her chances now?

On the other hand, Doug couldn't see his way any better than she could. And her years of badly impaired vision had sharpened her powers of hearing and smell, combining to give her a curious sense of nearness that had often saved her from bumping into things she couldn't see. She could *feel* her way in the dark. Doug couldn't. She would certainly overtake him.

So she plunged ahead, not running but walking rapidly, arms straight out to each side in case the sidewalk turned a corner or she began to wander from a straight course. Every fifteen or twenty feet she stopped to listen. Once or twice she thought she heard a distant footfall, and held her breath, concentrating fiercely in an effort to pluck sound out of the silence.

Distance and time were hard to measure, but she knew she had turned several corners and estimated that she had covered two or three city blocks when she finally stopped to rest. She admitted to herself how foolish she had been to chase after Doug in the murky maze of a decaying underground city. In any event, she had lost him and the only thing to do was to go back.

She reversed her course, still using her arms as a cat measures the size of a hole with its whiskers. The way back to the restaurant seemed much longer than when she was coming from the other direction. And more complicated. More turns, more narrow, irregular holes punched in walls separating the underground level of one building from the underground level of the next. At every turn she expected to see a thin stream of light from the Brasserie Pittsbourg. Minutes passed and the light didn't appear. She had lost Doug. And now she, too, was lost.

At first, Karen was more embarrassed than frightened. She knew that the underground city was about a mile and a half in circumference, and that only a small section had been made safe for guided tours. Apparently, she had had the bad luck to wander into the part that had never been cleared or repaired. But if she kept her head and didn't go around in circles, she was bound to find her way out.

The sidewalks were uneven, dipping unexpectedly where the underlying fill had sunk, rising suddenly where there were two or three steep steps between buildings. After some time, she sensed that she had entered a large room. Though she took several side steps to the right, then to the left, her hands didn't encounter a wall. The air was drier, and the sound of her leather heels was muffled as in an enclosed space. She paused, took one forward step, and bumped her forehead against something so hard her, "Ow!" echoed in the darkness.

Karen backed up, cautiously extended one hand and explored the object she had walked into. It was a wooden column, smooth to the touch and ringed in two or three places by an ornamental collar. She advanced a few more feet and found another column just like it. She was probably in a store of some kind, and the artistic woodwork suggested that it had been rather elegant in its day. Karen hoped fervently that there would be an entrance that would open onto the main sidewalk and to one of the sections that was illuminated for the benefit of the guided tours. But to find her way she needed *light*.

She knew there was no use dipping into her handbag for a book of matches. She didn't smoke and had no need for matches, except the big kitchen variety she used to light a fire in her Franklin stove. Suddenly she had a mental picture of herself doing just that only a few days before, when she had kindled a hearth fire on a rainy afternoon. The same visual recall showed her wearing the teal green cardigan she now had on. She searched the pockets anxiously. The first was empty but the second yielded two thick wooden matches. Two precious aids to ending an ordeal that was beginning to frighten her badly in spite of her resolve to keep calm.

She dropped to one knee and felt along the floor for a spot free of dirt, a little rough, and above all, dry. "Please God," she whispered as she struck the match, watched the thin fire bend before a draft and then rise in a small but steady flame. She got to her feet, one hand holding the match and the other cupped around it protectively.

In the faltering light she saw that she was indeed in a shop of some kind. One wall consisted of large empty frames where display windows had looked out onto the street. Peeling strips of fancy floral wallpaper clung to an inside wall. One small area was still covered with a few feet of the original oak flooring. But where was the main entrance, the one that would connect her with *today's* Seattle, the escape hatch from this crazy waffle of dark passages and ghostly caves?

Something her teacher had told the class came to mind—that in the fancier shops, the merchants had installed iron steps leading down from the new street level into sky-lighted wells. If steps led down . . . That was it, of course! Steps that go down, go up. To rescue herself she had to find such a staircase.

She saw it on the far side of the room just as the match flame burned her fingers and went out. She felt in her sweater pocket for the second match but changed her mind. Since she had already spotted the stairs, she could manage in the dark and save her one remaining source of light.

Her excitement at being so near to deliverance made her careless for the first time since she realized she was lost. The match had established the space between herself and the stairs and shown that it was clear. She hurried across the room, slowed as she felt for the first riser with the toe of her shoe, and then she eagerly began to climb, running the fingers of her right hand along the wall like feelers.

Her fingers anticipated the spiraling curve of the stairwell, but they couldn't warn her that around the bend the steps had crumbled and fallen apart. At that point she was so excited, so confident in her mental picture of what lay ahead, that she was almost running when the stairs ended abruptly. She dropped straight down into a hole three or four feet deep and lay on her side, gasping, while hot waves of pain traveled up from her ankles to blend with the stinging pain in her knees. "Stupid!" she said out loud, and then repeated it, "Stupid!" because anger at herself was easier to cope with than the fright she was feeling.

Gently she explored her ankles and knees. Her nylons were torn and the exposed knees were wet, probably with blood, but the pain was subsiding and when she pulled herself up and put a little weight on her feet, she was sure there were no broken bones or serious strains. She groped for her handbag, found it, and, grasping the rim of the pit, dragged herself up the side. With one hand against the wall as her guide, she ascended safely. Back to square one.

In the middle of the abandoned shop, Karen paused and tried to logically analyze her situation. The immediate question was what direction to take. Back the way she had come, or through the paneless display windows into a different area? There was a third alternative that hadn't occurred to her before—shouting for help.

Karen moved slowly toward the display windows, found an opening and instinctively lifted her feet to step through the empty window frame. Arms outstretched, she took two or three forward steps. This was as good a spot as any. After that first impulsive race to catch up to Doug, she had been plunging through the wilderness with almost no fear of what she might encounter. She had been lost without really feeling lost. But all at once the dark was filling the shadows with invisible horrors. She felt threatened by whatever lay ahead, and indescribably terrified by the thought of going back into the blackness from which she had emerged. Fists clenched, she filled her lungs with air, threw her head back and put all her strength into one shouted word: "Help!" She took another deep breath and yelled again. "Help! Help!" And again and again, until the blood vessels in her neck and throat seemed about to burst with the effort.

Panting, she waited for a response. None came. She must be in an area that was effectively blocked off from the modern city. She had to find a spot where there was a crack, an old vent, any sort of careless gap or incomplete construction. To spot such a place, she needed light.

After a few more steps, Karen stopped, removed the precious remaining match from her sweater pocket and struck it on the wall. By its pale flame she made a desperately fast examination of her surroundings. She saw that pipes were suspended along the retaining wall at her left, three or four of them of various sizes, the largest made of tile and the others of gray metal, some rusted at the joints. Those with rust were probably not in use, but the others might be. She didn't know enough about electricity or plumbing to guess what they housed. Conduits for cables? The municipal water system? In any case, they gave her an idea.

Before the match flame flickered out, she noticed that odds and ends of old boards were stacked against the retaining wall under the pipes. She ran her fingers over the stack until she found a short piece. She picked it up, lifted it over her head and began to beat a rhythm on the pipes. Tap tap tap, bang, bang, bang, tap tap tap. The three shorts, plus three longs, plus three shorts of the international code of distress, a bit of knowledge learned as a Girl Scout. She repeated it over and over again until her arms ached, waiting several seconds between each series to listen for a response. After what seemed an eternity, she dropped the board and the suffocating silence descended.

She moved ahead blindly, stumbling over rough spots, catching herself, going on until she reached what her exploring hands identified as a T-intersection where the sidewalk continued straight ahead but another branched off to the right. She turned to the right. At the far end of what seemed like an endless tunnel she saw a pinpoint of light. And with the light, the image.

The distant gleam grew brighter and brighter as the amorphous break in the darkness took shape and became the glittering point of the needle. Panic knotted deep in Karen's throat, blocking the hysterical screams that were trying to get out. Trembling uncontrollably, she stared at the image, waiting helplessly for its predestined advance and the merciless terror of the decending needle.

But the light remained at the end of the tunnel, pale and shapeless and immobile. Somehow this was different from the vision seen by Dickie Brewster's eye. It existed in the real and physical world outside herself, as tangible as the board she had picked up or the pipes she had struck with it. And though her pulse was pounding and her knees felt weak, she began to realize that her panic was something she could control. She *could* walk toward that light as common sense and her instinct for survival told her she had to do.

By plain force of will she walked unsteadily toward the light. With every fearful step she told herself that the light ahead had frightened her, not because she was seeing it with Dickie's eye, but because of its similarity to the way the other visions had begun. The image was an inner reality, which she alone could see and interpret. But the light up ahead came from a manufactured glass globe containing delicate filaments and connected with the underground electrical system, and that was all there was to it. Except that, being real, it could lead her to the way out.

She came to another intersection, and there it was—one single light bulb suspended from the ceiling by a rubberized cord. To her right were a series of broad brick arches, all cleaned and restored to their pristine glory into what she guessed would be entrances to a series of small shops. Ninety years before, wax mannequins in bombazine dresses might have posed in one of those windows. Now they were empty vaults, furnished with nothing but worthless debris and peopled by ghosts and scampering rats.

As she studied her surroundings, Karen heard a sound, so faint she thought at first that she imagined it. Tense and motionless, she gave all her attention to identifying it. It was a ticking sound, like a clock. She walked toward it and paused. Now it was more distinct. She went on, stepped through an opening into another building. Here, also, a single light bulb illuminated the sidewalk. The ticking object was on the wall to her right. A small, metal box with a movable indicator hand. A timing divice, similar to the manual gadget she used when she was baking. She was still wondering about its purpose when it stopped ticking and the light in the building she had left and the light over her head went out simultaneously. Once more she was lost in total darkness, but she felt like shouting with joy. The lights were controlled automatically by the timer on the wall. The only logical reason for turning them on would be to light the way for a guided tour. The little device on the wall was there to save power by turning them off after the tour had gone through. If the tour had proceeded in the direction from which she had come, surely she would have stumbled into it. Therefore, she thought, they must be ahead of me.

At first she kept a sensible pace, remembering how the sidewalks dipped and turned. Better to catch up slowly than to take another bad fall and not catch up at all. But when, at last, she saw another faint light ahead, Karen forgot caution and began to run.

Silently cursing the darkness, Dr. Adam Stewart's bungling and Big Toby's jitters, Doug came to a halt and once more threw all his power of concentration into picking up sounds. Ever since he had pursued Toby through the Brasserie Pittsbourg into the underground, he had stopped every few minutes and listened for audible clues to the informer's whereabouts. Twice he had heard distant footsteps. Shouting, "Hey, Toby! It's me, Doug!" he had increased his stumbling pace. But the pursued man moved faster than his pursuer. Doug's voice boomeranged off the walls of the deserted city, mocking the futile chase. A man who had been badly spooked, for whatever reason that had happened, wasn't going to stop and wait meekly to be overtaken.

The whole crazy mess seemed more senseless the longer Doug kept pushing his way through the pitch black maze. From whom was Toby fleeing? He already had been in a dead run when Doug rushed out of the alley behind him near Doc Maynard's.

After fifteen or twenty minutes something happened that increased Doug's confusion. The first time he heard footsteps the sound had come from up ahead, as he expected it would. But the second time, it came from behind. Had Toby doubled back, and was now fleeing in the opposite direction with the idea of escaping the underground as he had entered it, through the rear door of the Brasserie? That seemed impossible, unless Toby had found a passageway off the main sidewalk that Doug hadn't noticed. Or was a *third* person charging along these damp, dusty-smelling abandoned sidewalks, chasing or being chased? Ridiculous, Doug told himself. Toby was fool enough to hide in the underground and Doug Cooper was fool enough to come looking for him, but who else would join such a bizarre and potentially dangerous game of hide-and-seek?

Another ten or fifteen minutes had gone by when the sidewalk Doug was following reached a dead end. A somewhat narrower passage branched off at a right angle. With cautious steps, feeling his way along the wall, Doug rounded the corner.

In the distance, the length of a city block from the intersection, a pale light illuminated the sidewalk. As he walked toward it, a small figure burst out of the shadows from some passage or side street branching in from the right. As weak as the light was, Doug recognized Karen.

His first thought was that it would be better to overtake her than to shout and perhaps startle and frighten her. He quickened his pace.

But as suddenly as Karen had appeared out of a side street, a second figure emerged, a figure too dimly seen and shadowy to be identified except as a man of more than average height. Whoever he was, he was pursuing Karen.

Doug broke into a run, shouting her name. He saw the man lift his arm, saw Karen fall. Running blindly, Doug tripped over a bump in the sidewalk, fell, got to his feet and raced ahead. By the time he reached her, the man had disappeared and Karen was sitting up, looking around with the dazed expression of someone being aroused too quickly from a deep sleep.

He dropped to one knee. "Hey, are you all right?"

"I think someone hit me."

"Someone did. I saw it. Are you hurt?"

She shook her head. "Not really. I must have jumped to the side when you shouted, and the blow glanced off. I just feel a little bit, well, stunned. And scared. But I'm all right. I can get up."

"Okay, but slowly, and let me help you."

Doug put his arms around her, lifting her to her feet. "Why, Adam!" she exclaimed. "Why did you . . . when did you . . ."

Still supporting Karen, Doug turned around to face the blinding brilliance of the flashlight in Adam's hand. "Hey, aim that thing some place else," Doug said brusquely. "And pardon my curiosity, but what the hell *are* you doing here?"

"Trying to find Karen," Adam said coolly. "What happened, Karen?"

"Someone hit me. I was wandering along a dark corridor. I turned a corner and I saw a light way ahead in the distance, so I began to run. And then, it happened."

Adam swiveled his flashlight so that its beam moved along the wall and across the ceiling, stopping when it fell on a steel girder directly over the spot where Karen had fallen. "Could that be your someone?" he said gently. "You were running in the dark and you could have hit your head on that very solid piece of steel. Here, close your eyes. I want to take a look at your head."

"It wasn't a girder," Doug said angrily. "You might get her to believe that, but not me."

"I'm not trying to get her to believe anything," Adam retorted, examining Karen's scalp with the tips of his fingers. "But the girder is low, just the right height to hit her where there's a slight swelling on the top of her head. Maybe someone did attack her, but I just came from the direction he would have to have taken to get away unless he wanted to run right past you, and I didn't see anyone. Just a bunch of tourists listening to a guide recite the history of the underground—and not one of them was out of breath and carrying a blunt instrument. So let me ask *you*, Doug. *What* man attacked Karen, and where did he go?"

"It must have been the man I saw run into the underground. The man I've been chasing for the last thirty minutes. Toby. My contact."

"I don't think so," Adam said matter-of-factly. "Your informer is probably twenty miles away from here by now. He told me to tell you that he won't be available for a while."

"Jesus! What in hell happened?"

"He took one look at some thugs who came into Doc Maynard's and bolted. It's too bad that it happened before I had a chance to get any answers about Dickie Brewster. I gave him the two hundred dollars, but he panicked and ran out before he could tell me anything."

"Is that right?" Doug asked, though the question had the tone of a flat statement.

"That's right." Adam's voice was cold, dismissing the subject. To Karen he spoke quietly, showing concern. "I'm sorry, Karen. I know you're disappointed that nothing's come from this affair except a painful bump on the head. Come on, now. Let's get out of here."

Karen hesitated. She looked from Adam to Doug, caught Doug's barely visible nod and knew what he was telling her—Yes, go with him now. We'll talk this over later. "Yes, Adam," she said wearily. "Please take me home."

Sixteen

Karen imagined that when Adam said good-night at the houseboat door there was more warmth in his voice and manner than he had shown before. Not that he had said anything out loud. Perhaps the emotional intensity that registered so clearly on her sensory radar screen during the few minutes they were standing together in the dark had been nothing more than the concern he would show for anyone who had taken such a nasty bump on the head.

"The skin isn't broken but cleanse the whole area thoroughly with hydrogen peroxide. And you'd better take a couple of aspirin." These were hardly words of love, but somehow they had conveyed love, or at least enough affection that only her fear of rebuff kept Karen from asking him to come in. Now that he had gone, Karen regretted whatever chicken-heartedness or defensiveness had kept her from going a little more than halfway. The houseboat, her beloved refuge, her hearth and home, was suddenly a desperately lonely place.

Jennie's quick footstep and Jennie's pixie face peering through the French door brought the bad moment to an end. Karen welcomed her joyfully, rescued by Jennie's rapid-fire commentary on what Doug had been telling her since he got back from Pioneer Square, a recital punctuated by many hugs and mother-monkey inspections of Karen's bruised head. At length Jennie released her and said, "You don't look sleepy."

"Just the opposite. I'm all keyed up."

Jennie nodded sagely. "It figures. Want to have another go at the painting? That awful business in the underground might have stirred things up. The strange light down there, the attempt to kill you . . . all that might have jarred Dickie's eye. You know, might help bring something into focus. Anyway, shall we try? If nothing else happens, you'll be good and sleepy when you come out of the trance."

"How funny," Karen mused. "I do feel like painting. Even before you suggested it, I was thinking—I want to paint, I've got to paint."

"Good," Jennie said. "Now sit down in your chair and relax while I get Doug."

Jennie began this second session just as she had the first. The physical environment was the same—"Jennie's chair" facing "Karen's chair," the easel in the corner, and on the table beside it,

Karen's palette, tubes of paint, and a variety of brushes in a jar of turpentine.

Jennie closed the drapes and switched on a floor lamp near the easel. "Now we're ready," she said as she sat down facing Karen. "You're comfortable, aren't you, Karen? That's your favorite chair, and it's a nice one . . ."

Using her voice to project intimacy and confidence, Jennie repeated some of the preliminary explanation she had gone through before, moving much more rapidly this time into the actual induction. From the moment she began with, "Now it's time for you to go to sleep," she saw that Karen was even more susceptible to suggestion than she had been the first time. "Relax. Relax all your muscles. Your eyelids are heavy now. Now they're closing. Slowly, slowly . . ."

In fifteen minutes, Karen was in a genuine hypnotic sleep. Continuing with the same quiet confidence, but a little more softly, Jennie instructed Karen to open her eyes, to walk to the easel and to turn the canvas around.

Karen responded without hesitation. She seemed as relaxed and as confident as Jennie's voice.

"Now I want you to look at what you painted the last time. Look at it closely . . ."

The last time Jennie had taken a position outside Karen's range of vision to reduce her presence to a commanding voice. But now Karen was confronting her own artistic projection of the needle image, not a blank canvas. Jennie sensed that if she could see Karen's face, she would have a better chance of leading her past the moment of terror that had paralyzed her and had put an end to the first session. She was particularly concerned about Karen's reaction to the detail in the painting that had gone beyond what she had seen in her vision—the lonely disembodied eye, peering through the fog.

At Karen's side, Jennie said, "You're looking at the image. But it's not all there, is it, Karen? There's too much fog. Something is hidden behind that fog. You can't see it yet, but when you start painting, the fog will begin to lift. Look hard, Karen. Look at the bright light, and the shining needle. There's the sharp point of the needle. There are the fingers, holding the needle. Now look there, right there . . ."

On impulse, Jennie moved the floor lamp closer to the easel so that the light on the picture was suddenly more intense. "The lamp is shining on that one spot, Karen. There, coming through the fog. An eye . . . I want you to start painting, Karen, because now you can see something you've never seen before. Start painting, Karen . . ."

Karen responded to the extent of picking up a brush, but then she seemed immobilized. The hand holding the paintbrush hovered uncertainly over the palette while she stared at the painting. She appeared to be more confused than frightened.

"Yes, Karen. You painted that. That's what you saw when the vision came at night. That's what you saw when you were in the dentist's chair. I want you to look at the needle, Karen. *Think* about the needle . . . You are going to see something new, something that was hidden in the fog. Are you looking at the needle, Karen? If you are, I want you to nod your head."

Karen's head bobbed slowly, not once but twice, as if to tell Jennie she was really trying.

"Very good, Karen. Now look at the eye . . ." Again Jennie asked her to nod her assent, and once more Karen made a positive response. But there was still a block. To Jennie, Karen appeared to be emotionally detached from what she was looking at. Something was diluting her ability to concentrate on it, even though she was clearly in a state of hypnosis.

Should she give up, at least for now? Awaken Karen, and then make another attempt another day? That prospect was discouraging. There was still one idea that had come to her while she was planning this second session, and wild as it might prove to be, it was worth trying.

"Now I want you to relax completely, Karen. I'm going to leave you for just a few seconds and while I'm gone you are going to think about your painting, but you won't paint more of it until I ask you to . . ."

Jennie hurried into the bedroom, put a warning finger to her lips as Doug looked up from his magazine, and went into the bathroom. Having changed the dressings on Karen's operated eye, she knew exactly where to find a roll of gauze, adhesive tape and a pair of small scissors. Back with Karen, she cut two strips of adhesive and folded a length of gauze into a patch two inches square. Her motions were deft but deliberately unhurried. As she cut and folded, she explained exactly what she was doing and why.

"We've done this many times before, haven't we, Karen. I'm making this patch so that I can cover your eye, just as I did after you came home from the hospital. But now I'm *not* going to cover your *new* eye. This patch is for your *other* eye, the one we used to call your good eye. Hold still a moment . . ."

Karen blinked but didn't draw back as Jennie placed the patch over her right eye and taped it securely in place. It wasn't necessary to ask Karen if she could see through it; Jennie had been careful to use so many layers that that would be impossible.

"Very good, Karen. Now in just a minute I'm going to ask you to start painting. But first, there's something I want you to understand. We both know it's your *left* eye, your *new*, operated eye, that has the power to show you what Dickie Brewster saw when he died. Your right eye does not have that power. So when you were looking at your painting with both eyes, the right one kept telling you that there was nothing behind that fog, because *it* couldn't *see* through the fog. It kept you from concentrating. It was distracting your new eye, diluting it's power to see . . ."

Jennie paused and stepped back. With more emphasis than she had used at any time during the session, she said, "Now I want you to start painting. Your new eye isn't confused any longer. It's free, it can show you what it sees . . . Fine,

fine. Yes, put paint on the brush. The fog is beginning to lift. The picture is getting clearer and clearer . . ."

Karen worked slowly at first, with Jennie's continual reassurances like a verbal obbligato to the movements of her right hand. Then suddenly all her attention focused on the area around the eye and the tempo of her painting speeded noticeably. Jennie was so fascinated by what was emerging from the canvas that she forgot to watch Karen's face.

Karen's terrified cry came without warning. Her face was ashen, her eyelid closed. Her whole body swayed and would have fallen if Jennie hadn't been quick enough to catch her.

Jennie called urgently, "Doug!"

Doug carried Karen to her bed and Jennie covered her with a quilt. Sitting on the edge of the bed, Jennie recited the gentle commands that had awakened Karen from her previous trance. When Karen was fully awake, Jennie said, "You did beautifully. But now you're feeling very tired. So you're going to take a nap."

Karen smiled, closed her eyes and was asleep almost immediately.

Doug followed Jennie into the living room and while she closed the French door, in a rough masculine *sotto voce* asked, "Is she okay?"

"Sure. Feeling sleepy is the healthy aftermath of a hypnotic trance. You move easily and naturally from one kind of sleep to another. Come on, I want you to see what she painted."

Side by side, Jennie and Doug studied the unfinished picture in silence. At length Doug breathed, "Jesus! It worked."

"*It* worked?"

"Yes. Covering her right eye. Oh, I was listening. What do you expect from a veteran snoop like me?" He went back to the painting, examining it closely, then stepping back to see it from a different perspective. His expression was puzzled. "The face isn't really distinct but it's a helluva lot more than she got down before. It looks like the eyes and eyebrows are beginning to emerge. I guess it could be anybody, man or woman. Does it remind you of someone?"

Jennie shrugged. "I can't say that it does. What about you?"

"No. It isn't clear enough yet. Except I get the feeling that if she ever does get the whole image onto that canvas, I'm going to yelp louder than she ever has."

Jennie whispered, "You know what you're saying, don't you? You're saying you believe Karen's right. That her operated eye *is* actually imprinted with an image and if she can see it clearly she'll know who killed Dickie. Now you're a believer, huh?"

"I don't know," Doug said soberly. "But I keep asking myself—why did covering the right eye make such a difference? Was it simply because Karen *thought* it made a difference? Because she swallowed your line about letting the new eye do all the seeing? Or did more of the image come clear to her because that trick of yours actually did help her new eye penetrate the fog?"

"I'm asking *you,*" Jennie said drily. "You're the hard-boiled skeptic. I'm only a hard-boiled romantic. After two of these painting sessions, watching the way she goes at it—it's almost like automatic writing—well, after watching it happen, I'm awfully close to thinking something is going on that can't be explained scientifically."

Doug nodded slowly. "So we go ahead on that basis, right? That Karen's vision is some sort of phenomenon, physical, psychological, or whatever. And if she's willing, we keep her working on this painting."

They had trapped him. They had effectively cut off the only route from her front deck to the shore. They hadn't seen him, though the man had glanced at the deck as he crossed over to her houseboat.

When someone pulled the drapes, he felt safer. He still couldn't escape, for one of them would surely see him as he passed the uncurtained French door, but he didn't really want to give up, to fail again, to leave without doing what he had come to do.

And so he hugged the shadows, cramped between two large planter boxes, commanding his sense of hearing to screen out the soft lapping lake water against the float and all other exterior sounds and to concentrate on voices inside the houseboat. The man wasn't speaking at all. The women's voices came to him as a continuous murmur from which he could pick up only an occasional word. As the isolated bits of speech collected, a pattern of meaning began to emerge.

After fifteen minutes he knew what was happening.

His stomach lurched and pain burst open in his temples. She had been hypnotized and she was painting, while her friend's voice, rising now to a clear confident monotone, urged her on, promising her again and again that Dickie's eye was ready to show her the face of the man who had killed him.

"It's getting clearer and clearer, isn't it, Karen. Your brush is moving through the fog, finding the face . . . Fine, Karen, fine! Keep painting . . . Dickie's eye is showing you what to paint. Dickie's eye sees . . ."

Dickie's eye, Dickie's eye . . . The man retched violently as the killing headache took possession. Blind with pain, his whole being screamed for release from that terrible eye. His ears faithfully reported the sounds on the other side of the window and his mind remained coherent enough to tell him when the hypnotic session ended and when the man's voice insisted that Karen was in no state to be left alone overnight. A little later, the lights in the houseboat went out and all three emerged and crossed to the other houseboat.

In a few minutes some invisible switch was flipped and the patio lights went out as well. The man crouched in the shadow between planter boxes, removed his shoes, slowly rose to his feet, and ran soundlessly along the dock to the shore. Safe in the grove of balm of Gilead trees at the foot of East Sutherland Street, he stopped to catch his breath. Panting, he turned to look back at the scene of this last and most bitter defeat. She had escaped tonight. He could not let that happen again. His time was getting shorter with every stroke of her paintbrush.

Seventeen

As Karen and Adam approached the entrance to the Drakes' late Victorian mansion, Karen said, "Do you realize I've never actually seen Dr. Drake? Except as a pair of dark eyes peering out between a face mask and white surgeon's cap. He won't look the same at a cocktail party."

"He's seen *you*, and he definitely liked what he saw. He called you beautiful. The man's daft, of course."

"Dr. Drake has seen me? You mean in the operating room."

Adam shook his head. "No. He doesn't really 'see' someone during surgery. Not the whole face, that is. Only the eyes. But he has seen you twice since. The first time was one afternoon when you were leaving our office. You wouldn't remember that—it was the day you panicked at the dentist's and you were still badly upset. He saw you again at the hospital, when you were warming up for your burglary of the Eye Bank office." Adam pressed the doorbell.

The door opened instantly. A woman in a maid's uniform said, "Come in, please."

The spacious hall opened onto a large living room already humming with the curious blend of sound produced by forty or fifty voices speaking in different keys, and all at the same time. As Karen and Adam entered, a maid took Karen's blue linen coat and seconds later a man wearing beautifully tailored casual clothes detached himself from a small cluster of guests and approached them with a glass in one hand.

"Dr. Drake," Adam said. "But I don't think he's looking at me."

The doctor switched his glass to his left hand, extended his right to Adam, all the while smiling at Karen. "You said you were bringing someone, Adam. I'm delighted with your choice."

"Karen, this is the man behind the surgical mask. Frank, this is Karen Thorndyke."

Drake signaled to a young man in a black suit and black bow tie carrying a silver tray. "It's rare for me to have the pleasure of offering a drink to a patient. This one will come in a glass, Miss Thorndyke, not through a tube. Adam, you know most of the people here this evening. May I turn you loose while I greet some newcomers?"

The young man with the tray was standing at attention.

"Yes, sure, Frank. Karen? Scotch?"

When the waiter had gone to the bar in the adjoining sunroom, and Dr. Drake to his guests,

Karen's attention shifted to the roomful of strangers, all chatting amiably, all with glasses in hand. It had never occurred to her that she would see someone she knew at a cocktail party in a Broadmoor mansion, unless some of the guests were patrons of the arts who might have attended the opening of her show at the Frye Museum. But here in the Drake home she *did* know someone, someone whose presence gave her a hollow sensation in the pit of her stomach. Martha O'Donnell, Dickie Brewster's sister, whose stricken look she would never forget, was standing with two men near the French doors leading to the sunroom. She was listening attentively to a tall, angular man in a tweed sports jacket, the only man in the room as tall as Adam, who was emphasizing his remarks with strong gestures of his free left hand. Martha O'Donnell's expression was relaxed and amused. At a particularly dramatic gesture, she laughed delightedly.

Karen said urgently, "Adam!" In her own ears, his name came out of her throat like a shout. But it couldn't have, for he was waving to someone on the other side of the room and steering her through the crowd. Toward the door into the sunroom! Toward the tall man with the emphatic left hand and his eager listener, Martha O'Donnell.

Mute and painfully aware of the blood rushing to her face, Karen went through the trial of introductions. Adam's friend was the third member of the trio, Dr. Rob Dennis, a short, balding man with a fluffy rim of orange-red hair encircling his pate like a hedge. He accepted Karen's hand, pumped it vigorously, and introduced

Martha O'Donnell, who looked at Karen without any expression and said coolly, "We've met." As if Karen didn't exist, she gestured toward the tall man and addressed only Adam Stewart. "Do you know Henry Garner, Dr. Stewart?"

Karen, with her eyes fixed on Adam to avoid looking at Martha O'Donnell, saw Adam's start of surprise. "Henry . . ." he said as they shook hands. "My pleasure. You're an attorney?"

Garner smiled and said drily, "Does it show? Or perhaps we've met before. Except for statutes and legal codes, I've got a rotten memory."

"No, I don't believe we've met. But your name is familiar." Adam had brought the startled expression under control as quickly as it flashed across his face. His tone was casual, almost joking. "Perhaps I heard it from one of my colleagues. If you handle malpractice suits."

Somehow Karen muddled through the next few minutes, speaking only when silence would have been an even worse breach of cocktail party protocol than serious conversation. To her relief, Adam seemed as anxious as she was to leave these people. After a brief conversation with Rob Dennis, they moved away through the crowd.

At the far side of the living room Karen said quietly, "Adam, what jolted you when you were introduced to Henry Garner?"

Adam shrugged. "Not really jolted. Just a little surprised at a coincidence. The name that appeared in the Eye Bank files as Dickie Brewster's attorney of record and legally appointed next of kin was Henry Garner. Which is why Garner was the one the Medical Examiner's office contacted when they wanted to get formal permission to remove Dickie's eyes. That was in the file, too. It makes sense. Martha O'Donnell was Dickie's only relative, but since she lives in Dublin, it was natural for Dickie to name the family lawyer in case of an emergency."

"How curious," Karen mused, looking back at the trio still in conversation near the sunroom. "I mean, the connection between Garner and Dickie and Martha O'Donnell."

"He's their family attorney. What's odd about that?"

"Perhaps nothing. But while we were talking a few minutes ago, I gathered that Martha O'Donnell had never met either Dr. Drake or his wife until tonight. She came to the party the way I did—as the guest of a friend of the Drakes, and apparently a close one. Are you with me?"

Adam's smile was distinctly patient. "You like plots, don't you, Karen. Drake's friend Garner was Dickie Brewster's lawyer and close friend. Neither Garner nor Drake know the name of the donor of the eye Drake used for your transplant operation, or that it happened to be available only because Garner gave permission to use it." He looked down into Karen's upturned face and added drily, "Did I miss anything?"

"I'm afraid you did. Martha O'Donnell knows the answer to that question, thanks to my effort to tell her about my vision. This all gives me a funny feeling, Adam, a link between me and Dickie Brewster."

"Karen, let's just admit that it's a small world after all, and go get ourselves a drink."

Karen smiled in agreement, though somewhere in the back of her mind an unformed thought still struggled to take shape. She lost track of it a few minutes later when a second familiar face appeared in a group of new arrivals. "Madeleine Cartright!" she exclaimed to Adam. "She was my art teacher when I was a child. I haven't seen her for years."

"Why don't you go talk to her before she gets swallowed up in the crowd," Adam suggested. "I'll go have some necessary shoptalk with Frank Drake which would bore you silly. By the way, Karen, I have a theory about couples at a cocktail party. They should split after the first drink and fly solo until it's time to thank their host and hostess. That way you can repeat the same cute story a dozen times without putting your date to sleep. Besides, it's bad manners to monopolize the prettiest girl in the room."

Karen laughed. "Well said, Dr. Stewart. All right. We've had our first drink. You find Dr. Drake and I'll go trade memories with Madeleine. After that, when our paths happen to cross, I'll give you a brisk salute as I pass by."

"Don't get lost."

Karen waved gaily and left.

At last the host had performed all the necessary introductions. Meanwhile, his guests drew together in small groups, chatted with animation, then slid apart smoothly to form new groups.

Dr. Franklin Drake noted that even Priscilla appeared to be enjoying herself. During the first hour, she had greeted strangers with a wooden smile and rigid back, hostility blazing in her eyes when the arrival was a woman younger or better-looking than herself. This relentless scouring had finally ceased, thanks perhaps to the dry Manhattans the butler refilled so efficiently. Was she drinking too much? So be it, if that's what it took to convert a suspicious wife into an amiable hostess. And it was time to allow himself a second drink. He had been nursing a half-empty glass for an hour, his chosen technique for drinking little without making his guests self-conscious.

Carrying a fresh drink, Drake crossed the room to where Henry Garner and the woman from Dublin were standing, deep in conversation.

"Am I interrupting?" he asked as he joined them.

Garner said emphatically, "To the contrary, Frank. I intended to haul you over here as soon as you were free. Martha and I have been discussing a patient of yours." He turned, addressing Martha O'Donnell. "Go ahead, Martha. Tell him what happened. I think Frank will find it interesting."

It had been relatively easy to describe the experience to Henry, adding details she hadn't mentioned on the telephone, for they had known each other for many years. But Martha's voice faltered as she began to tell Franklin Drake about her encounter with Karen Thorndyke.

She had said very little more than her name when Drake nodded and said, "Oh, yes, I know the case. My assistant, Adam Stewart—you've met him, of course, you were just talking with him. Adam told me about her strange obsession. He's doing his best to help her."

Drake's voice was reassuring. "But please, Mrs. O'Donnell, I didn't mean to interrupt. After all, the woman is a patient of mine. I am anxious to hear about your meeting with her."

"I know I shouldn't allow myself to be so upset. I'll start again. . . ." His searching dark eyes made her uncomfortable. Martha turned her head just a little, directing her gaze to a spot on the wall behind Henry Garner. "You see, my brother died last month. I had come over from Dublin because I was worried about him. His body was found . . ." her voice broke off.

Garner put in quickly, "You don't have to go into that part of it, Martha. It's beside the point. The point," he said, addressing Drake, "is that her brother was an eye donor. About a year ago he came to me and told me what he wanted to do. I signed his Eye Bank donor card. My secretary was the second witness. Of course, we had no idea what was done with his eyes after his death."

Martha burst out, "I didn't *want* to know. And then that woman came. Karen Thorndyke. She came to my brother's apartment. I was there, trying to sort out things, so of course I was in an emotional frame of mind even before she arrived. It was hard being in my brother's home, to look into the closets and see his clothes, and open his bureau drawers, and go through his desk. . . ."

Martha stopped abruptly. "Excuse me, I'll be all right in a minute." It wouldn't do to burst into tears. Or to lose all control, as she had when that woman . . . she sucked in her breath, exhaled slowly, and then managed to get through the story about the girl who claimed the eye for her corneal transplant had come from Martha's brother, and that now his eye was seeing what he had been looking at when he died.

As she spoke, Drake nodded from time to time, seemingly in recognition of a detail he had already heard from Adam Stewart. Once he murmured, "A bizarre case . . . please go on, Mrs. O'Donnell."

When she finished, he appeared to be deeply concerned, even agitated. "I'm glad you spoke to me about this, Mrs. O'Donnell. Adam's account was not nearly as full, nor as specific." He paused, looking into Martha's face with such intense concentration she felt as if she had become the "bizarre case" rather than Karen Thorndyke. At last he said thoughtfully, "Tell me—what was your impression of Miss Thorndyke? Would you consider her to be a truthful person, under normal circumstances? Did you give her story any credence?"

"She's insane!" Martha exclaimed, looking straight into Drake's narrowed eyes. "Do you know what she claimed? That my brother was murdered. *And that his eye had shown her how it was done!* Dr. Drake, that woman is mad!"

"By the way, Frank," Garner interrupted, trying to direct the conversation to a less emotional topic before Martha broke down completely. "You and Martha haven't met before, but she was born and brought up in Seattle. I think you've met members of her family. She was Martha Brewster."

"Brewster?" Drake repeated. "Sorry. No. But I'm glad you came today, Mrs. O'Donnell. And grateful to you for telling me about your experience with Karen. So her cornea was donated by your brother. But what a difficult way to learn about it. However, forget about her. Such an extreme reaction is rare, but a good many open-eye patients suffer some sort of post-operative trauma. They get over it. She will, too. In any case, I'll follow up on this. In fact, I'll have a talk with her this evening, just to see if I can be of any help." With a cordial smile for Martha and a nod for Garner, Franklin Drake moved purposefully through the crowd, not stopping until he reached Karen.

In the eyes of Priscilla Drake, glaring furiously at her husband from another corner of the room, the conversation that followed was entirely too long and too intimate.

"Don't cover up for my husband!" Priscilla Drake's voice was so shrill several of her guests turned around to stare and, embarrassed, quickly looked away.

Henry Garner grasped her elbow and led her away from the crowd into the entrance hall. "I want you to calm down, Priscilla." His tone was sympathetic but commanding. "All right. That's better." He released her arm and said quietly, "If this was the first time you accused Frank of being involved with another woman, I might believe you. Come to think of it, the first time, I *did* believe you. As it turned out, the charge was absolutely groundless, of course, but in the meantime you put me in the position of siding against a friend. It won't happen again."

"You've never been a friend to me!" Priscilla Drake's thin face was flushed. Though she spoke to Garner she was looking past him, her pale eyes resting on the infuriating sight of her husband expending his charm on a young and beautiful woman. "I've been wondering for a long time who she was. He doesn't want to have anything to do with *me*, you know. That's the way you can tell."

"Goddamnit, did you ever consider that there's nothing very attractive about a woman who keeps nagging a man?"

She answered as if she hadn't heard. "Look at her. Smiling at him. Listening to him as if every word fascinated her."

"Frank's an intelligent guy and he's charming. Women like him. So what? Why shouldn't they? Listen, Priscilla, please . . ." Garner put his hands on her shoulders and forced her to face him with her back to the living room. "Believe me, Frank's only mistress is his work."

"I could kill her!" Priscilla Drake's thin lips barely moved. "I mean it. *I could kill her.*"

"Oh Christ! If you really want to turn your husband off, keep making childish threats like that. Now go back to the party."

His hands dropped from her shoulders. Without another word she walked away. Garner watched her uneasily, and felt enormously relieved when she went straight to the bar rather than toward the spot near the windows where Drake was still engaged in conversation with Karen Thorndyke. Apparently Frank wasn't aware of how close his wife had come to entertaining the guests with an all-out, no-holds-barred scene. But Drake ought to be warned. He'd better talk to him before he left the party, and maybe they could have lunch together sometime soon. Dammit, he didn't like lies, and the situation was buzzing with them. It was a good and loyal thing to do, to calm a jealous wife in defense of an old friend. But if he himself had doubts about the truth of what he was saying? And then there was the fact that less than thirty minutes ago, Frank had lied, forgetting that there was one person who could spot the lie, and that was his old friend Henry Garner.

What price loyalty, Garner thought. *Then if my friendships break and bend, There's little need to cry, The while I know that every foe, Is faithful till I die.* God bless Dorothy Parker. . . . Garner sighed, went back to the living room, and signaled to the young man with the silver tray.

The drink had steadied him, plucking him from the vortex of a whirlpool where distorted faces and screeching voices had been spinning around him, closer and closer, faster and faster, until the first burning gulp of liquor slowed the speeding wheel. He was still close to the edge of disassociation. He could still feel the pull and hear the banshee cries, but he was safe. The crowd around him was no longer a whirling blur of grimacing mouths and gaping eye sockets, but a collection of socially acceptable Seattle Brahmins who never said shit at a cocktail party. Those had been Dickie's words, Dickie's way of describing the people he revered, mimicked and manipulated.

He had always been repelled by Dickie's malicious commentary, but in spite of himself, it had amused him, too. And Dickie, now dead, still would not be silent. Of all the beastly voices in the mental whirlpool he had just escaped, Dickie's had been the loudest. Even now, made whole again by three ounces of straight whiskey, he couldn't mingle with these well-bred people without imagining what Dickie would say about them behind their well-bred backs.

"La dee da! Wasn't she Miss Prissy when I asked her what she thought of Erica Jong! A filthy book, says she. How did she know? Because she read it, says she. If fuck is filth, she could have stopped reading on page three."

Or about the portly corporation executive who had been explaining to a rapt audience of men why a woman should never be elected governor of the state of Washington: "He doesn't like Dixy because she's got more macho than he has. You wouldn't like her either if you had to squat to pee."

The man's eyes moved around the room, dwelling on faces Dickie might have selected for a flight of malice, while goading his mind to invent something Dickie might have said. Time slipped away. He caught himself on the edge of losing track of it completely. He had been keeping too much to himself. As Dickie had once quipped, "To be a success at a cocktail party, save your charm for the people you despise, and your best lines for people who haven't the wit to top them, and, above all, be sure that when you talk, you don't say anything." Standing alone with an empty glass was a sure way of arousing curiosity, and curiosity would be dangerous to his plan. Today of all days, he must not be remembered as having acted strangely.

Mingle, chat, smile, nod. . . . He could do it. He was doing fine. He was handling himself very well. She was coming toward him, but he was ready now. She would never know that while he smiled, chatted, and nodded, inside his head he was rehearsing what he was going to do to her, step by step, again and again, in an obscene litany of the deed-to-be.

After their stilted conversation in the sunroom, Karen had succeeded in avoiding Martha O'Donnell. In her solo flight, as Adam had expressed it, she had navigated around and away from Dickie's hostile sister by taking a quick check on the other woman's position before she changed her own. The game made her feel miserable in the midst of genteel revelry. When Adam rejoined her and asked if she thought they should say thanks and depart, Karen responded all too eagerly, "I'll get my coat."

Light-headed with relief, she flew down the hall to the bedroom-powder room where the maid had deposited the women's coats. To her dismay, Martha O'Donnell was sitting before the dressing table mirror, applying fresh lipstick.

Karen came to a halt as if she had suddenly reached the end of a tether. Martha was equally as startled, for Karen's reflection had burst into view in the mirror.

Karen tried to think of something to say that wouldn't sound either apologetic or vacuous, and quickly gave it up. In silence she sorted through the coats on the bed, found her own and would have retreated without putting it on if Martha hadn't stopped her.

"Miss Thorndyke. Karen . . ."

Karen turned around. The older woman was standing now, with her back to the dressing table. Her face was pale, her expression strained. The chin was high but the mouth trembled. "I want you to know . . . this is difficult for me to say. Everything about my brother has been so emotional, so . . . ambivalent. I talked with Dr. Drake this afternoon. He gave me some insight into the nature of your . . ." she paused, the perfect lady trying to say something offensive in an inoffensive way.

Karen said quietly, "Into the nature of my post-operative trauma."

"Yes, yes." Martha O'Donnell was clearly relieved, but apparently had not yet fully discharged whatever statement she wanted to make. All at once Karen felt strong in comparison to Dickie Brewster's sister. Dickie haunted her, too. Everything about Dickie had been "difficult." But Martha didn't have the strength to face and accept her conflicts. Her aggressive indignation, her accusation, "You're mad!" had been a kind of self-defense. "Yes, Mrs. O'Donnell?" Karen asked. "What did you want to tell me?"

"I hope, I hope sincerely, that Dr. Drake will be able to help you. That is, it's not always easy to accept help. I do hope you will. I understand he is a very fine doctor."

"He's not a psychiatrist," Karen said flatly. She felt no malice for this unhappy woman, but neither did she feel duty-bound to make her comfortable, while Martha was in effect calling her insane.

"Oh, of course. But I'm sure . . . he explained that it's not really unusual." She paused and added lamely, "Perhaps he will refer you to someone."

Karen slipped into her coat. At the door she said, "Thank you for your concern. I may be as crazy as you think. But I don't believe I am. I'm slowly discovering the key to my so-called obsession. Your brother was murdered. I know that, and I think you do, too. You say I need help. *You* could help me, if you would, by talking to me honestly about your brother. But in any case, with or without your help, I'm going to discover who killed him. Sometimes I have the feeling that I'm getting very close. I had that feeling several times this afternoon. You see, I'm not afraid to say it, even while you're calling me mad."

Martha O'Donnell was about to reply when Karen heard someone outside the door. Another departing guest, coming to pick up a coat? The footsteps were softened by carpeting, but were audible nevertheless, and the presence on the other side of the half-closed door was so near that Karen could hear the faint sound of breathing. She stepped aside automatically to allow the newcomer to enter. Seconds ticked away, but no one appeared.

Curious, Karen went into the hall. No one was there, but she was in time to see another door, fifteen or twenty feet down the hall, shut with such force that it slammed.

Her pulse leapt and her throat constricted. She wheeled around to see that Martha O'Donnell was right behind her. Forgetting everything but the menace of an eavesdropper who ran to hide—*to hide so as not to be recognized*—Karen whispered, "Someone was listening."

Martha was staring at her, lips parted as if to cry out once more—"You're insane!"

Without a word Karen walked away. She did not need another scene with Dickie Brewster's sister, especially one that might be witnessed by other guests. Her final statement to Martha O'Donnell—or tirade, as some might see it—had been indiscreet, or considering her growing reputation as a mental case, downright foolhardy. She had said too much too loudly. But she could not call it back. Her claim that soon she would identify Dickie's killer was already stored in someone's mind and that person could not be far away. Danger was hidden behind any door, or behind any of the civilized masks on any of the faces in the crowd of casually chatting men and women. She must find Adam and get away from here without revealing to him or to anyone how badly frightened she was.

Neither Drake nor his wife was on hand to say good-bye. "We don't need to wait any longer," Adam said after ten or fifteen miuntes of futile searching. "I last saw Priscilla standing alone at the bar. She put away a drink in two or three gulps and immediately demanded another. She's apt to do that under stress, and I guess that for her a party is a stressful situation. Anyway, Frank is probably trying to put her to bed without being too conspicuous about it. Shall we take off?"

"Yes, please," Karen replied, glad that Adam was as eager to leave as she was.

The sky had been overcast when they came, but now rain was falling steadily. Sparrows and Oregon juncos huddled under the protection of the ornamental shrubbery on both sides of the porte cochère.

"Those birds have the right idea," Adam said. "You stay under cover while I get the car."

Karen watched Adam stride up the hill and disappear around the corner at the first intersection. Having been among the last to arrive, they had had to park several blocks away. Karen listened anxiously for the sound of an approaching car. Two or three came down the hill, sped noisily by and then the hush fell again, enveloping as fog, pure quiet except for the soft spatter of rain on the carriage-port roof.

Karen wasn't wearing her wrist watch, but Adam seemed to be taking a long time. What was keeping him, should she start out for the car, what time was it . . . . Such trivial questions began to harass her as her vigil stretched on. She became more and more uneasy, unreasonably so, she told herself, but she felt threatened, as fearful of leaving her refuge as she was of staying in it, alone and somehow terribly exposed. And then the quiet was shattered by gunfire. One sharp, explosive report that put several startled birds to flight.

Karen froze. Then blindly she groped for the brass knob on the massive oak door. It gave way suddenly as it was opened from the inside and she fell forward into the foyer. Someone caught and steadied her. A man's voice said, "Easy, easy . . ." and a woman exclaimed, "Henry! What happened?"

Henry Garner's hands were supporting her. Martha O'Donnell was in front of her, her eyebrows drawn together in a worried frown.

"There was a gunshot," Karen gasped. "It came close, very close."

"A shot?" Henry Garner looked concerned but skeptical. "Are you saying someone shot at you?"

Karen shook her head helplessly. She could read it all in Martha O'Donnell's horrified eyes. Another psychotic episode. One more invention of her paranoid mind. "I don't know," she said. "I just don't know."

"You don't know," Garner repeated.

Karen realized too late that she had convicted herself. Martha O'Donnell's expression was still shocked, but Garner was plainly satisfied that her wild story needn't be taken seriously. "Probably a car backfiring. The sound is the same."

Martha asked curiously, "Where's Dr. Stewart? Isn't he taking you home?"

"He went for the car. I was waiting . . . ."

"We'll wait with you, won't we, Henry." Martha's tone was firm. Like a concerned big sister she led Karen out the door and Henry Garner followed. Under the porte cochère she asked Karen where she had been standing, but after that neither she nor Garner attempted any sort of conversation. They were either comforting her or restraining her, and Karen was too shaken to argue or to justify her fright. When

Adam finally appeared, explaining that he had had trouble starting the car, she caught Garner's meaningful glance at Martha and knew he had condemned her, too. Trouble starting the car, clogged exhaust, backfire. It was a reasonable explanation that didn't make waves. One just didn't say, "Someone tried to shoot me" at a cocktail party in Broadmoor.

Karen was grateful for one thing—they didn't tell Adam. Because her mini-scene in the foyer had embarrassed them? Because they thought there was nothing to tell? No matter, she thought wearily. Maybe even Doug and Jennie will have a hard time with this one. I certainly won't try it out on Adam.

As Adam's car swung into the street and turned down the hill, Martha went to the spot where Karen had been standing when she heard what sounded like the report of a gun. "She would have been looking at the road," Martha said thoughtfully. "So she would have been facing this way. As I am now, with her back to the bushes."

"I suppose so," Garner agreed. "Though I don't get the significance."

"She wasn't waiting in the doorway, which is recessed, and where she would have been more or less lost in the shadows. She was out under the porte cochère, with the light behind her, clearly silhouetted."

"A perfect target?" Garner looked at her curiously. "Is that what you're thinking? Martha, do you believe that girl's story?"

"I don't know what I believe. I wish she

had been standing against a wall or a fence. Then a bullet, if there was one, would be imbedded there. But, look . . ." She gestured toward the wide expense of lawn that stretched out for two or three hundred feet beyond the porte cochère, a smooth green slope bordered by rhododendrons, weeping willows and flowering cherry trees. "It's hopeless to try and search for it out there."

Garner shook his head. "You're a riddle, Martha. In the past half-hour you seem to have undergone a complete change of heart, or at least a change of attitude. Something must have happened that I don't know about."

In careful detail, Martha described the incident in the bedroom.

"But don't you see, Martha?" Garner protested. "Somebody in hiding, spying on the girl, listening to your conversation, and then 'escaping,' so to speak, before he or she was caught. Don't you get it? Karen Thorndyke is paranoid. She admitted she didn't see anyone. And whatever she claimed, I don't believe she heard anyone either."

"Oh, yes," Martha replied earnestly. "I *know* she heard someone. I *know* someone was hiding behind the door. Because, Henry love, I heard it, too."

At the door to the houseboat, Adam said, "The party wasn't much fun for you, was it? You've been under a strain from the moment you spotted Martha O'Donnell. Look, I'm going to give you a sedative. Sleep is what you need."

"You've gone doctor on me."

"Right. So I'll wait in the living room while you get ready for bed, then I'll give you a shot and be on my way."

Concerned but professional, warm but aloof —it was the same old story, Karen reflected, and though he is asking to come into my bedroom, he will do exactly what he has just said he will do, and no more.

When she was in bed, she called and he came in from the living room. He had removed his necktie and stuffed it into his coat pocket, but other than that he was dressed and ready to leave. He sat down on the edge of the bed, felt the inside pocket of his coat and pulled out a small leather case. He smiled reassurance. "Don't worry. This is onc needle that will give you pleasant dreams." He picked up the silk blouse she had hung over the back of the chair beside the bed and handed it to her. "Hold this over your eyes. And no peeking."

Karen felt the wad of cold, wet cotton as he scrubbed a spot on the inside of her left elbow, and then the sting of the hypodermic needle. She heard a small click as he turned off the bedside lamp, and the faint ripping sound as he closed the zipper case. "You can come out now," Adam said. He took away the blouse and lay it across the chair. She murmured, "Good night, Adam . . . ." She felt the faint brush of his lips against hers, and then he was gone.

She heard the sounds of his departure only vaguely. The careful closing of the bedroom door, the swish of the French door as it slid open and shut. . . .

How long she slept she did not know. She only knew that she was suddenly awake, jerked back to consciousness by a sound she was too confused to identify. She lay absolutely still, listening intently, struggling against the pull of the sedative. Drugged, disoriented, she still knew that the sound had been close to her. And then it came out of the dark. The vision of the shining, deadly needle. But it was only too real—a very real hypodermic needle, more terrifying than any that had haunted her before. She sat up. Half-asleep, half-hysterical, she struck out, trying frantically to push the vision away. Her arm hit something cold and solid. She saw the needle soar into the air, heard it drop to the floor.

With a helpless cry, she fell back against her pillow, eyes closing against her will as the narcotic sleep reclaimed her. Her sense of hearing was the last part of her to give up the struggle. It picked up the hollow ring of footsteps fleeing down the wooden walk to the shore.

The orange glow of midmorning sun filled the bedroom when Karen opened her eyes. She blinked against the light, sat up, and looked around at the beloved and familiar objects that assured her this was the real world. The night was gone. The drugged fog had melted in the sunshine. The vision was only a vision and had fled back to its nightmare world. Reality lived in the things she could see and touch. Her old oak dresser, the lemon-yellow curtain with the hem that needed to be mended, her favorite landscape, hanging on her own wall because she didn't want to sell it, her silk blouse, the one she had worn to the cocktail party. But it wasn't on the chair, it was on the floor. She leaned over the side of the bed to pick it up. In one glance, she saw them both. The broken hypodermic syringe, and beside it, Adam's tie, the tie that had been stuffed into his coat pocket when he said good night.

Eighteen

Karen threw her blouse over the shattered syringe, leapt out of bed and ran out of the bedroom in panic-stricken flight from the deadly needle. Sunshine was streaming through the picture windows and the living room had captured its heat, but her naked body was gripped by violent shudders. Sobbing, she stumbled across the room to the sofa, wrapped herself in a brushed wool lap robe and huddled there, staring at the open bedroom door as if the hideous object she had fled from had the power to pursue her.

Gradually, the sun's warmth and the clear, clean light of a spring day drove out the chill. Her fear of the needle lingered, but her pulse slowed, her body relaxed and thoughts broken and scattered by the winds of terror began to settle into a coherent whole.

The vision that had broken into her drugged sleep was not a product of her imagination—proof of that lay on the bedroom floor under her blouse, a physical reality as solid as the sofa on which she was sitting. The image produced by Dickie Brewster's eye could be dissolved by a police officer with a kind voice, by Doug and Jennie holding and comforting her. It came on like a seizure, shook her until she was almost senseless and then vanished, leaving no trace except the memory of a nightmare. But last night, even during the few minutes she was awake before blacking out, she had sensed that this time the "image" wasn't an image at all.

A real person had been in the bedroom last night. Someone had loomed over her and would have succeeded in giving her an injection if she hadn't come awake and knocked the syringe out of his hand. He was so undeniably real that her memory had recorded the hollow sound of his footsteps as he had fled down the wooden walkway to the shore.

Karen rested her head on the back of the sofa and closed her eyes. When Adam had seemed intent on blocking her search for the identity of the eye donor, she had wondered about his motives. But he had come around, hadn't he? He wasn't blocking her now. On the contrary, he was trying to help her. He had been willing to meet the informer at Maynard's; he had even insisted on paying the fee. But half-formed suspicions had been lurking in the background, feeding themselves on any word or act of Adam's that could be interpreted in more than one way. Karen told herself wearily that it was no use trying to ignore them. The only way to overcome them was to bring them out into the daylight and face them squarely.

All right—start with the proposition that the man in the bedroom was Adam with a hypodermic syringe in his hand. He might have forgotten it and come back to the houseboat later to pick it up. She hadn't actually seen him put it into its leather case, or return it to his coat pocket. The sedative he gave her had put her to sleep so quickly that she remembered nothing after the sound of his opening and closing the French door as he left the houseboat. It was as simple as that. He had tried to steal back into the bedroom to retrieve the forgotten syringe, and in the dark had bumped into something and awakened her....

Karen frowned uneasily. Such an explanation demanded more explanations and only increased the torment of suspecting him. How could he have re-entered the houseboat without a key? To Karen's vast relief, the answer came easily to mind. The first time they went out, she had forgotten her key ring and Adam had seen her take the extra key from the flowerpot beside the door.

But why would he come all the way back to Portage Bay at three or four o'clock in the morning just to pick up a syringe? He had mentioned that he had to be in surgery at half past seven. But surely the hospital could supply any instrument he needed.

Karen halted her flow of thought and backed up to another "why?" Why was she assuming that he had returned to the houseboat several hours after he had left it, which would indeed be hard to explain? He may have gone no farther than his car parked at the foot of East Sutherland when he realized he had left the syringe in the bedroom. When she had awakened, she felt as if she had been asleep for a long time. But she was under the influence of a strong sedative, and only partly conscious. It could have been minutes, not hours, since Adam had said goodbye.

All perfectly simple, perfectly clear . . . but it wasn't. With a strange prickle of fear, she recognized that the big question remained, as if it had been hiding in the wings while lesser doubts were raised, examined and dismissed. A sound had broken into her drugged sleep. She had seen the needle. She had reacted violently, as she had to every appearance of the image, striking out with both arms and crying hysterically. If Adam's presence in the bedroom had been as innocent as she was trying to believe it was, why had he fled? Wouldn't he have stayed to comfort her and see that she got back to sleep? Unless, of course, there was some reason he couldn't.

Wrapped in the lap robe, Karen returned to the bedroom and began to dress. Once more she was feeling both angry and ashamed for having allowed herself to doubt Adam, and more determined than ever to put her faith in him even when questions arose for which there were no ready answers. With all her anguished soul-searching she had proven nothing, and she had wandered a long way from the starting point—that little bit of metal and broken glass, still hidden under the silk blouse she had been wearing last night.

She pulled a red sweater over her head, picked up her grandmother's silver-backed hairbrush and began to run the brush through her long copper-brown hair. The trouble with suspicion, she told herself firmly, is that tolerating the presence of even a small one is to open up a Pandora's box. She had begun by wondering why Adam opposed her search for the identity of her eye donor. She had allowed that issue to draw her deeper and deeper into a dangerous flirtation with a flock of groundless suspicions. To the pale face and wide, anxious eyes reflected in the ornate Victorian mirror, she said—Wipe the slate clean.

Karen put down the hairbrush, applied lipstick and started for the kitchen and a pot of good strong breakfast tea with milk and fireweed honey. Like Lot's wife, she could not prevent herself from stealing one last backward glance. There it lay, the deadly seed of suspicion. And not just the syringe but the necktie. An involuntary shudder rippled through her body. She wasn't quite ready to remove the blouse. She would call Adam. Just talking to him would surely dispose of her doubts for all time.

With the dream-like motion of a sleepwalker, Karen returned the telephone's receiver to its cradle. The voice of Adam's answering service had been imperturbable even when asked for the third time to repeat the message. Dr. Stewart was out of town. Yes, Dr. Stewart was out of town. Yes, Dr. Stewart . . .

Karen broke in, "But I was expecting him to call me!"

"I'd be glad to take your name."

Karen said unsteadily, "He knows my name," and lowered the receiver.

She sat by the telephone, numbed by the force of suspicions that the cryptic message was reopening like wounds only partially healed over. Scenes of the past few days lighted up in her mind like a series of tableaus caught by a candid camera. Of Adam the night he walked into the Eye Bank director's office just in time to prevent her from reading the files. He had never told her how he knew she would be there, except to say he had guessed, and guessed right. But earlier that evening one of Adam's technicians had seen her. Wasn't it possible that Adam had also spotted her, pretended not to and then followed her to find out what she was up to?

Her thoughts jumped ahead to the Drakes' party, where she had discovered that Dickie Brewster's attorney, Henry Garner, was a friend of Dr. Drake. She remembered how Adam had startled her by anticipating her revelation before she had said more than a few words. As a personal friend, as well as Drake's assistant, Adam had undoubtedly been invited to their home many times. And since Henry Garner was a longtime friend of the Drakes, odds were that Adam had known him before. Why had he pretended to be meeting Garner for the first time?

Henry Garner had brought Dickie's sister to the Drakes' party. That had been Martha O'Donnell's first meeting with the Drakes, not surprising since she had been living in Dublin for many years. But Dickie lived in Seattle. Henry Garner, close friend and family lawyer, might have introduced him to the Drakes, and to Dr. Adam Stewart . . .

Karen's hands trembled as she filled the tea kettle and put it on to boil. Now she was really letting her mind go wild, and it was headed straight for the madhouse maze of paranoia. What if Adam *had* met Dickie Brewster? It might have been so long ago, and so casually, that Adam had honestly forgotten the name. To suspect that they had known each other was to suspect that Adam had been the professional who had given Dickie clean, hygienic injections, and from there to suspecting that Dickie and Adam had been lovers. Hero, dear Hero . . . and now she was searching for Leander. If Adam was Leander—but how *could* he be?—he had killed Dickie Brewster, and now he must kill her.

He saw the news item in the newspaper by accident. He always read the morning paper thoroughly but efficiently, his quick mind skating past the trivial to absorb and catalogue what he considered worth remembering. Since Dickie's death, he had been reading the paper erratically, often so distracted by his own thoughts that he skipped from one section to another and back again, remembering nothing he read, head throbbing in the effort to concentrate.

This morning he was having more trouble than usual. Clutching a cup of coffee that tasted as bitter as bile, he could scarcely bring the words into focus until her name shrilled like a siren from a headline in the art and entertain-

ment section. KAREN THORNDYKE OPENING AT THE NEW LOOK. *Today from noon to five. Wine and cheese. The talented young artist on hand between two and four . . .*

He could feel the fever in his mind lifting and the poison corroding his body drain away. He was suddenly strong, clear-headed, whole. It was a command, a signal. Today. You can do it today. You will think of a way, you will succeed, and peace will come in the morning.

The bicycle was Jennie's idea. Karen had resisted at first. A city built on seven hills is a steep course for a green biker. Today however, she was glad she had followed Jennie's suggestion. Sunshine, fresh air and exercise might dissolve the terrors of the night and put the distorted suspicions of the morning into proper perspective. The route from her houseboat to the art gallery was not too difficult or heavily trafficked, and her tailored jeans and turtleneck sweater were just as appropriate for an appearance at the New Look as they were for peddling a ten-speed bike.

She set out determined to forget everything but the joy of life on a lovely afternoon in May, with Lake Washington glistening in the sunlight and the misty purple snow-capped Cascade range stretched out along the eastern horizon. There was joy, too, in a day that celebrated her work, if only in a modest way, for which George Manzo, the New Look's black-eyed, bearded owner had apologized, saying, "The cheese is Wisconsin and the wine is California, dear heart, but if your stuff keeps moving as it has been, next year it will be Beluga and Mouton-Rothschild."

At the New Look, George greeted her warmly. "By the way, there's a message for you from Dr. Stewart's secretary. She said the doctor had just phoned from Portland and wanted to let you know he's been called there for a three-day conference. He told her that if she didn't get you at home, to try here because he knew today was your opening. Okay?"

"To be honest, I don't know. I mean, thanks George, for giving me the message."

"Got something going, have you? Why don't you fall for an art gallery director instead of a doctor? Oh well, come on. Let's see what we've got in the trap."

During the next two hours he was both host and stage manager, guiding her progress around the gallery, signaling with a subtle lift of one shaggy eyebrow when he was introducing a serious collector. The afternoon went quickly and well. By four o'clock she was so stimulated that her mind was singing with ideas for new paintings and new painting techniques. The mood was too lively, too creative, to be wound down right away. She had already decided to go from the gallery to the Space Needle, where she would make some rough sketches for a mural she had been commissioned to do for the restaurant, when Martha O'Donnell came through the door.

She walked directly to Karen, showing no interest in the paintings she passed as she crossed the room. Karen's initial impulse was to avoid her, but of course that was impossible, and when Martha reached her the thought of ignoring her died.

There wasn't a trace of the hostility Karen had come to expect from Dickie Brewster's sister. Her eyes were troubled as she said, "Forgive me for injecting myself into an afternoon that must be a happy one for you. I'm flying to Dublin early tomorrow morning. Last night I decided I couldn't leave Seattle without offering you an apology, and I have always felt that an apology over the telephone, or even worse, by letter, is an act of cowardice. When I went to your houseboat, your neighbor—Miss Karras, is it?—told me where to find you." A hesitant smile softened Martha's tense expression. "She also suggested that considering one thing and another, as she put it, I shouldn't spoil your day by showing up here until you were about to leave. So I hope that at least my timing is right."

"I was on my way out when you came in."

"Then can we talk outside? I won't take long. In fact, I asked the taxi driver to wait for me. Perhaps I can take you someplace."

"Thank you, but I have my bicycle. Mrs. O'Donnell, you don't have to apologize. I understand your feelings and considering the way I approached you and what I asked you to believe, I think I'm the one who should be apologizing."

"It's more than that," Martha O'Donnell said earnestly. "You said last night that I could help you by talking honestly about Dickie. There *is* something you should know."

"I'll say good-bye to George and then we'll go outside."

They sat on a stone bench in a small courtyard next to the gallery. Martha O'Donnell spoke rapidly, eyes averted and fingers playing nervously with her handbag. "This is painful. Forgive me, I'll get it all out as quickly as possible. . . ."

About a week after Dickie's funeral, she had realized that she could no longer put off the disposing of his clothing, furniture and personal possessions, so she began taking inventory. Thinking there might be something among his papers of importance to settling his estate, she had begun with his desk.

Three drawers were unlocked. They contained receipts, a carbon of his will, an address book—what might be expected of a young bachelor with many friends, everything neatly sorted and arranged, for Dickie, she recalled, had always been obsessively neat. Even when he destroyed things as a child, he saved and hid all the pieces. . . . One drawer was locked. A search of his bureau drawers uncovered a small ring of keys. Two of them appeared to be keys to a safe deposit box, one or two to luggage. An ornate brass key opened the fourth drawer in the desk, and that's where she found the letters.

They were obscene, they were depraved. They were the outpourings of Dickie's lover, describing what they had done together, pleading letters that sometimes cried out so loudly that they sounded threatening. They were addressed to Hero and signed Leander, and one of them ended, "Would you love me if my precious presents ceased? If the light by which you guide me blew out in a storm I would surely drown in the sea." Though Martha O'Donnell remembered the Greek myth of the priestess of Aphrodite in Sestos, and knew that Leander had been the lover who nightly swam the Hellespont to see her, the truth stared at her from every letter. Dickie was Hero, the girl of the legend, but these fervent appeals from Leander had not been written by a woman but by another man.

The revelation of Dickie's homosexuality had shocked her almost as severely as his death. She had long suspected and worried that he was involved in drugs. That had been her reason for flying over from Dublin, for she was his only close living relative and as his older sister felt responsible for him. But playing sweetheart to another man . . . She was too ashamed to mention it even to Henry Garner. She was ashamed that even after she realized the nature of the letters, she kept reading them. Then she put them back together and tied them as they had been with a gold velvet ribbon. She returned them to their hiding place, slammed the drawer shut, hurried into the bathroom and washed her hands. But she left the key in the lock.

The consequence of forgetting about the key came clear several days later when she entered Dickie's apartment to find the desk had been ransacked. The contents of all three unlocked drawers had obviously been inspected in great haste. The fourth drawer was empty. Nothing else had been disturbed in any of the rooms, but there was a large wet spot on the Chinese rug in the living room.

She considered reporting it to the police or

telephoning Henry Garner, but that meant she would either have to lie about the letters or admit that she had read them and could guess why they had been stolen. The instinct to conceal what she considered a disgrace to the family won and she didn't report the break-in to anyone. But the knowledge gnawed at her. The implications became clearer and clearer until last night, an interminable and almost sleepless night, she finally gave up and looked at them squarely.

Leander must be a desperate man who knew he would be destroyed by the discovery of his handwritten letters to Dickie. Socially and professionally destroyed—that, of course, but perhaps even more literally. There had been a threatening quality to many of the letters; they had been written by a man so obsessed by his passion for Dickie that he might often have been on the edge of violence. And Martha O'Donnell knew her brother. He could be cruel. He enjoyed playing with people. Even as a child, he had known how to torture in subtle ways. Perhaps he had gone too far, and "Leander" . . . Martha's voice broke and she covered her face with both hands.

Karen put an arm around the other woman's shoulders. "Now you know that your brother was murdered. I don't want to cause you unnecessary pain, but I must ask you—Do you still think I'm insane?" Martha's hands dropped into her lap as she turned to look directly into Karen's eyes. "Oh, no," she said quietly. "You're not insane. But someone else is."

It happened so quickly. She was pedaling along a quiet residential street, her mind so occupied by her conversation with Martha that she was paying little or no attention to what was going on around her. She kept well to the right, a foot or two from the gutter except to swing out occasionally to go around a parked car. Several cars had come up behind her, slowed a little and then passed by; she hadn't even looked up. And then the sound of an automobile at her back invaded her consciousness because its driver accelerated suddenly and the roar of the motor bore down on her. Frightened and confused, she turned the handlebars sharply to the right. The wheels skidded and hit the cement curb. Like a bucking horse the bicycle threw her onto the grassy strip between the sidewalk and the street and fell beside her, one pedal slamming into her left leg.

Gasping, Karen struggled to a sitting position and watched the car speed away. It was a model like millions of others—a pale blue sedan. The frame around the rear license plate bore the name of a rental company, but in that brief and dazed glimpse she didn't catch the license number and the name of the rental company didn't register.

She got to her feet, dusted off her jeans and righted the bike. The street was deserted. No other driver or pedestrian to witness what had happened. Was it possible that she had swerved to the left and into the path of the car? In any case she couldn't just stand on the street or go knock on someone's door and ask them to believe this latest episode in the Perils of Karen-Pauline.

The sensible thing to do was to get back on the bicycle, proceed with her plans for the afternoon and ignore that hysterical little voice that was insisting the hit-and-run driver who missed her by inches had really meant to kill her.

Nineteen

It was Doug Cooper's day off, and on such a beautiful spring day he would normally be spending the afternoon on the green slopes of the Snoqualmie Falls golf course. But he had other fish to fry. He had already done his homework and his pocket notebook contained the name and address of the only authorized Triumph dealer in the city of Seattle.

In Charley's Cycle on 12th Street, Doug presented his credentials to an affable young man who introduced himself in one unbroken sentence as Bill-What-Can-I-Do-For-You-Today?

"Got a few minutes?" Doug asked. "Or maybe you want to steer me to someone else?"

Bill grinned. "Well, if you want to start at the top, the owner's out and won't be back for awhile yet. But I'm the service manager and salesman. If you think I can do you any good, let's go into the office."

In the cubicle at the rear of the showroom, Doug sipped on a mug of strong black coffee and explained that he was trying to identify the owner of a specific model. Referring to his notebook, he recited serial number and general appearance. "Silver, with red, white and blue stripping. Wheels are chromed. Chrome cylinder head."

Bill was nodding enthusiastically. "That red, white and blue striping is hand-painted. The pin stripes on the wheels are done by hand, too. The only custom paint job that Triumph ever put out."

"You recognize the model?"

"Sure. That's the limited edition. Bonneville Silver Jubilee. Only a thousand made in honor of the Seventy-fifth anniversary. Five-speed transmission. Front and rear disc brakes. High speed Dunlop racing tires. Nitrogen gas shock absorbers. 750 C.C. engine. Most dealers only got one of them. We got three. So far we've sold two. You want to see the last one?"

Doug said wryly, "On a cop's pay? I can't even afford to look at it. So you had three, and one's left. With something that special, maybe you can remember who bought the first two."

"Sure. Those babies are all serialized. Each owner gets a plaque with his name on it and serial number of the bike."

"When does that happen?"

"You mean, when does he get the plaque? The day he buys it. Want me to look up those names? I guess it's all right. Nothing confidential about buying a bike."

"Yes, thanks."

"I don't need to look one of them up. The first special we sold went to a guy named Edgar Burns. I already knew him because he's been coming in for repairs on his old Triumph." Bill opened a desk drawer, removed a ringed notebook and after a few seconds found the page he wanted. "Here it is. The second special. I sold that six months ago to a Dickie Brewster, Westminster Apartments."

"Dickie Brewster," Doug repeated, but that was a name he already knew and not the one he was trying to uncover. "That's the name of the *owner*, right? The name you put on the plaque."

"Right, right. Come to think of it, he had us haul the bike to the Westminster and leave it in the carport."

"The same day he bought it?"

"Damn right. He led the way, watched us take it out of the truck. Like we couldn't find the Westminster without him, or maybe we'd get careless and drop it off someplace else."

"Okay. So it's Brewster on the plaque, and I suppose Brewster on the application for registration you sent to the DMV?" As Bill nodded assent, Doug went on to the key question. "The owner and the buyer wouldn't necessarily be the same person, right?"

Bill shrugged. "No."

"In other words, the man you saw might have been buying the bike for Brewster."

Bill's face flushed with a mixture of surprise and understanding. "Jesus, that explains it. Somehow, I couldn't quite *see* that guy on a bike. You know what I mean? I couldn't even see him in a pair of jeans. He was a real formal dude."

Doug grinned encouragingly. "Now we're getting somewhere. What was *his* name? The guy who *bought* the special?"

"Beats me."

"But he paid for it, right? How? Personal check?"

"That's another thing. He paid cash. I can't brag about my memory, but in this shop that's something you don't forget. With more than five thousand of good old U.S. currency in my fist, I don't need any ID. If his name wasn't Brewster, it's nothing to me."

"Let's forget about his name. You noticed his clothes. Why?"

"Like I said, smooth, custom made, expensive as hell. But conservative, you know what I mean? The kind of clothes you'd be wearing if you could shell out that much cash the way I dig into my pocket for bus fare."

Doug nodded. "I get the picture. Now listen, Bill. You said your truck delivered the bike to the Westminster and he led the way. Whoever was driving the truck would have had a good look at his car. That didn't happen to be you, did it?"

"Oh, no. Mike made the delivery."

"But maybe you saw the car when he pulled in here?"

The salesman shrugged. "Sure, I saw it, but it was nothing special."

"Come on," Doug said. "A good bike man

is a wheels man, whether it's two or four. The guy impressed you, right? All that beautiful *cash.* So naturally you're going to be curious about what kind of a car a guy like that drives."

"Well, yes, sure I was. But that's just it—he was driving the kind of package you don't look at twice. A light blue Ford, with a rental license plate."

"A rental? What outfit? Hertz, Airways, Avis?"

Bill shook his head. "It wasn't one of the big ones. God, man, rent-a-car outfits are sprouting up like dandelions. Maybe I saw the name, but it's gone now, and most of those outfits don't mark their cars anyway. All that hunk of tin meant to me was that the guy was from out of town."

"Maybe so," Doug said thoughtfully.

"Say, you really want to locate him, don't you? If he comes in here again, I'll get his name and give you a call."

Doug grinned. "Do that, Bill. But don't expect him to give it to you."

"It's a long chance, anyway, that the guy who bought the bike would be the one to bring it in for repairs. This guy Brewster is the one who's riding it."

"Not any more," Doug said. "Brewster's dead."

Bill's friendly eyes opened wide. "Is that right! God, I'm beginning to catch on. You've *got* to track that buyer, don't you. You going to try the rental car offices?"

"Yes," Doug said glumly. "All fifty of them."

The man gambled on the chance that the bicycle "accident" had happened too fast for the girl to get a good look at the car. He parked on the street above East Sutherland as the familiar feeling of excitement mixed with nausea began to stir. He realized that there was no way she could escape without his seeing her.

He sat in his car, trying to extract coherent thoughts from the churning, disjointed sound track inside his head. His right hand slipped into the pocket of his sports jacket and stroked the small zipper case. The feel of the leather soothed and reassured him. The hypodermic was his best weapon. The innocent little white pills he had been carrying lately were seldom deadly, but might be useful in another way.

Lost in thought, he was startled when she left the houseboat and walked in the opposite direction from his car. She had changed from the jeans and sweater she had worn to the art gallery into a dress of sea-green silk and she was carrying a large thin folder—an artist's sketch pad.

She waited at the bus stop, not even looking his way. When the bus pulled to the curb, he started the motor. His excitement mounted as he followed its slow, methodical progress around Lake Union and on to the Seattle Center at the foot of Queen Anne Hill. At the bus stop near the Space Needle, she was among a dozen passengers who got out and went to the tree-lined promenade leading to the tower.

Sweating now, he swung his car into the parking lot across the street, fumbled in his pocket for the right change, dropped quarters into the slot and joined a cluster of tourists on their way to the Needle. He held back until he was sure she was going up the tower rather than past it. All the while bits of a plan were taking shape. When she got in line at the ticket window, the pieces fell into place.

Forty-three seconds to ride to the top of the six hundred-foot Needle, traveling at eight hundred feet per minute . . . The restaurant turns a full three hundred-sixty degrees each hour and is so well-balanced only a one horsepower motor is needed to power it. . . .

Karen and thirty others were herded into the glass-walled elevator by a smiling guide. Hugging her sketch pad, Karen looked at the attendant and thought—Bless her for her charm. If she believed someone was trying to kill her, would she still manage to smile?

The elevator whisked past the restaurant and disgorged its passengers on the observation level. Karen strolled through the circular lobby and went out to the open deck.

It was a glorious day, just right for getting a feel of the mural she had been commissioned to do for the restaurant below. Sunlight bounced off the halo of gilded solar sensors and warmed the enamelled gray walls that enclosed the deck. Karen hadn't visited the Space Needle for at least five years, for as her vision failed, she had avoided places that were particularly frustrating reminders. But she remembered this outer deck well enough to recognize that something had been added to it, and with an involuntary shudder, remembered why. After two suicide leaps, horizontal cables strung from vertical L-shaped girders had been installed outside the promenade.

Karen turned her back to the sunshine and the soft air and walked down the two-level stairway to the restaurant.

In the ring-shaped restaurant, Karen chose one of the banquette tables facing the windows so that she could watch the slowly shifting panorama without turning her head. She gave her order to the waitress and leaned back against the rust-colored leather bench.

For her, the hour-long circuit was starting with a view to the north. Karen's first impression was of water all around—the salt water of Puget Sound to the left, of Lake Union to the right, with the steep barrier of Queen Anne Hill rising up between the two.

Karen's concentration on the scene outside was interrupted by two women at the table to her right, who were exclaiming over the dessert a waitress had just set before a girl of six or seven. The child, wide-eyed, stared at it with both small hands clamped over her mouth.

Karen laughed inwardly, for she had reacted the same way when first acquainted with a "Lunar Orbiter." The edible part was nothing more than a strawberry sundae, but it was served on top of a huge brandy snifter half filled with brilliant blue liquid that steamed furiously because a chunk of dry ice had been dropped into it. White clouds rose around the dessert dish and continued to billow as the little girl recovered, picked up her spoon and, grinning ecstatically, set out to demolish the sundae. Karen opened her sketchbook and used a few swift pencil strokes to capture the quality of that syrupy grin.

It was the first time since she had slid in behind the banquette table that her attention had been drawn to any of the other occupants. With her mind fully concentrated on the world beyond the windows, the people inside became faceless presences passing along the curving corridor at her back or intercepting her view for a fraction of a second as they followed a waiter to their table.

Even when she left her table to make a telephone call, she was moving in a private world, recording impressions from which she would select her material for the mural. On her way to the telephone booth, she walked past a number of people without noticing that one man turned away quickly as she approached.

Back at her table, Karen sipped her cocktail absentmindedly as she looked southward toward the glittery forest of steel, concrete and glass structures that is Seattle's highly concentrated downtown, making mental notes of the contrasting shapes and shades.

Suddenly feeling drowsy, her gaze settled on the old L. C. Smith tower, once the tallest building west of Chicago but now pushed into the background by a dozen daring architectural upstarts. Vainly, Karen fought an overwhelming sense of drowsiness. Her last sleepy thought was that the grand old building was like the aging symphony musician who has gradually been demoted to the very last seat in the violin section but still keeps on fiddling. Then she closed her eyes, drooped to one side and slid unconscious off the seat onto the carpeted floor.

He allowed himself to be among the first eight or ten people who gathered around the girl, but he didn't appear to be anything more than one of the curious who knelt or stood beside the unconscious form while the waitress initiated a search for a doctor and an anxious head waiter hurried to his office to call the Center's first aid station.

His hand slipped into his pocket. Fingers closed around the syringe he had taken out of the case and filled in the protection of the men's room. He drew it out slowly, palming the glass tube so that everything but the last half-inch of the needle was concealed by his hand. In spite of the throbbing pain in his head, he felt calm now that he had reached the critical moment in the series of acts he had rehearsed so carefully. He kneeled beside the body and lifted Karen's arm with his left hand, the needle in his right hand. A child's piercing voice exploded above the murmur of spectators. "Hey, Mister, what's that thing in your hand?"

He looked up and directly into the face of a little girl with sticky traces of whipped cream smeared on her chin and upper lip. "What are you going to do to the lady?" the child insisted, bright eyes fixed not on the prostrate form but on the visible tip of the hypodermic needle.

To the man, that shrill voice was the only sound in the room. His hand drew back and scuttled for the safety of his pocket. He got to his feet, muttered, "Excuse me. . . ." and pushed his way through the crowd. With the last measure of his self-control, he walked away casually, up the steps to the reception area, through the door that led to the stairs to the rest rooms and observation deck.

At their table by the window, the little girl's mother dipped the corner of a napkin into her glass of water and began removing the traces of the strawberry sundae from her daughter's face. "Did you notice that man?" she asked the other woman. "The one Charlene was talking to?"

"No, which man?"

The first woman shrugged. "I can't really describe him. But it's funny. Now that I think of it, I'm sure he stopped at the table where that poor young woman was sitting. She was gone for a few minutes and he just stood there, as though waiting for her to come back. But by the time she did, he was gone. I remember thinking —her black folder was right there so he must have known she was coming back, so why didn't he wait a couple of minutes?"

The second woman laughed good-naturedly. "You and your imagination, Tina. You could make a mystery out of a woman walking out of the Safeway with a bag of groceries."

Karen had agreed that another attempt to paint the image should be made as soon as Doug and Jennie were through work for the day. She had called Jennie as soon as she got home from the Space Needle. The waitress at the Needle had been kind and obviously concerned about Karen, assuming that she had had a severe reaction to the "Cloud Buster." Karen had done nothing to disillusion her, and after much fuss and innumerable promises to take better care of herself in the future, she had escaped into the solitude of a taxicab.

Karen didn't know what had caused the blackout, but she suspected that the fall from the bicycle might have hurt her more than she realized at the time. She decided not to say anything about it, unless it happened again.

Twilight was casting long shadows and the lake echoed the brilliant pinks in the western sky when Doug and Jennie appeared at the French door, Jennie with a bag of groceries and Doug with a narrow paper sack that could only contain a bottle.

"Beware of the gift-bearing Greek," Doug said, a blunt thumb waggling in Jennie's direction.

"Beware of smart-aleck cops," Jennie retorted cheerfully, passing Karen on her way to the kitchen. "After our painting session, I'm going to make egg and lemon soup and stuffed tomatoes. Or is that what you had for breakfast?"

Karen laughed. Jennie lifted her spirits as no one else could. "Nope. And it sounds wonderful."

"First, a glass of wine," Jennie announced as she opened the refrigerator and deposited several small packages. "Then we'll get down to business and Doug will remove himself from the scene."

"Why do I always end up in the bedroom?" Doug said.

Jennie's sea-green eyes were wide and innocent. "Would you prefer the kitchen?"

The session went much as the others had, but Jennie was aware that this time Karen seemed to be too tired to concentrate fully on the painting. Jennie brought her out of the trance after only half an hour, and the two women stood observing the progress that had been made. The eyes were more distinct and the bridge of the nose was beginning to emerge. But neither of them could recognize a familiar face from the image on the canvas.

"There's no rush," Jennie said, heading into the kitchen to prepare dinner. "One of these times we're bound to hit pay dirt."

Twenty

Priscilla Drake was sitting at her dressing table when she heard the muffled sound of the electronic garage door lifting and riding along its metal tracks. At last he was home. But now that the moment had arrived, could she summon the courage to go through with the act she had been preparing for all day?

She pulled out the top drawer and saw that the cocktail glass, concealed among her meagre assortment of cosmetics, was almost empty. She drained it quickly, returned it to its hiding place and closed the drawer. Could she get to the bar, refill it, and return to the bedroom in less time than it would take Franklin to get from the garage to the living room? Perhaps, but it was risky. Too risky. If Franklin caught her, his silent scorn would exhaust her pitifully small reservoir of confidence, and right now she needed it all, and badly.

She leaned forward to study her reflection for several seconds. Three hours in an Elizabeth Arden salon had been well spent. A clever hairdresser had given some style to the drab gray hair. A complete facial had put color into her cheeks, softened the wrinkles and accented the too-small, too-pale eyes. The mirror image was a little indistinct because she wasn't wearing her glasses. She picked them up and quickly put them down again. They belonged on the face of Priscilla the plain, Priscilla the gray, not the daring Priscilla who today had bought a ridiculously expensive hostess gown because the sales clerk had called it "Glamorous! *Le dernier mot!*"

She got to her feet carefully, steadied herself, and surveying her full length reflection, slowly ran her palms down her body, shivering a little as they cupped her breasts and went on until they rested, pressing the velvet fabric of the gown into the soft triangle between her thighs. Franklin must be in the sunroom now. Probably pouring himself a carefully measured Scotch. She turned her back to the mirror, hesitated like a sky diver looking down through an open hatch, and then resolutely walked out of the bedroom and down the hall to the living room.

As she had anticipated, Franklin was in the sunroom. Glass in hand, he turned, recognized her presence with a nod and a murmured, "Hello, Priss," and raised the glass to his mouth.

Priscilla advanced, watching his face hopefully. Halfway across the room she stopped, consciously posing, silently begging for his attention. But the new, the beautified Priscilla didn't arouse anything but a slight frown and a wary, "Can I make you a drink?"

He offers, she thought bitterly, because he wants to control how much goes into it. She said stiffly, "No, thank you," though her eyes fixed themselves hungrily on his glass. Like a polite robot, she asked, "Did you have a hard day, dear?"

"Awful," he said just as mechanically. "I've got a raging headache. Yours?"

"Oh, mine was pleasantly different. I went to Frederick's. I spent a lot of money. That ought to make you happy."

"You may buy whatever you like," he replied. "I think I've made that clear many times."

She heard a warning note of irritation she always seemed to arouse when she was trying hardest to be amusing and to please. "Oh, yes, Franklin," she said hurriedly. "I was just . . . well, my sense of humor . . ." she paused, trembling like a child in her velvet gown, knowing she had offended, mutely awaiting absolution.

He shrugged and took a sip of his drink, but over his glass he was looking at her as if her appearance had registered for the first time. "That what you bought?" he asked. "It's lovely. I like the color. Purple, is it?"

"Plum."

"Sorry. Plum. What do you call that kind of dress?"

"It's a hostess gown."

"Very nice." He sat down on the sofa,

placed his glass on the cocktail table, leaned back and closed his eyes.

Stranded in the middle of the living room, Priscilla struggled desperately to silence the inner person who was crying, so you don't know what to call this kind of dress? What does *that* girl wear when you go to see her? Nothing, perhaps? What does she do, take off all her clothes the minute you walk in?

The inner voice grew shrill as she stared angrily at a husband so far from being aroused by Elizabeth Arden's Priscilla that he might have fallen asleep. "Franklin . . ." Quietly at first. Then, "Franklin?" louder now as the emotional pressure kept building. And finally, close to hysteria, "Franklin, look at me!"

He opened his eyes, sat up, appraised her coolly and reached for his drink. "I'm tired, Priss," he said. "Sorry, but I don't feel like talking."

Her fingers fumbled with the wide sash of pink satin, loosened the knot and dropped the sash at her feet. They found the little bow at the top of the front zipper, grasped it and slid it down very slowly, inch by inch from her throat to the end just below her navel. Still in slow motion, the trembling fingers lifted, pulled the gown off her shoulders and released it. It settled around her ankles in a soft ring of plum velvet and she stood before him naked, nipples hard and swollen, hands clutching each other uncertainly just above the dark nest of pubic hair.

"Oh, for God's sake, Priscilla!" Drake jumped up, carried his glass to the sunroom and refilled it at the bar

Choking, Priscilla gasped, "Don't you *care* at all? Am I so repulsive to you that you can't even look at my body without turning your back? What happens when you go to bed with that girl? Do you make her lift her skirt so you can do it to her with her clothes on? Doesn't she have a body, Franklin? Breasts and a belly and thighs and buttocks? Or is she only a damp hole you find between her legs when you make love in the dark?"

"You're drunk," Drake said coldly. "Put your clothes on immediately or I'm leaving the house."

Even the threat was spoken without emotion. "What do you do to her?" Priscilla screamed, and he turned his back. Frantic, she ran into the sunroom, grabbed his free hand and pressed it against the aching valley between her thighs. "There," she said hoarsely. "*There.*"

Drake swept her hand aside and walked past her. He paused beside the vivid puddle of her clothes long enough to say, "It's a lovely gown. Put it on. You look better in it." He continued down the hall to his study. The heavy oak door closed behind him.

Priscilla stood in the sunroom, shivering uncontrollably. Then she walked carefully to the crumpled hostess gown, dropped to her knees, picked up the gown and methodically began to rip it to pieces.

Henry Garner listened patiently to the hysterical monologue coming to him over the telephone. Priscilla Drake was so drunk she was incoherent.

"Look, Priscilla," he said, raising his voice to break into her tirade. "It's late. Everything looks worse at night than it will in the morning."

"Won't someone believe me? Henry, you're the only one I can talk to. My dear husband has locked himself into his study where he intends to spend the rest of the night. *Henry!* I'm going to *make* you listen. Are you there, Henry?"

"I'm here," Garner said wearily. "But you did wake me up, Priss."

"I followed him."

"Followed him? Frank?"

"Yes. Franklin. My beloved husband. The fine, admirable, successful, rich, popular, butter-wouldn't-melt-in-your-mouth Dr. Franklin Drake surgeon of reknown. The night after the cocktail party. He thought I was asleep. I knew what he was going to do, so I pretended I was sleeping. He got out of bed, he went into his dressing room, he came out a few minutes later and sneaked out of the bedroom. All that time I didn't move. But then I jumped out of bed and I followed him. He didn't know it! Isn't that wonderful, Henry? Wasn't I smart? Oh God, oh God . . ."

"Enough, Priss. Calm down. Honestly, you shouldn't be telling me all this."

"But I can prove it now. About that girl. That girl Adam Stewart brought to the party. You thought she was Adam's girl, right?" Priscilla's voice rose in a harsh laugh. "Ha! Franklin wasn't out of the driveway before I was in my car. I backed out the minute he turned the corner. He hadn't gone two blocks before I caught up with him. But I stayed back, way back, and

I kept following. From Magnolia to Lake Union, all around the lake. When he turned onto Boylston I almost lost him, but I caught up. He stopped. I watched him park, and get out of his car and walk down the hill . . . ."

Garner sighed deeply. He had often reflected that if Drake were not his oldest and closest friend, he wouldn't suffer through even one of Priscilla's jealous binges. "Okay, so he parked and went down a hill. What did *you* do?"

There was a brief silence, and then Priscilla said in a voice that was deadly calm, "I drove home. Because I am a prude and a priss, as you and Franklin have no doubt agreed many times, and I was afraid someone might see me in my nightgown."

Or didn't really want to catch her husband *in flagrante delicto*, Garner thought. Or maybe the reverse—was afraid of discovering that he *wasn't* keeping a tryst. "Good night, Priscilla," he said firmly. "I'm tired. I've listened, but there's nothing I can do. Go back to bed, please."

Firmly, he replaced the receiver and flipped off the bedside light. His last waking thought was that he wouldn't blame Frank if he was having an affair, and if he was, poor Priscilla would at least have the satisfaction of being right.

Somehow Priscilla had gotten through the night. She picked up a piece of buttered toast, stared at it and dropped it onto her plate. She could put it into her mouth, she could even force herself to chew it, but she knew she would choke when she tried to swallow. The memory of last night's scene was a hangover as nauseating as the one caused by too much liquor.

Groveling in her misery, she watched the man on the other side of the breakfast table as he picked at his scrambled eggs and drained his third or fourth cup of coffee. He had been part of their ugly scene and he had spent the night on the sofa in his study, but apparently he didn't think either breach of their marital bonds was worth mentioning, far less "settling," as she so urgently needed to do.

"Franklin?" she said tentatively. "I'm sorry. Can't you understand . . . ."

He lifted a silencing hand. "It's all right, Priss. I understand. Let's not start the day on an unhappy note."

"I'm not a fool, *or* a mental case."

"I agree," he said as he pushed back his chair. "Not everyone would. Now excuse me, please. I've got to make a phone call." With that he left the kitchen and crossed the hall to his study.

Priscilla heard the study door close. The voice of suspicion, never silent for long, began to whisper that her husband had shut the door because he was going to make a telephone call he didn't want her to overhear. As if the action were predestined by a force far stronger than herself, Priscilla rose from her chair and walked to the extension telephone in the kitchen. Using both hands so that lifting the receiver would not make the clicking sound Franklin would detect, she put the receiver to her ear.

The telephone call from Dr. Drake came while Karen was sipping a cup of strong breakfast tea. He explained that he had just gone over the results of her last tests and had discovered a serious problem that Adam had apparently overlooked. He reassured her quickly. The problem could be corrected. He was confident the condition hadn't developed to the point where any lasting damage had been done. But it was imperative, he said earnestly, that she check into the hospital right away. Only immediate surgery would prevent her body from rejecting the transplant. He had already scheduled the operation, a hospital bed had been reserved.

Karen packed her bag quickly, wrote a note for Jennie and put it into her mailbox on her way to the taxi waiting for her at the foot of East Sutherland. Adam had "overlooked" the results of the tests! That was Dr. Drake's generous interpretation, but not necessarily hers. The possible implications made her tremble. Had Adam deliberately withheld the results? Did he *want* her body to reject the transplant? On the way to the hospital, one prayerful thought dominated all the frightened and shocking thoughts struggling for recognition. Thank God for the conference that took Adam to Portland, if that was where he really was, and for whatever suspicion or impulse that had made Dr. Drake review the results of her tests.

Garner had known that, drunk as she was when she called him in the middle of the night, Priscilla wouldn't forget that he had hung up on her. But there was no undertone of reproach in her voice this morning. She spoke urgently, hardly referring to their conversation the night before except to apologize for awakening him.

At length she said, "Believe me, Henry," and then, "Good-bye." And that was that, except that when he went back to the brief he had been working on, he couldn't concentrate on it.

The things she had told him made him uneasy, as if they had tripped a mental switch that activated a train of thought he didn't want to pursue. Garner had assured Priscilla that there was nothing to worry about, but his own mind clung tenaciously to questions that could not be silenced by hanging up the receiver.

He had often quipped that, to lawyers and writers, nothing is real until it is written down. Like the pious seeking the confessional, or the neurotic the couch, he reached for a yellow, blue-lined legal pad. He wrote for some time. Sentences, parts of sentences, a few words, sorting out his thoughts, trying to separate those that were conscious and accounted for from those that were subconscious and repressed. At length he paused. He felt as if all the pieces of the human puzzle were there, needing only the flash of insight that would make everything fall into place.

The first and simplest element was the Other Woman—or "That Girl!" as Priscilla had called her. That Girl was the same woman Martha O'Donnell had accused of being insane, and her name came to him quickly. To confirm it he opened a desk drawer, took out the Seattle directory and turned to the T's. Priscilla said she had trailed her husband's car until he parked it on East Sutherland Street. There it was, the right name, the right address. Karen Thorndyke, 134 East Sutherland. The girl with the gray-blue eyes and classic profile—Adam Stewart's friend at the Drakes' cocktail party, the current target for Priscilla's jealous fury, once the cause of hysteria in the normally kind and level-headed Martha O'Donnell.

Perhaps that was what bothered him. Martha's attitude had done a complete about face. She had recanted on the question of the girl's sanity. Her last words when he put her on the plane for Dublin had been, "I have to go home, Henry, but please don't dismiss Karen Thorndyke as a bothersome crackpot. Don't even dismiss her belief that this vision of hers is meant to help her identify Dickie's killer."

"Nonsense," Garner had answered. "Killer? We know Dickie died of an overdose of narcotics."

"Of course," Martha had agreed. "But why is someone trying to kill Karen Thorndyke?"

Garner focused on one of the shortest items he had jotted down. Frowning, he picked up his pencil and underlined it. *Death by O.D.* He had refused to consider the possibility that the overdose had been deliberate rather than accidental. Had they all been lulled by a careless assumption? Someone other than Dickie could have administered that last deadly injection . . . . Nonsense! Garner told himself again. If he was to believe that, he'd soon be sharing the notion that Karen Thorndyke's transplanted cornea was imprinted with the image of the murder weapon. At that point he'd be as mad as the girl herself.

What troubled Garner was that, crazy as she sounded when Martha described her visit to Dickie's apartment, when he saw Karen Thorndyke in person at the Drakes' party he had been impressed by her intelligence. All right. Dickie *could* have been murdered.

He scanned the pages of notes and paused thoughtfully, reading and re-reading the question, "Can Priscilla be right?" Poor Prissie had been haunted by so many imaginary Other Women that until now he hadn't considered the possibility. At the cocktail party, Frank *had* given a great deal of attention to Karen. That had been the spark that ignited Priscilla's half-drunk diatribe in the foyer. But why conclude that Frank's interest in Karen was anything more than a surgeon's professional concern for one of his patients?

On further reflection, something else struck Garner as odd. He had seen Drake greet Karen when she and Adam Stewart arrived. He had spent a minimum of time with them before he went on to other guests, and his brief welcome had been directed at Adam rather than the girl. Why the sudden awareness . . .

The indefinable uneasiness that settled over Garner during Priscilla's phone call came to a peak as he remembered the scene. Drake joining him and Martha O'Donnell. Drake's eyes as he absorbed every detail of Martha's story about Karen Thorndyke's obsession. It was after that conversation that Drake had shown intense intense interest in the girl. And it was during the same conversation that Drake had lied. An unnecessary lie, as transparent as the explanation Drake had offered a few days later when they had lunch together.

"Something's been bothering me, Frank. When I introduced you to Martha O'Donnell at your party last week, I told you she was Martha Brewster before her marriage. You denied knowing anyone in her family."

"Well?"

"Have you forgotten that you met Dickie Brewster at my place?"

Drake had responded with an offhand laugh and, "By God, I did, didn't I? I guess he didn't make much of an impression." Both the laugh and the tone of voice dismissed the subject, and Garner could not pursue it without calling Drake a liar for a second time.

An hour ago, Drake had lied to Priscilla, if that unhappy woman were to be believed. Eavesdropping on the kitchen extension, she heard him talking to Karen Thorndyke. Nothing personal about the conversation, she had admitted. He was talking about a recent eye examination, telling her he had discovered a serious problem Dr. Stewart had overlooked . . . . There was more, none of it bearing on Karen's role as the Other Woman, so Priscilla couldn't remember it. Instead she had pounced on the way the conversation began.

"Miss Thorndyke? This is Franklin Drake. I'm in Adam Stewart's office where I've been checking his report on your recent examination . . ." A lie. A pointless lie, unless it was used deliberately because nothing short of it would get the girl into the hospital during Adam Stewart's absence.

Like the keystone in an arch, the central truth of the human tragedy was falling into place. Through the kaleidoscope of memory, the all-important forgotten image came slowly into focus. Garner recalled that lonely human being, standing in the rain beside Dickie Brewster's grave. Like all the mourners, that faceless figure had been wrapped in rainclothes and shadowed by a roof of umbrellas. Now Garner thought he knew who it might have been.

He propped his elbow on the desk, rested his head in his hands and closed his eyes. He felt nauseated, he felt betrayed. He felt as if he could weep forever, like a father grieving for a dead child. When he regained a measure of self-control, he told his secretary he would be gone for awhile, perhaps for the rest of the day, and took the elevator down to the garage and his parking space in the basement.

Twenty-One

Anxiety was so foreign to Adam Stewart's nature that he hadn't recognized it until it bedded down with him at the Portland Hilton. Sleep came in small ragged patches, filled with such disturbing dream images that he welcomed the sleepless periods in between. Lying wide awake in the vacuum of night darkness, he reviewed the case of Dr. Adam Stewart while hour by hour the vague uneasiness he had felt about leaving Seattle kept swelling and growing until it was like an invisible presence, perched at the foot of the bed and mocking him.

Adam Stewart, professional to a fault, tearing himself away from a woman because he was afraid her feeling for him was the brief infatuation he had seen many women patients have for their doctors—an infatuation that usually disappeared with their symptoms. But if that's all it was, why was he running from it like a frightened virgin? He had kept his distance, even to the point of rejecting Karen's open appeal when he wanted so much to make love to her that his body ached.

—But any normal man, he told himself, in fact any doctor, would find it hard to undress a young and beautiful woman without being aroused.

—Ha! His alter-ego replied. Last night wasn't the first time you wanted to touch her. This thing has been building for a long time. Why didn't you leave her at the door? Why that sudden desire to show her what a great omelet chef you are?

—You don't get nutritious food at a cocktail party, and she's too thin.

—Balls!

The dialogue continued fitfully, interspersed with visual bits and pieces of Karen in Eye Bank headquarters, Karen in the hospital cafeteria, Karen in his office after her flight from the dentist's chair—scene after scene in which she had tried to convince him that her new eye possessed supernatural power. And more recently, since the eerie incident in the underground city, insisting that someone was trying to kill her. First light was just beginning to penetrate the darkness of his room when the sleep of exhaustion overtook him.

He awoke suddenly, the haunting anxiety of the night coupled now with an indefinable sense of foreboding. Six-fifteen. It was too early to call the program chairman but he was going to do it anyway. He hadn't been pleased by Franklin Drake's sudden decision to send his assistant to the conference in his place; in fact, he wouldn't have agreed if Drake hadn't insisted. It went against the grain to read another man's paper, even a paper as brilliant as Dr. Drake's. Since Drake wasn't presenting it himself, what difference did it make whether his stand-in was Adam Stewart or someone else? The program chairman could handle it. *He* was going to get back to Seattle on the first available flight.

When Doug began to canvas the car rental agencies, he had two specific bits of information to work with. One was that the special edition Triumph motorcycle had been sold and delivered to Dickie's apartment on October fifth of the previous year. The other was the fact that the purchaser had paid cash, the probable deduction from that being that he was concealing his name and identity. A police badge would open all doors and file cabinets, but even with the full cooperation of clerks and managers, Doug began the search for the name of Dickie's jealous lover with the feeling that he might as well have volunteered to count the sea gulls in Elliot Bay.

He made his first stop early in the morning, to be greeted by a wide-awake blonde with a fanatic respect for company policy. She showed him, without meaning to, how valuable that second clue was.

"Oh, we *never* accept payment in cash, Mr. Cooper. Company policy. We require a major credit card, preferably our own. Even a big advance payment would be only a fraction of the cost of replacing a car if the leasee absconded."

The list of rentals for October fifth told him nothing. None of the names were familiar and, as far as he knew, none had had any connection with Dickie Brewster.

He thanked the conscientious blonde for her trouble and added truthfully, "It's been at least ten years since I rented a car. Do the other agencies operate the same way you do?"

"In regard to accepting cash? Yes, indeed. All of the, well, *reputable* companies."

His most boyish grin and another round of thanks-for-your-trouble, and the girl set him up with a desk, a telephone and a cup of coffee. He started at the top of the list, asking, "Do you ever rent a car to someone who doesn't have a credit card but can pay cash in advance?" In ten calls, he heard ten "No's," one lecture on the importance of establishing credit, and one lament over how much rental income is lost by the time a stolen car is recovered.

One company admitted that under some circumstances, cash was acceptable. "If you are an established local resident, working someplace where we can verify your employment, yes, we'll let you have a car, after we've checked your credit rating." For a man like "Leander," meeting such requirements would be even more dangerous than presenting a credit card.

But the calls went quickly, and Doug was just starting on his second cup of coffee when he hit pay dirt. He had been assured by the pretty blonde that *all* agencies have a no-cash policy if they are *reputable.* His twelfth call was answered by a sleepy male voice that said, "Sure, sometimes. Come on over and I'll see what I can do for you."

It took fifteen minutes to get to the presumably disreputable rental agency, ten to locate the log for October fifth. There had been one cash rental on that day.

"Does your record show the name?"

"Oh, sure. We don't insist on a credit card—that's a risk we take if we have to. But we don't let anyone drive off our lot until he shows us a driver's license." He turned the rental agreement around and pointed to the top line.

"Jesus God," Doug breathed. "Thanks, buddy, thanks a lot." With that and a quick wave, he bolted through the door and ran to his car.

Adam parked at the foot of East Sutherland and hurried down the path to the floating dock. The aroma of balm of Gilead came up to meet him, evoking the image of Karen's smile and the laughing quality of her voice the night they had returned from the opera. The mental picture was so vivid it frightened him, as if the real and living Karen had slipped away and her wistful ghost were trying to reassure him. He was unreasonably happy to see her houseboat at the far end of the pier, and slowed his pace a little so that he wouldn't arrive at her door looking as anxious as he felt.

He knocked on the door, waited several seconds, and knocked again. No answer nor sound from within. He pulled back the cuff of his sports jacket and looked at his wrist watch.

Nine-twenty. Even if she were still asleep, it was not too early to wake her up. "Surprise!" he'd say when she came to the door, hair tousled and sleep in her eyes. "I came back a day early."

Better yet, he'd wake her up himself. He dug fingers into the flowerpot beside the door, retrieved the hidden key, inserted it in the lock and stepped inside. The living room and little yellow kitchen were as silent and still as a painting. He walked softly across the living room and down the hall to the bedroom.

She wasn't there. Sheets and blankets were carelessly heaped at the foot of the bed and one pillow lay on the floor. The door to the clothes closet stood open and the closet light was burning. The whole room was off-key.

The blue silk blouse on the floor beside the bed struck him as particularly out of character. He recognized it as the one she had worn to the Drakes' cocktail party. Obviously Karen had left in great haste. But why?

The question troubled him in a way he couldn't define. Automatically, because throwing clothes on the floor was unlike him, too, Adam picked up the blouse, intending to hang it in the closet. A hypodermic syringe lay on the carpet. He stared at it, disbelieving the sight of it, stunned by its implications. Nothing emerged clearly from his chaotic thoughts except that Karen must have used the blouse to conceal it. And that in itself made him apprehensive.

He knelt to examine the syringe carefully. The glass tube was broken. Its contents had soaked into the carpet, and the size of the stain suggested that little, if any of it, had been injected before it was smashed. The needle, a very real and deadly needle . . .

The sound of the French door sliding open brought him to his feet. He wheeled around, calling, "Karen?" and hurried into the living room.

Jennie, in jeans and T-shirt, was just inside the door. "Hello," she said. "I saw you from my kitchen window. Aren't you supposed to be in Portland?"

"I came back early," Adam said tersely. "Look, Jennie, what happened to Karen?"

Jennie's green eyes blinked. "Happened to her?" she repeated. "Why, nothing. I mean, nothing wrong."

"Are you sure?"

"Well, sometime during the night—not last night, the night before, after the party at Drakes —Karen claims someone came into her bedroom and tried to give her a shot."

"There *is* a needle. On the floor beside her bed."

"Yes," Jennie said quietly. "I know. I've seen it. I wanted to take it away but she wouldn't let me."

"Why not?"

Jennie hesitated. How much should she tell a man Karen was afraid to trust? But the vibes she was getting from Adam were good, and as Doug had often told her, you might as well trust your intuition when you don't have a logical mind. "She wouldn't say much about it. Only that she wanted to leave the hypo where she found it until you got back from Portland. Let the owner reclaim it, so to speak."

"For God's sake, Jennie!" Adam said indignantly, "It certainly isn't mine."

Jennie stared at him, mouth open as if she had been stricken in the middle of a sentence. "Not yours?" she echoed. "Not the one you used to give her a sedative?"

"No. Tell me quickly, Jennie. Where did she go?"

"To the hospital. She got a phone call about an hour ago. The doctor told her to check in immediately."

Adam shouted, "*I'm* her doctor, for God's sake!"

"I know. But it was Dr. Drake, and he said it was urgent."

"Why did he want her to go to the hospital?"

"She was tearing out of here so fast we didn't talk much. She said something about the last tests being incomplete, or imperfect. Tests you made, I guess, when she went to you for an examination last week. Dr. Drake said he had been checking them and discovered something wrong that had to be corrected immediately." Her eyes narrowed, "You know, it's funny. I remember how happy Karen was when she came home from that examination. Everything seemed to be going so well. I wonder what happened. Does it make any sense to you?"

"It makes no sense at all. Or else it makes too much sense," Adam said grimly. "I've got to get to the hospital right away!"

Jennie said impulsively, "Wait a minute, Adam. I want to show you something." She went quickly to Karen's easel, turned the painting around and stepped back. "She's been trying to paint the image. It's still indefinite, but there's almost a face there. I don't think it's someone I know. But how about you? Does that face remind you of anyone?"

"Yes it does!" Adam said. "God, yes. Jennie, I've got to hurry."

"You go ahead. I'll lock up," Jennie said, but he was already running down the pier.

It would be over soon. He had outwitted Dickie. The eye would be destroyed. Poor girl, poor girl. The damaged eye would slowly die until it was as shriveled as a raisin—he knew only too well what the tiniest surgical error could do. A slip of only a hundredth of an inch, so small and done so quickly that no one in the operating room would have the slightest suspicion. He could do it because he was a brilliant surgeon—even beautiful wicked Hero had said it many times. "My Leander! My famous, my renowned, my best-in-the-West eye surgeon. Kiss me, Leander. Kiss me more, more. . . ."

He had never really wanted to murder the girl. Perhaps that was why he had failed every time he tried. Those maddening headaches had stopped from the moment he made his decision to blind her accusing eye rather than kill her. Poor girl, poor girl. But it wouldn't hurt. In time there would be no pain in the shrunken and empty eye socket. Soon, soon, it would be all over. Soon . . .

Twenty-Two

As Adam approached the eighth floor nursing station, one of the nurses exclaimed, "Dr. Stewart! I thought you were in Portland. Dr. Drake said you'd be gone for three days."

"My plans changed. Where's Dr. Drake?"

"He's with a patient. Karen Thorndyke. I gave her the preliminary injection."

"Preliminary to *what?*" Adam shouted into the nurse's startled face.

"To—to surgery, of course, Doctor," she stammered, a touch of wounded dignity appearing in both her voice and posture. "Dr. Drake is very concerned about her."

"For God's sake, what happened? Was she injured? Has she been in an accident?"

"I don't believe so. Evidently some problem developed suddenly. In the operated eye. An emergency. That's all Dr. Drake told me." Her moment of pique ended abruptly as she recognized the significance of Adam's expression. "Is there something wrong, Dr. Stewart?"

"You were with Dr. Drake a few minutes ago? In surgery?"

"Why, yes, doctor. Dr. Brae was about to begin preliminaries to anesthesia."

For an instant Adam's reactions were paralyzed. Then the terrifying truth exploded in his mind. Pursued by the nurse's protests, he raced down the corridor. In sports clothes, without mask, gown, or cap, he skirted the wash-up area and plunged through the swinging doors into surgery.

Karen lay on the table. Drake was leaning over her. Indignant objections sounded from the white-masked surgical nurse as Adam brushed her aside to get to Drake. With a glance he saw that Karen's eyelids were drooping from the effect of the preliminary sedative. But she was still conscious, and her eyes brightened slightly with recognition.

Over the top of his mask, Drake's dark eyes glared at Adam. "What the hell do you think you're doing?"

"What are *you* doing, Frank? I examined this patient less than a week ago and there was absolutely nothing wrong with her eye."

"This is an emergency," Drake said coldly. "I don't have time for explanations. Get out!"

"Goddamn it, what kind of an emergency?"

Drake's eyes blazed with anger but his voice was desperate. "She had an accident. She fell off her bicycle. The fall broke several stitches."

Adam looked down at Karen's face, seeking confirmation. Without a high-powered microscope, he could not be sure whether the eye was damaged, but at least she might be able to tell him if she had, indeed, been in an accident. The words she was murmuring were too fuzzy to be understood, but her eyes spoke volumes. Wide with fright, they were fixed on Drake's masked face in horror.

"Get out of here!" Drake's voice was high-pitched and shook as if it was beyond his control. "Get out before you contaminate my instruments!"

For a paralyzed moment there wasn't a sound in the room. Then Karen spoke through drug-induced drowsiness, this time clearly enough to be understood.

"Yesterday—bike . . . no one knows . . ."

"I understand," Adam said softly. "I saw the painting, Karen. Now I want you to look at Dr. Drake. Concentrate. Don't be afraid, I'm right here." His hand darted at Drake's face and tore off the surgical mask. "Look hard, Karen, and let Dickie's eye tell you—Is this the face in that painting?"

Karen's terror-stricken voice whispered, "Oh God. Oh yes. . . ." Just before she slipped into a drugged sleep, she murmured, "Adam, please help . . . I'm so afraid. . . ."

Drake's eyes flashed. "She's insane! You know as well as I do that this girl is mad. Now get out of my way!"

Adam's hand shot out and grabbed Drake's wrist. "Leander," he said quietly. "Leander, it's all over."

An animal cry rolled up from Drake's throat. "I only wanted the eye. I wasn't going to kill her. Poor girl. Poor girl. I *had* to kill the eye." He swung around, dropped the instrument he had been holding and ran out of the operating room. Adam was on Drake's heels as they burst through the door and into the corridor.

Not ten feet ahead, the tall angular figure of Henry Garner was hastening toward them, trailed by Doug Cooper.

Drake halted. Speechless, his face gone ashy-white, he stared at Garner while Adam grasped his arm and signaled to Doug. "I'm glad you're here."

"I've got something to tell you, but it looks like it can wait."

"About the rented car?"

Doug nodded. "But I guess you already know who it is."

"Yes. I know. Doug, can you take Dr. Drake to his office? Last door on the left. And stay with him, please, until I come."

"Sure." Doug put a hand under Drake's elbow. "I'm sorry, Doctor," he said. Drake offered no resistance and the two men walked slowly down the hall, not speaking, while curious nurses turned to stare.

Adam saw the same mixture of shock and grief in Garner's face that he was feeling himself. "God, Garner. You and Frank have been friends for a long time. I know how you must feel. But I'm as sure as I've ever been of anything in my life that he killed Brewster, and that except for incredible luck, he would have blinded Karen's eye."

Garner sighed deeply. "Poor tormented Frank."

Adam looked at him curiously. "I guess we both know what happened. Or you wouldn't have come here today."

Garner nodded. "I wasn't sure. I am now. You know, he really did love Priscilla in his way, at least at first. But for most of their married life, he was impotent. He tried, he really tried. Until Dickie came along. God, to think I introduced them. Dickie must have overwhelmed Frank."

"And Frank killed him." Adam looked down the hall to the office where Doug Cooper was standing guard over the man he, Adam, had once so admired. "I've got to call the police."

Garner lifted a hand in protest. "What have you got to tell them, Doctor? That Dickie Brewster died of an overdose? They know that. That Frank gave it to him? You can't prove that. No one can. Are you going to testify that you know Dickie's death was murder because Karen Thorndyke received a vision through a transplanted cornea? I don't need to tell you how that would sound in court."

"But I know that Drake murdered Dickie. And so do you."

"I'll admit that. And I still say—who can prove it?"

"But I'm equally sure that Drake intended to blind Karen. He must have believed that she would eventually uncover his relationship to Dickie. He would be destroyed, not just financially, but in every way, if it became known he was a homosexual."

"*Known?*" Garner said earnestly. "Because

Karen Thorndyke says so?" He shook his head. "Believe me, Adam, Karen has no credibility. Don't call the police too soon, Doctor." He paused. In a voice that seemed about to break, he said, "I think that you know, and I know, the nature of the tragedy. Adam, Franklin Drake has been my close friend since we were kids. . . ." He cleared his throat. "You're a physician, and I think that girl in the operating room needs your attention. You take care of your patient, Doctor, and I'll take care of my friend."

Doug left the office at Garner's request. The two old friends were now alone. Drake was standing by a window that looked out over the tops of leafing trees to the peaceful waters of Lake Washington. As Garner walked up behind him, Drake neither moved nor spoke.

Garner stood beside him, feeling the room's silence like a weight. Side by side, Garner was several inches taller than Drake. He looked down, numb with grief, and put a protective arm around Drake's shoulders.

"You know why I did it, don't you, Hank? You do what you have to do." Drake spoke quietly. The anger, the desperation and the madness had drained out of him. "Remember that painting I showed you a couple of months ago? The one by Jake Burck that I bought for my office. A woman sitting on a chair, weeping, with her hands over her face, and some other figures, police officers, maybe, standing over her, looking down. It's a great painting, but I think it was the title that hit me so hard. 'She killed him because she loved him.' But I don't need to explain to you."

"No, Frank. I understand."

"Do you suppose Adam ever will? He's a fine surgeon, you know, Hank. He's been loyal, almost too loyal, and I think maybe I've held him back. You might talk to him sometime, Hank. Tell him how highly I thought of him."

"Let's go home, Frank. I'll take you."

Drake turned and looked searchingly into Garner's face. "Home? Why, no, Hank. I'm not going home."

"No one here will stop you. No one's going to bring charges, because they can't be proved."

For a moment something close to a smile trembled at the corners of Drake's mouth. "Look, old friend. Forget that you're a lawyer. I don't need one." He resumed his watch over the lake.

Garner, knowing the answer, asked, "What are you going to do?"

Drake didn't seem to hear. "See that yawl over there?" he said. "I've been watching her because she reminds me of the *Clementine*, the one my father had when you and I were kids. Remember Dad with his visored cap pulled down to meet his eyebrows, yelling, 'Goddamnit, you two, when are you going to learn? The mainmast is forward. The mizzenmast is smaller and it's abaft the rudder post!"

"Sure I remember."

"Keep an eye on this one. She's a beauty."

From his post by the window, Garner studied the graceful lines of the yacht. The sounds behind him were barely audible, but carried so much meaning that they pounded on his mind like drumbeats. A desk drawer was pulled out and then closed, a zipper case opened, a pause, soundless except for a faint rustle of clothing . . . and at last, silence, while on the lake below, the yacht's sails suddenly filled with the west wind and she slipped across the rippling lake and disappeared.

Garner turned around slowly, seeing the room dimly through the tears he could no longer control. Drake was in his desk chair, arms outstretched with forearms resting on the desk. A small phial and a hypodermic syringe lay beside the open zipper case, both of them empty.

Drake's head lifted slowly. "You see, Hank," he whispered, "I've always paid my . . . my debts." Like a child too tired to stay awake, he leaned against the desk, slowly bent his head and closed his eyes. Garner stood beside his chair and, weeping helplessly, waited for his old friend to die.

In Room 811 of Mathews Memorial Hospital, Karen lay very still, peering up at the pale blue ceiling as she tried to sort out what Adam had been telling her. The day now drawing to a close had the quality of a horrible fantasy. Doctor Drake's telephone call summoning her to the hospital might have taken place in some earlier life on another planet. Her only vivid memory was of the surrealistic moment on the operating table when the image had emerged from the eerie mist that in all previous visitations had hidden the human presence lurking behind it. It happened when Adam's voice called her name and Adam's hand tore off Dr. Drake's surgical mask. Like the climax of a magician's act, the concealing mist had evaporated. Staring into the surgeon's face, she had known even through the sedative that Dickie Brewster, dying, had been looking into those dark and angry eyes.

Karen shivered involuntarily and reached for Adam's hand. It was reassuringly warm and real. Adam, sitting beside the hospital bed, Adam's deep and comforting voice—that's what would send the fantasy packing. She gave his hand an impulsive squeeze. "Adam, there are so many questions, so many pieces to the puzzle."

"And you want to fit them all neatly together. So do I. It's something we have to do, we have to do it together. But let's not tackle it this afternoon."

"No, no, of course not. I just . . . well, I'm not sure that I'm happy about being Dickie Brewster's instrument of revenge. If only I hadn't gone to the Eye Bank, or seen Martha O'Donnell. . . ."

"Don't do this to yourself. Franklin *did* kill Dickie. And he tried to blind you. Instead of feeling sorry for him, try to think of his death as a welcome release from the hell his life had become. The important thing is that Dickie's eye isn't going to terrorize you any more. The visions are over. And the eye has healed in spite of your leaping in front of cars on Fourth Avenue, diving into Lake Washington in the middle of the night, getting bonked in the Seattle underground, and being thrown from your bicycle. So I say it's a damn good eye. In a few months, I'm going to patch up its partner and you'll have a full house."

"When I think back . . ." Karen mused. "Everything that happened seems so bizarre, like looking at things through the wrong end of a telescope. So mysterious . . ."

Adam moved to the edge of her bed and held her in his arms. "This isn't a mystery story, Karen. It's a love story." Then he kissed her, gently at first, then hungrily. And he didn't leave Room 811 for a very long time.

A NOTE ON THE AUTHOR

Charlotte Paul grew up in Seattle and was graduated from Wellesley College. She has held a variety of jobs, including a stint as an Arthur Murray dance instructor. She served as assistant foreign news editor and foreign correspondent for the Chicago *Times*, and later became a member of the Washington State Parole Board and the U.S. Board of Parole. Miss Paul has now returned to her first love, writing, and lives with her husband on the island of Lopez, located off the coast of Washington. Her two most recent books, *Phoenix Island* and *A Child Is Missing,* were national bestsellers.

MORE FICTION FROM CORONET

		JOHN SAUL	
☐	22687 0	Suffer the Children	£1.50
☐	24262 0	Punish the Sinners	£1.25
☐	25548 X	Cry For The Strangers	£1.50
☐	26680 5	Comes The Blind Fury	£1.50
		JUDITH ROSSNER	
☐	20818 X	Looking for Mr Goodbar	£1.50
☐	23030 4	Attachments	£1.25
		ALEXANDER CORDELL	
☐	20515 6	Rape of the Fair Country	£1.60
☐	17403 X	The Fire People	£1.00
☐	23224 2	This Sweet and Bitter Earth	£1.50
☐	26675 9	To Slay the Dreamer	£1.75

All these books are available at your local bookshop or newsagent, or can be ordered direct from the publisher. Just tick the titles you want and fill in the form below.

Prices and availability subject to change without notice.

CORONET BOOKS, P.O. BOX 11, Falmouth, Cornwall.

Please send cheque or postal order, and allow the following for postage and packing:

U.K.–40p for one book, plus 18p for the second book, and 13p for each additional book ordered up to a £1.49 maximum.

B.F.P.O. & EIRE–40p for the first book, plus 18p for the second book, and 13p per copy for the next 7 books, 7p per book thereafter.

OTHER OVERSEAS CUSTOMERS–60p for the first book, plus 18p per copy for each additional book.

Name ....

Address..

....